## *"You have exactly three seconds to leave."*

The duke ran a finger down her cheek, his gaze lingering on her mouth. "I advise you to leave."

Charlene lifted her chin. "I can stop you any time and throw you to the floorboards, remember?"

"Is that a challenge?" His green eyes grew smoky and intense. "I've never been able to resist a dare."

"I'm not afraid."

A wicked smile played over his lips. "You should be."

Oh, he was arrogant. He thought his kiss would overwhelm her. He had no idea.

"One." He tugged on her shawl until it pooled around her feet.

"Two." He stroked his thumb across her lower lip, slipping inside until the tip touched her tongue. She tasted cinnamon from the drinking chocolate and salt from his skin.

One small, unspoken word echoed in the space between them.

This wasn't the right time. This would be madness.

"Three," she whispered.

**By Lenora Bell**

HOW THE DUKE WAS WON

*Coming Soon*

IF I ONLY HAD A DUKE

# LENORA BELL

# How the
# Duke
# Was Won

 The Disgraceful Dukes

AVONBOOKS

*An Imprint of HarperCollinsPublishers*

This is a work of fiction. Names, characters, places, and incidents are products of the author's imagination or are used fictitiously and are not to be construed as real. Any resemblance to actual events, locales, organizations, or persons, living or dead, is entirely coincidental.

AVON BOOKS
*An Imprint of* HarperCollins*Publishers*
195 Broadway
New York, New York 10007

First Avon Books mass market printing: May 2016

Avon Trademark Reg. U.S. Pat. Off. and in Other Countries, Marca Registrada, Hecho en U.S.A.
Avon, Avon Books, and the Avon logo are trademarks of HarperCollins Publishers.
HarperCollins® is a registered trademark of HarperCollins Publishers.

Printed in the U.S.A.

10 9 8 7 6 5 4 3 2 1

*For my knight in sawdusty Carhartts.*

# Acknowledgments

No dream ever came true without tremendous love and support from family and friends. I'm so very grateful to my husband for the wood fires, home-cooked meals, and strong, slow-burning love. I'm thankful my parents ensured their offspring would be lifelong bookworms and artists by filling our house with literature and music. My siblings, especially my dear Amelia, are my creative consultants and constant inspiration.

I've been blessed with the most incredible writing friends and critique partners: Tessa, Courtney, Kerensa, Laura, Rachel, Lisa, Maire, Delilah, Darcy, Meljean, Piper, Pintip, Sheri, Evelyn, Patty—I owe you everything.

Enormous thanks to my fantastic agent, Alexandra Machinist; my miracle-working editor, Amanda Bergeron; and her awesome assistant, Elle Keck. All my gratitude to the entire team at Avon Books, including Carrie Feron, Pamela Jaffee, Tom Egner, Karen Davy, and Nicole Fischer. There's truly no place like Avon and being with you is my over-the-rainbow.

Hugs to the Nonfiction Vixens for all the Malbec,

chocolate, late night/early morning Skype dates, and for being kindred spirits. It's my turn to keep the traveling journal.

Finally, I'm honored to be a member of the talented 2014 Dream Weavers community, whose support and encouragement have meant so much. And a very special thank you to the Romance Writers of America®, especially Carol Ritter, for offering the Golden Heart® contest to unpublished authors, giving hope and a golden opportunity to the scribblers, the dreamers, and the believers.

# How the
# Duke
# Was Won

# Chapter 1

*Surrey, 1817*

**S**he will do.

James aimed at her gold-kissed curls and serene smile and launched his dagger. Right on target. Dead center between her placid blue eyes.

"An excellent choice, Your Grace." Cumberford pushed his spectacles up his narrow nose and consulted a ledger. "Lady Dorothea Beaumont, eldest daughter of the Earl of Desmond."

Lady Dorothea. A thoroughbred groomed to bear champions. "What do you think of her, Dalton?"

The only answer was an inebriated snore. James's friend Garrett, Marquess of Dalton, was stretched out on a sofa, arm dangling off the edge, still clutching an empty brandy glass.

James selected another dagger from the leather case and perused the pastel sketches he'd commissioned anonymously from a newspaper illustrator.

*Thwack*. His blade pierced a delicate swan neck. *Thwack*. He skewered an aristocratic nose.

Cumberford recited pedigrees, edging as far from the knives as possible.

James downed more brandy.

How had it come to this? He was the family disgrace, the exiled devil-may-care spare. He should be hacking a path through a West Indies jungle, not choosing duchess candidates.

Marriage had never been in the plan.

His next throw wobbled east, narrowly missing Cumberford's nose, and stuck in the burgundy leather spine of *The Life and Times* of his venerable forebear, the first Duke of Harland.

If Cumberford disapproved of James scarring the mahogany-paneled library walls, he didn't let on. He'd been the Harlands' man of business far too long to betray emotion.

"Damn!" said James.

"Wassat?" Dalton finally lifted his head off the sofa cushions.

"Almost chose Cumberford."

"Quite all right, Your Grace," said Cumberford.

"Almost *what*? Why have you got a knife in your hand?" Dalton groaned and threw his elbow over his eyes. "Where am I?"

James inclined his head, and a footman poured Dalton another drink.

Dalton closed his bloodshot blue eyes. "I'm going to be sick."

"None of that." James hauled his friend off the sofa and curled Dalton's fingers around a knife handle. "Make yourself useful."

Dalton stared at the dagger. "You're right. Once

you're caught in the matrimonial trap, I'll be one of the Last and Final Hopes. It'll be hideous. I should end it all now."

"Not *you*, idiot." James spun him to face the lineup of paper lovelies. "One of them."

Three knife-riddled ladies glared back. They didn't much like being pincushions. James swore Lady Dorothea's wide eyes had narrowed.

"You haven't thought this through," Dalton said. "They'll be on you like a pack of wolves. Warbury Park will be swarming with conniving females. I have to leave. Now." He took an unsteady step.

James propped him up. "Since you arrived unannounced, you could at least stay to help evaluate the candidates."

"If you must audition a wife, why not wait until the season, like a civilized fellow?" Dalton smacked his forehead with his free hand. "Oh, wait. I forgot. You're *never* civilized. You do know what they're calling you in London? *'His Disgrace.'*"

"I've been called worse."

"At least consider cropping that barbaric beard. Makes you look like a pirate."

"Just throw the knife."

Dalton squinted at the row of drawings fixed to the library walls. "All the same anyway," he slurred. "Soft lips and fluttery lashes. Until they snare you. Then it's harpy tongue and Medusa stare. Turn a man to stone for glancing at another girl. No fun, I tell you. None at all."

James shrugged. "It's the fathers I'm really wooing. Cumberford assures me these are the most influential men with eligible and refined daughters."

"Ah ha!" Dalton clutched James's cravat. "If it's the fathers you want, invite *them* here. We'll ply 'em with your excellent brandy and negotiate like gentlemen. You won't even have to meet the daughter until the wedding."

James shook his head. "I want to choose my bride. I need a sensible business partner. Someone gracious, genteel, irreproachable . . . all that I'm damn well not."

"Best of luck with that, then."

"When did you become so cynical? You were always waxing eloquent about Beauty and Aesthetics at school."

"Life." Dalton brandished the knife. "Life happened, old friend. Disappointments too numerous to name. Certain you won't reconsider?"

"Impossible. You know the score."

"I know, I know." Dalton made a wry face. "Must produce heir. Preserve the Harland legacy. Open your precious manufactory. All that nonsense. Bloody rotten business if you ask me."

"I don't like it any more than you do. Marriage is the last thing I want. I don't need more complications." James drummed his fingers on his thigh.

He didn't want any of this. The dukedom or the society bride.

He'd spent the last ten years roaming the world, living by his own rules, and he wasn't about to move back to cold, restrictive England and become a narrow-minded tyrant like his father. Instead, James would find a blameless virgin to sacrifice to the gods of Reputation and Respectability, one with a father of ample means and solid political connections, and leave as soon as possible.

He swept a hand toward the pastel sketches. "One of these lovely ladies is sure to be duchess material. A demure, mannerly—"

"Medusa!" Remarkably, Dalton managed to sink his blade into the edge of one of the drawings.

Cumberford permitted himself a small sigh of relief. "Another superb choice. Miss Alice Tombs, daughter of Sir Alfred Tombs, rumored to have amassed a fortune of over—"

"That's four now," said James. "Deliver the invitations, Cumberford. I want this bride business concluded as swiftly as possible."

It was already August. The mourning period for his father and brother had kept him in England too long. He must set sail for the West Indies before the hurricane season made ocean crossings more dangerous. He would stay here in England only long enough to sire an heir and ensure the success of his new cocoa manufactory.

"Very good, Your Grace." Cumberford bowed. "I shall personally deliver the invitations to the fortunate ladies tomorrow morning."

James nodded his dismissal, and his man of business practically sprinted for the door, eager to distance himself from the drunken target practice.

"It's not too late." Dalton raised a fist. "Call off the hounds! Stop the hunt!"

"Four ladies. Three days. How bad can it be?"

Dalton sighed. "You've no idea. Don't say I didn't warn you, Duke."

*Duke.*

The duke was dead.

James helped Dalton back to the sofa and poured himself more brandy.

He could still see the silver-handled coffin disappearing into the dark crypt beneath the black-draped family chapel. Could still smell death and sickly sweet lilies. The English rain had soaked through wool and linen, turning his skin to ice.

James jammed a blade deep into the smooth mahogany of his father's desk.

*I'm the last of my line. I never wanted this. I never wanted to be the duke.*

His brother, William, had been the consummate family scion. Steady, sober, obedient . . . law abiding. But he'd died in the same carriage accident that had left their father mortally wounded and claimed his life six months later.

James tugged at the noose society called a cravat, craving air. He'd never been any good at following rules or treading a prescribed path. But there were so many people depending on him now.

Not only tenants and workers. He thought of the little girl upstairs in the nursery. Her dark, sad eyes and rebellious screaming fits. Such an unexpected responsibility.

But she would be safe in England with an elegant, blameless duchess to protect her from society's inevitable scorn and oversee her development. He knew it was a lot to ask of a debutante.

He took a sip of brandy and contemplated the sketches.

He wasn't cut out to be a duke, but he could choose the perfect duchess.

Cumberford had gathered a predictable batch of English roses. No doubt they had the blinkered eyes and fettered souls of a respectable aristocratic upbringing.

James had been uncharacteristically celibate since arriving in England, but he was certain that society debutantes would be too timid to tempt him, which was for the best. He couldn't afford any distractions. This was a business arrangement, not a love match.

He emptied the brandy bottle and raised a glass to Lady Dorothea's innocent eyes and beatific smile.

She'd have to be a bloody saint to marry the likes of him.


Some nights Charlene Beckett didn't feel like being a saint.

When her back ached and her fingers were red and raw from the washing. When her head pounded from staring at figures that never seemed to add up to what they needed.

Some nights it was difficult to smile, give comfort, be strong.

Tonight was one of those nights.

Every footfall dragged heavier than the last as she climbed the stairs to her room. All she wanted was to crawl into bed and pull the counterpane over her head. Shut out the sounds drifting down from overhead.

Soft giggles. Blustery male voices. A tinkling pianoforte.

Trussed up in rose-colored velvet and plumes, floating on laudanum to suppress the cough that grew worse every day, Mama was holding court upstairs in her discreet bawdy house known as the Pink Feather.

Charlene rested against the wall for a moment. The sound of her mother coughing made her wince. Tomorrow she'd find a way to convince her mother to stop working. Tonight Charlene needed to sleep.

The door to her room was ajar.

"Lulu?" she asked as she opened the door, thinking her younger sister might be waiting for her.

An aquiline nose above a gleaming white cravat emerged from the gloom.

Charlene's heart clenched. The moment she'd been dreading for more than a year was finally here.

*Not tonight. Please, not tonight.*

"I've been waiting for you, pretty bird." Lord Grant rose from where he sat near the window.

"Lord Grant." She managed to keep her voice steady despite the panic clawing at her throat. "We didn't expect you for several months yet."

"I couldn't leave my flock alone so long, now, could I?"

He stepped into the light of the oil lamp, and Charlene swallowed back revulsion. He peeled off gray kid gloves and set them on the table. Ran a hand through wavy brown hair, thick with orange-scented pomade. He might have been handsome if she hadn't known the deep streak of cruelty beneath the polished façade.

Grant's assessing gaze swept her body. "Still beautiful, I see, even in that drab gown."

Charlene opened the door wider, searching the hall for movement. They were alone.

She stopped herself from flinching as he approached.

His finger brushed her cheek. "I've dreamt of this moment."

So had Charlene. Only in her dreams, it was bright daylight and she burned with enough keen-edged hatred to slice through this suffocating fear.

"We need more time," she said.

"More time?" He cupped her chin in his palm. "I don't understand."

"To raise the funds. We need more time."

Charlene's mother, known as Madame Swan, had opened the exclusive bawdy house with gifts from a grateful benefactor, but she was too soft-hearted for this business. Most of the profit went to her employees. She'd accepted a loan from Lord Grant, a frequent patron, and now he was here to collect.

He laughed and framed Charlene's cheeks with his hands. She twisted her head away, but he jerked it back into place.

His fingernails were half crescents of white, buffed to a shine. He wasn't one to get his hands dirty. She was surprised he hadn't brought one of his guards tonight to subdue her if she proved troublesome. Which she would.

"You never learn, do you," he said. "Life doesn't have to be complicated. It's very simple." He rested his forehead against hers. "I want *you*, nothing else. You're all the payment I require."

He nipped at her earlobe, the heavy, bitter-orange scent of his hair clogging her senses. "I'm willing to forgive and forget."

Charlene stilled. *He* was willing to *forgive*. She fought a swell of anger that threatened to swamp her control. The last time she'd seen him, he'd been wielding a blazing brand, preparing to mark her with his family crest. Induct her into his private harem.

He dipped his head to nuzzle her cheek. "Don't make this unnecessarily difficult."

She would never forget the moment when he'd held the glowing brand above her shoulder. Her world had been separated, like the whites of an egg from the yolk. Before, she'd believed that life held promise, maybe even the possibility of love. Afterward, she'd known that wealthy, titled gentlemen had a core of evil. She would never fall in love. Never give anyone even a modicum of power over her.

The timely arrival of Kyuzo, the bawdy house guard, had helped her escape before Grant had branded her, and the baron had left for Scotland the next day. In the intervening year, she'd practiced defending herself, preparing for Grant's return.

*Remember your training, Charlene.*

*No anger. No fear. Only a gentle, flowing river.*

*He has no idea that you're ready this time.*

An arm snaked around her waist. He pulled her against his unyielding length. "Don't fight me, pretty bird," he whispered in her ear.

He kissed her neck.

"Let me go."

"Don't you want the things I can give you?" He sounded genuinely puzzled. "Aren't you tired of wearing sackcloth and smelling of lye? I'll bring you to live in luxury. You'll have silks and French perfume."

And she would be owned, kept for a man's pleasure. She would never let that happen.

"Let me go," she repeated, staring him straight in the eye.

"No. I've waited too long for this."

*Wait until his energy is full.* Kyuzo's words echoed in her mind. *Use his energy against him. In that way you have the strength of two.*

She turned her face to avoid his kiss. He clamped one large hand around her throat and forced her back to face him.

*Soon.*

*Wait. Breathe.*

*Now.*

Swiftly, she stepped back, following Kyuzo's instructions. *Place both hands around the hand that holds your throat. Bend backward, away from harm. Twist his wrist. Lock your elbow above his elbow. Right foot to left foot. Force him down.*

"What the devil?" Grant's right knee hit the floor. He grunted in surprised pain, his arm bent at an awkward angle.

She could snap his elbow from this position.

*Breathe. No anger.*

She applied more pressure to his weak, extended elbow, forcing his other knee down to the floor. "I'm not yours for the taking."

"You don't decide that," he gasped, struggling against the arm lock.

"Charlene." Kyuzo burst into the room. "I heard a noise."

Charlene released the baron.

Grant stumbled to his feet, cradling his elbow and wrist against his chest. He glared at Kyuzo. "I see you still have your mongrel protector."

Kyuzo's arms crossed over the formidable chest that had convinced her mother to hire him as a guard. "Miss Beckett said you were leaving."

Charlene gathered the baron's top hat, gloves, and overcoat, and thrust them into Grant's arms.

Kyuzo took the baron's elbow, but Grant wrenched free. "Don't touch me." His brown eyes turned nearly black. "I'll be back to collect my due."

"I'd think twice about coming back if I were you," Kyuzo growled. "Go on with you then." He steered the baron out the door ahead of him.

Charlene's spine remained rigid until she heard them descending the stairs. She staggered against the wall, her knees buckling.

Grant would be back.

Even with taking in washing and selling Lulu's paintings, they hadn't saved nearly enough to repay the loan and the exorbitant interest he'd charged.

As her breathing returned to normal, Charlene searched her mind for a solution. She must find a way to settle their debt, close the house, protect Lulu from Grant.

She'd find a way.

She had to.

# Chapter 2

**S**haking out her skirts and smoothing her hair, Charlene took the lamp and headed back downstairs. Kyuzo had resumed his post by the front door.

"Impressive." Kyuzo's eyes crinkled up around the edges. "You used *Ude Gatame.*"

Charlene smiled. "I had an impressive teacher."

Fifteen years ago, Kyuzo had escaped from the Dutch merchant vessel that stole him from a fishing village in Japan and forced him into unpaid servitude. He'd survived on the streets of London with only his wits and fighting prowess to earn a living.

It was his knowledge of the traditional Japanese art of *Jujitsu* that had secured him the position of guard. Over the years, Charlene had helped the older man improve his English language skills and, in return, he'd taught her basic defensive techniques to safeguard herself against the unwelcome advances of the titled gentlemen who came to the Pink Feather for sport.

Charlene drew a shuddering breath. "He'll be back, Kyuzo. And he won't come alone."

"I know. We'll be ready. Don't worry."

There was a knock at the door. Charlene's breathing quickened. "Grant again?" she whispered.

Kyuzo shook his head. "He wouldn't knock."

Charlene slid the viewing panel open and peered out at the tall, imposing man and black-cloaked woman standing on the stoop. Their clothing was expensive and their demeanor impatient. They were nobility, and unaccustomed to being kept waiting.

"May I help you?" she asked.

The man spoke into the open panel. "We have a private matter to discuss."

Not a threat, Charlene decided, unlatching the door.

"Miss Charlene Beckett?" the man asked.

Charlene paused. How did they know her name? "What brings you here?"

"You," the woman said.

Beside her, Kyuzo's shoulders stiffened.

"I'm not available." Charlene was so weary of clients who assumed she was one of the commodities for sale.

The woman lowered her hood, and Charlene's heart hammered into her throat. She recognized the stern profile and pale blue eyes. Lady Desmond. Her mother had pointed her out one day when they'd been shopping on Bond Street.

"You know who I am," the countess said. It wasn't a question.

Charlene nodded.

"Come here."

The imperious order carried Charlene toward the countess before she knew she was moving.

Lady Desmond gripped her chin. "Dismal light in here." She turned Charlene's face toward the tallow candles burning in sconces along the hallway. "What say you, Jackson? Will she do?"

"It's uncanny, your ladyship. She could be Lady Dorothea's twin."

"Precisely." The countess squeezed Charlene's cheeks until her mouth popped open. "All her teeth. And passably white, too. I must say I am surprised."

Charlene jerked away and stood next to Kyuzo.

"She's a bit fleshier, though." The countess cocked her head to one side, measuring with her eyes. "But I'll be able to squeeze her into Dorothea's gowns. She'll do, Jackson. She'll do."

"I really must bid you good evening, your ladyship." Charlene sketched the barest of curtsies and gestured to the door.

When they didn't move, Charlene glanced at Kyuzo and tapped one finger to her wrist—their signal that these visitors were unwelcome.

Kyuzo took a step forward.

The countess held up her hand. "Send your guard away. We need privacy. I have a matter to discuss that could prove extremely lucrative for you."

"Anything you have to say you will say now, and Mr. Yamamoto stays."

Kyuzo eyed Jackson and widened his stance. "I stay."

"Very well." The countess extended one elegant, white-gloved hand toward Charlene. "I know you are unhappy here. Let me help you."

Charlene hugged her arms to her chest. "You don't know anything about me."

"On the contrary, I make it my business to study all of my husband's by-blows. The ones he acknowledges, and the ones he does not." Lady Desmond inhaled sharply, as if the subject pained her. "You are of particular interest because you are nearly identical to my own daughter, Lady Dorothea."

The earl's legitimate daughter. Her half sister. Charlene had often thought about Lady Dorothea and wondered what her life was like in her fashionable house in St. James's, worlds away from the chaos and grime of Covent Garden.

"You have put up a brave struggle," the countess said. "But it's only a matter of time before you are forced to follow in your unfortunate mother's footsteps. Sell yourself. Become a bawd. And Luisa, such an artistic child. What will be her fate? Have you thought about that?"

Of course Charlene had thought about it. Lulu was still an innocent. She lived in a world of her own creation, intent on the miniature portraits she loved to paint, blissfully unaware of their home's improprieties. Charlene would do anything to keep her from learning the truth.

Countess Desmond reached inside her reticule and extracted a thin, rectangular piece of paper. Candlelight caught and held gold-embossed words and gilded edges. "This is your golden opportunity. An invitation from the Duke of Harland, issued to only four young ladies in all of London."

"How is that relevant?"

The countess handed Charlene the paper. "The invitation is for Lady Dorothea, who happens to be on a ship returning from Italy." She narrowed her pale blue eyes. "I refuse to let the trifling fact that she is not here ruin my daughter's chance of becoming a duchess. You were born to play this role, my girl. You will use your . . . *arts* . . . to snare the duke. He will be forced to marry my daughter. She will become a duchess."

Charlene suppressed a hiccup of disbelieving laughter. "You want me to seduce a duke? While pretending to be your daughter?"

"If you must put it so crudely, then yes. It's really very simple. Three days of acting for enough coin to achieve your dreams. What is it you want most?"

That was easy. "Pay our debts, close the Pink Feather, and open a respectable boardinghouse." Her mother's health was worsening. She couldn't sustain the long hours she worked. Charlene would run the boardinghouse. Save vulnerable young girls from prostituting themselves, save them from predators like Grant. "And I want to purchase a painting apprenticeship for my sister."

"Well then," said the countess with a slight smile. "Is that all? Jackson."

Jackson drew a packet from inside his coat.

"Her ladyship has anticipated your requests. Here is a letter of introduction for your sister to Mrs. Anna Hendricks of Essex, an elderly miniaturist whose eyesight is failing and who has need of a gifted young apprentice."

His gaze traveled to the countess for a moment, as if he were giving her time to stop him. When she did not, he continued. "This is in addition to the one thousand pounds her ladyship will settle upon you should you succeed."

Charlene gasped. The countess must truly be desperate. They'd have the wherewithal to pay Grant and open a boardinghouse in a decent neighborhood.

How did they know so much about her and Lulu? It was downright sinister.

"Well?" asked the countess.

Charlene shook her head. "I was raised for . . . *this life.* I can't pass for a lady."

"No matter how you were raised, the blood of emperors flows in your veins, however tainted or diluted."

Charlene squared her shoulders. She'd already booted a baron. She refused to be cowed by a countess. "If I am so *tainted*, how do you expect to fool the other ladies, who, I assume, are acquainted with Lady Dorothea?"

"Only one of them knows her, and not well. The other two have never met her."

"And the duke? Surely he's met Lady Dorothea before?"

"He's been living abroad for a decade and only

recently inherited the title. They say he's brutish, more pirate than gentleman. But I daresay you're adept at handling difficult men."

This was all too preposterous. Charlene held out her ungloved hands. "Do you see these? I earn my keep in this house doing the bookkeeping and some of the washing. Can a girl with these hands entice a duke?"

"Pish," countered the countess. "People see only what they expect to see. A duke is no exception. A few days under my tutelage will suffice to transform you."

The determination in her icy blue eyes made it clear that the countess believed herself omnipotent.

Kyuzo gestured for Charlene to walk a few steps with him. He turned his back on the countess and whispered in Charlene's ear. "Ask her what are the terms if you fail. If the duke doesn't propose. You need to be paid either way or it's not worth the risk."

"You're right," Charlene agreed. They returned to Jackson and the countess.

"What are the terms if I don't secure a proposal?" Charlene asked. "What then?"

Jackson set his lips disapprovingly. "Her ladyship has established terms that you will find more than satisfactory. One hundred guineas now, yours to keep even if you fail to procure a proposal."

He shook the purse. There was the metallic sound of coin against coin. The music that ruled her mother's world. The sound of a girl being sold.

"If you succeed, the full payment. Contingent upon the promise that you will never contact her ladyship, or any member of her family, and will accompany Miss Luisa to Essex for the period of at least one month after the conclusion of the contract."

Charlene wavered. This could be the answer to her prayers.

"It's only five days, Miss Beckett," urged the countess. "We must begin your training this very night. You may send your family a letter of explanation in the morning, making no mention of my name or your mission, of course. I require absolute secrecy."

"You there, Yamamoto, is it?" Jackson tossed a smaller purse to Kyuzo. "Here's something for your silence. If I hear you've been spreading tales, you'll answer to me."

The lines around Kyuzo's mouth deepened as he examined the contents of the pouch. "You call this a bribe, Sir? Twenty guineas? I could win twice that at the gambling tables tonight."

Charlene had to grin at the shocked expression on Jackson's face. Clearly he hadn't expected any resistance.

"I highly doubt you have the wherewithal to command such large sums," Jackson said disdainfully. "You'll be happy with what I gave you."

Kyuzo pretended to reconsider the offer. Then he smiled. "I wonder. Do you think The Times might be interested in this little story?" The smiled dropped off his face. "Fifty guineas and count yourself lucky."

"This is outrageous," Jackson exclaimed.

Kyuzo shrugged. "A man's got to save for retirement."

"Oh just pay him, Jackson," the countess said impatiently. "Come along, Miss Beckett, we haven't a moment to lose."

There was a noise from the stairway. Lulu appeared at the top of the stairs, fragile and pale, her long red hair, so different from Charlene's blonde locks, covering her thin shoulders. "Charlene? Are you coming to bed?"

Charlene hurried to the foot of the stairs. "Go back to bed, sweetheart. Everything is fine." She smiled reassuringly. Her sister appeared so much younger than her fourteen years.

"It's late." Lulu's hazel eyes were filled with concern. "Who are these people?"

"Come along, Miss Beckett. We must leave," Jackson said.

Kyuzo joined Charlene. "Don't worry. Luisa will be safe."

"What if Grant returns?" Charlene whispered.

"I'll hire another guard while you're gone. Go now." Light danced in his eyes. "That poor duke doesn't have any idea who's coming for him. You can do this."

She *had* to do this. There was no other alternative.

She took Lulu's hand. "Sweetheart, I'm going on a short journey. Nothing to worry about. I'll be home in a matter of days." She forced herself to look away. The questions in her sister's eyes would have to wait.

Kyuzo guided Lulu back up the stairs.

Charlene closed her eyes, just for one heartbeat, then followed the countess and Jackson to the waiting carriage.

She could act the lady if she had to. She'd been groomed to become an exclusive courtesan, and even though she'd rejected the role, she spoke French, played the pianoforte, and knew the proper forms of address for titled, pleasure-seeking gentlemen.

She glanced back at the house. Candlelight flickered in the upstairs windows, outlining the curvaceous silhouette of Dove, her mother's favorite. Mama was there as well, oblivious to her daughter's desperate bargain.

As Charlene settled onto the carriage's opulent silk cushions, she ran a finger over the gold lettering on the invitation. *The Favor of Lady Dorothea Beaumont's Company is requested at Warbury Park by His Grace. . .*

The Duke of Harland.

He probably wore stays to control a rotund belly, oiled his moustache, and had a custom snuff blend. And because he was born to privilege and obscene wealth, he thought nothing of ruining and discarding females as casually as he changed coats for dinner.

The same egotistical, autocratic bully she'd dealt with so many times.

But what alternative did she have?

They traveled the short distance to St. James's in silence. Before they reached the front gate of the earl's town house, Jackson rapped on the carriage ceiling and gestured for Charlene to follow him out. He took her around to the servant's entrance and smuggled her up the back stairs, shrouded in the countess's black cloak.

"This is Lady Dorothea's room," he whispered, glancing up and down the hallway before bringing her into the chamber. "Lady Desmond will be here soon." He handed Charlene a leather-bound copy of *Debrett's Peerage*. "Study this," he said, and left.

It was a feminine room, with a profusion of floral prints. There were pink roses and blue forget-me-nots on the carpet. An embroidery sampler depicting the wildflowers of England hung on walls sprigged with delicate white lily of the valley. A silk canopy the color of a rosy summer sunset covered a large wooden bed overspread by a white counterpane embroidered in intertwining vines and floating thistle flowers.

Charlene formed a picture in her mind of her half sister, as soft-edged and feminine as the room, a butterfly flitting among her flowers.

Charlene used to construct elaborate fantasies about the earl acknowledging her, and inviting her and Lulu, no matter that she was not one of his, to live in this grand house.

Now she was a usurper trespassing in Lady Dorothea's privileged world. Charlene wondered what her half sister was thinking about in her luxurious chambers on the ship back from Italy. Did she even know Charlene existed?

The countess marched into the room, followed by a slender lady's maid dressed in black, with a frilly white apron and cap. "Now then, Miss Beckett. Your speech is tolerable, but we'll have to correct your posture. Unfold yourself if you please. Ladies never sit in that manner."

"I'm not a lady," Charlene countered.

"You will be able to emulate one when I'm through with you," the countess said grimly. "I won't have you embarrassing me. Take off that cloak, Miss Beckett."

Charlene unfastened the cloak and laid it on the chair back.

"Your hair is in a deplorable state," announced the countess. She turned to the lady's maid, who'd been eying Charlene as if she'd seen a ghost. "Blanchard, stop gawking and fetch a hairbrush. There's much work to be done. Find the hand salve as well. Her hands need softening."

Blanchard hurried away.

The countess unfolded a square of blue velvet on the dressing table in front of Charlene, positioning glasses of varying shapes and sizes alongside a row of silver forks and spoons.

"Which glass is for sherry?" the countess asked.

Charlene chose a thin glass at random.

"Wrong. That is for cordial." The countess launched into a lecture on glassware.

Blanchard returned and unpinned Charlene's hair, brushing it with a gleaming silver brush.

The countess paused for breath.

"If I'm to impersonate Lady Dorothea, shouldn't I learn about her, as well as table etiquette?" asked Charlene.

The countess set down the fork she'd been wielding. "Lady Dorothea is a paragon of virtue. She never speaks unless spoken to, never takes more than one biscuit, something you would do well to emulate," she said as she glanced significantly at Charlene's waist.

Charlene had never been able to resist sweets when she'd been able to afford them.

"She devotes her free time to embroidery and charitable concerns." The countess indicated the wildflower sampler hanging on the wall. "One of her earliest pieces."

Needlepoint was Charlene's sworn enemy.

"Despite my daughter's many virtues," the countess continued, "for some unfathomable reason, she wasn't the instant success I'd hoped in her first two seasons. There was an . . . unfortunate incident. I sent her to Italy to visit an aunt and acquire more polish. If I'd known a duke would take an interest in her, I never would have allowed her to travel."

"But what are her mannerisms? For example, how does she laugh?"

The countess frowned. "I don't know, how does anyone laugh?"

"Is her laughter high, or low, does she chortle, or squeak?"

Lady Desmond turned to the maid. "What does Lady Dorothea's laugh sound like?"

"It's high pitched, my lady, more of a giggle than a laugh. I think she giggles when she's nervous. Which is . . ." Blanchard glanced at the countess.

" . . . all the time." She spoke with a slight French accent.

"Never mind what her laugh sounds like, it doesn't signify. You only have to be her for three days," said Lady Desmond. "It will be best if you keep speech to a minimum. I suspect the duke isn't searching for brilliant conversation. What he needs is a refined lady to polish his tarnished reputation."

Silence had never been Charlene's forte. She was far too opinionated. "Are you certain I'm right for the role?"

"You were trained by your mother, were you not? Use your *skills*. Be affable . . . be *accommodating*."

In other words, encourage the duke to take liberties. Flirt, flatter, and entice him into a compromising situation.

No brilliant conversation required.

The countess continued her dinner etiquette dissertation. Charlene had difficulty keeping her eyes open. It had been a long day, and Lady Dorothea's sumptuous bed beckoned. It would be soft and comfortable. She could pull the embroidered counterpane over her head. Forget the dangerous mission for a few hours.

"Miss Beckett, do try to pay attention," said the countess. "I will not have you embarrass me at the duke's estate."

Blanchard gave Charlene a sympathetic smile when their gazes met in the mirror.

Finally, the countess exhausted the subject of

proper dining. "We'll continue your lessons in the morning. You may sleep here tonight. You should become accustomed to Lady Dorothea's sensibilities." She swept from the room without a backward glance.

When she was gone, Charlene stood. "What's your name?" she asked the lady's maid.

"Manon Blanchard, milady."

"Oh, come now. I think you can tell I'm no lady."

Manon smiled.

"Tell me about Lady Dorothea. Do we truly look alike?" Charlene asked.

The maid nodded. "You could be twins." She helped Charlene remove her gown and don a fine cambric nightdress. "She's a sweet girl. Obedient and demure. But she's not . . . what did her ladyship say? A paragon? She's not a paragon. Just a girl."

Lady Dorothea was becoming a real person in Charlene's mind, not some mythical princess from the pages of a fairy tale. It had to be quite a trial having a mother with such impossible expectations.

As Charlene climbed into bed and finally pulled the whisper-soft counterpane up to her chin, her eyes pricked with unshed tears. She'd never been away from Lulu, not even for one night. Even though they were five years apart and had different fathers, they were best friends.

Lulu was approaching the age Charlene had been when she'd learned the truth about their life.

At fourteen, Charlene's life had seemed normal,

genteel even. Until the evening when her mother had taken her upstairs, to the Aviary. Where she'd never been allowed before.

She remembered the scene so clearly. The girls she'd known only as friends swinging from silken perches and performing feathered fan dances for leering peers in the secret top floor room. Nightingale, Dove, Linnet, Swallow. They all had bird names. And, in one moment of awful realization, Charlene had understood why.

She'd fled from the house into the shock of a frozen winter's night, trying to outrun her destiny. She'd had to go back, rather than risk the streets of Covent Garden in winter. But she'd refused to become a courtesan. She preferred doing the washing.

Charlene never wanted her sister to learn the sordid truth. Lulu was more than simply innocent, she was almost willfully blind to their circumstances. She was always painting romantic scenes in miniature, precise detail. Picturesque ruined castles crumbling in fields of orange poppies. It was almost as if she didn't see the real world, the soot and grime of London, preferring to live in an imaginary world of her own creation.

Charlene would do whatever it took to preserve her sister's innocence.

Seducing a duke was better than living life as Grant's prisoner.

# Chapter 3

James caught his valet's wrist. "Not too short."

Pershing gave a wounded sniff. "I'll leave curls around your neck. Your Grace will be fashionably tousled and poetic, and the ladies will swoon."

"Just not too short." James had seen too many men sheared like sheep. To keep the lice away. To brand them as prisoners.

The prisoner in the mirror stared back. Dark hair falling around shoulders broad from chopping trees, hoisting logs. Cutting his hair was his one concession to the female onslaught that was about to begin. The rest of him was disreputable enough.

Pershing hovered and darted in to snip like some scissor-beaked hummingbird.

Hair fell in piles around his feet. A neck emerged. Thick and bullish.

He hadn't cropped his hair these ten years.

A memory saturated his mind like ocean spray over a bowsprit.

Shimmying up the spire, Cambridge dwindling below, his friends watching from the shadows as he climbed and kept going, even when fear and cold numbed his fingers and he no longer remembered why he was climbing.

Higher and higher. Fifty feet, sixty feet, the flag stuck in his teeth. Hanging on with one arm while he lashed the flag to the spire, his stomach lurching.

In the morning light, the black flag streamed above King's College, a skeleton spearing a heart and raising a glass to the Devil.

Blackbeard the Pirate's emblem.

*Show no quarter. Have no fear.*

It had been so important to him to rebel in those days. Disavow his father's ruthless legacy. Declare his independence.

He'd been sent down for his prank, of course. And his back still bore the scars of the old duke's retribution.

*If you insist on playing the pirate, I'll send you to sea. Teach you fear of God and Family.*

He'd shipped James to their ailing sugar plantation in Trinidad the next day.

That first year, thirty men on his father's plantation in Trinidad had died of yellow fever. James had nearly been one of them. While he'd been in the sweat-soaked throes of the fever, he'd hallucinated that his mother was still alive. Felt her cool hand on his brow, a touch he hadn't known since she'd died giving birth to a stillborn baby when he was fourteen, and away at Eton.

As the thirst had raged and he'd vomited black liquid over the bedclothes, he'd seen her soft blue eyes pleading with him not to die.

He'd lived. Grown a beard. Vowed never to return to England and the father who had shipped him off to die.

James had closed down his father's brutal sugar plantation and left the West Indies to travel the world, earning his own way with sweat, gambling, and wise investments.

After several years he'd returned to the West Indies and, using no funds from his father, he'd invested in cocoa cultivation by other small farmers who farmed marginal cocoa lands in Trinidad and in the country of Venezuela.

Scissors attacked his beard.

When they finally captured the notorious Edward Teach, known as Blackbeard, and shot him dead, they catalogued his wounds. He'd been shot five times, carved by knives over twenty.

When James received the letter telling of the carriage accident that killed his elder brother instantly and left the old duke dying, he thought of Blackbeard, of cataloguing not the wounds his father had received but the ones he'd inflicted.

It would be a long litany. He'd been a cruel man who'd only valued people for what he could bleed out of them. William had learned the art of obedience from their faded, silent mother, choosing survival over independence, while James had chosen to fight.

He'd never stopped fighting.

The crooked nose in the mirror told the story. Too many reckless challenges in dark taverns, too many brawls when he'd been outnumbered but had provoked a fight all the same. He'd never learned to be silent in the face of injustice, never learned to keep his mouth shut.

Pershing smoothed something that smelled like a pine forest over his jaw, and a sharp blade scraped against his skin.

James clenched his fingers, battling the instinct to reverse his vulnerable position and flatten the valet against the wall with a fist at his throat. "Enough," he said, waving Pershing away and sweeping the towel from his shoulders.

The valet plucked two striped waistcoats from a shelf. "The crimson or the jade, Your Grace?"

"It's no use, Pershing." James rubbed the towel across his jaw. "You'll never make me respectable." He angled his head, taking in his reflection in the mirror. "I'll still frighten the poor ladies."

Hell. He looked like his father. He flung the towel against the mirror, obliterating the unsettling truth.

He had to escape. Every day he stayed in England, the memories grew more oppressing.

The thought of taking his place in the line of Harland dukes whose harsh faces haunted the gallery walls made his jaw lock with anger and frustration.

He couldn't don a gaudy silk waistcoat and stand on the front steps of the house he despised, welcoming polite society to pass judgment on him.

He had no choice, of course.

Producing an heir required a bride. Even if that bride would be repulsed by his brutishness.

Pershing proffered another waistcoat choice. "What about this cerulean blue—"

James leapt from the chair, startling the valet.

One more hour without the eyes of the *ton* assessing him, finding him lacking, as they always had.

"Robert," he said to the young footman standing at attention near the door.

"Your Grace?"

He was narrower in the shoulders, but it would work.

"I need your coat, Robert."

The footman unbuttoned his coat and handed it over without so much as an eye twitch. Delaying the inevitable for an hour would also give James the chance to observe the ladies' arrival in anonymity.

"I won't be needing those waistcoats, Pershing," James said. "Not just yet."

*D*amn, *the coat was tight.*

James stood in line with the other footmen, hunching his shoulders to loosen the tug of the constricting wool.

Dalton ambled down the front steps. "Have you seen Harland?" James heard him ask Hughes.

The butler tilted his head in James's direction, unwilling to voice the unthinkable, unconscionable truth. That his master, James Edward Warren, seventh Duke of Harland, Marquess of Langdon, Earl of Guildford, Baron Warren and

Clyde, was, horror of horrors, standing in a line of servants garbed as a common footman.

Albeit a very tall, very irritable footman.

"What the . . ." Dalton walked over. "Is that you, Harland?"

James nodded. The idea of passing as a footman during his initial encounter with the ladies had seemed clever. In his chambers.

Dalton raised an eyebrow. "It *is* you. Damn near didn't recognize you without that pirate beard. You look like the old duke."

"I know," James spat, the old helpless hatred pressing on his chest. "But I'll never become him. I swear it."

Dalton raised a hand. "Of course not. Didn't mean to suggest it. What the devil are you wearing? Is it a prank?" He'd been James's accomplice at Cambridge on too many occasions to be startled.

James gestured to the row of carriages winding up the stately drive. "A woman never shows her true nature to a potential mate. I'll assess them incognito. Gather information about their suitability."

Dalton nodded. "Haven't changed, I see. Never been one to do anything the conventional way."

"I don't intend to change." James wiped a trickle of perspiration from his forehead. "This wasn't a good idea. Think I'll go inside and take off this coat."

"Too late."

The first carriage stopped, the Selby family

crest emblazoned with such a blinding amount of gold leaf that it left no doubt as to the occupants.

"I'll think of something to tell the ladies," Dalton whispered. He returned to the front steps.

Nothing for it but to continue the charade. James helped Lady Vivienne, eldest daughter of the Marquess of Selby, descend from the carriage.

Without a glance in his direction, she and her mother, the marchioness, glided toward the house, fastidiously lifting the hems of their cloaks, bonneted heads held high.

When the next carriage stopped, he helped a trim lady swathed head to toe in white velvet down the steps. When her small feet hit the earth, she stumbled and fell against his chest.

"My my, you *are* solid," she purred. "What have you been lifting?" Her gloved hand remained on his chest for several seconds and drifted suggestively lower.

"Lady Augusta," huffed her mother, Lady Gloucester, a stout woman in matching white velvet. "Come away this instant."

Lady Augusta sashayed off with a flirtatious glance over her shoulder.

Good Lord, she had a penchant for footmen. Not exactly sacrificial virgin material.

He'd asked Cumberford to round up a virtuous lot. Must have been some misunderstanding with that one.

Miss Tombs arrived in an ostentatious carriage with twice the normal number of postilions and footmen, the better to advertise the staggering wealth of her father, a baronet. She gazed up at War-bury Park's impressive expanse of sand-colored stone with determination in her aquamarine eyes. Then she smiled slyly, revealing two deep dimples on either cheek.

"Stop smiling, Alice," said her mother. "There are to be no games this time. No eccentricities. No ridiculous talk of frugivorousness."

Frugivorousness? James had no time to contemplate what that could mean, because he caught sight of a pair of blue eyes glinting from inside a carriage window.

At last. His serene saint, Lady Dorothea.

When James helped her down from her carriage, *he* was the one who nearly stumbled.

The pastel sketch artist hadn't captured her at all. There was absolutely nothing pious or prim about her.

An oval face with a slightly too-sharp chin. A nose that flirted with snub. Opulent honey curls visible beneath her bonnet.

She smiled, only a slight twitch, but it was enough to call attention to extravagantly curved lips that begged to be kissed. And those blue-gray eyes. They weren't innocent at all. Hell, they sparked with enough delicious wit to tempt a cleric to sin.

Maybe it was because he'd constructed such an elaborate fiction about her saintliness when he'd been in his cups, or maybe it had been far too long since a woman had warmed his bed. Whatever it was, her features had an off-kilter harmony that hit him with a physical force.

Blood rushed to body parts that signaled danger. This was supposed to be a business arrangement.

Practical.

*Bloodless.*

She would *not* do.

James nearly bundled her straight back into the carriage and shut the door.

Lady Dorothea glanced down, then tilted turbulent eyes up at him.

*Dark clouds rolling in. Wind from the north. Wooden planks pitching beneath his boots. Men shouting, alarm bells ringing.*

"You seem to be . . . holding my hand," she said.

Her throaty contralto thrilled all the way to the soles of his boots. It made him want to keep her talking so he could float away on that voice.

*Damn.* He dropped her tiny hand. "Begging your pardon, my lady. You . . . remind me of someone I once knew."

A slight frown wrinkled her brow. "I'm quite sure we've never met." Dismissing him with a curt nod, she stepped away. James found himself facing Countess Desmond, who harrumphed and gave him a quelling glare as she allowed herself to be helped to the ground.

James retreated into the line of footmen unloading the baggage. He swung one of Lady Dorothea's heavy trunks onto his shoulder.

*You thought timid society debutantes wouldn't*

*tempt you, you ass.* Mentally, he kicked himself for being so wrong. Dead wrong.

There was no room for unbridled lust in his carefully laid plans.

How many hours were left? Forty-six if Lady Dorothea stayed until Sunday evening. Less if he chose a wife quickly and sent the others home. But that would be unforgivably rude, even for an uncivilized lout like him.

Or . . . he could find a way to make her leave early.

Frighten her away.

Scandalize her so thoroughly that she fainted and had to be confined to a bed. In London. Far away from him.

Obviously, that was the only course of action. The footman's uniform would serve the purpose.

But he should have kept the pirate beard.


The rude footman caught Charlene's eye and winked.

*He knew.*

There was no other explanation for his insulting familiarities.

Charlene swallowed a lump of terror. It was all over. He must have seen her at the Pink Feather on one of the occasions when her mother had been too ill to play hostess and Charlene had been forced to assume the role. It was possible that a duke's footman might have been a customer. He could certainly pass for a nobleman.

But wouldn't she remember him? He was over six feet of solid muscle that wouldn't be easy to forget, with shoulders so wide that she would have suspected padding if his coat hadn't been so tight the seams were ready to split. No doubt all the parlor maids swooned over those shoulders.

He had the telltale bent nose of a tavern brawler. He wouldn't be easy to dissuade if he wanted to make life difficult for her.

Before he disappeared toward the back servant's entrance, he winked again, and this time the countess caught him.

"Well," exclaimed Lady Desmond. "Such impudence. I shall certainly have a private word with the duke about that footman."

"I would like to have a private word with that footman," Manon whispered from behind Charlene.

"I heard that, Blanchard!" said the countess.

"Lady Desmond, Lady Dorothea, welcome to Warbury Park." A tall man whose hair glowed copper in the afternoon sun bowed over Charlene's hand. The duke? Hadn't someone said his hair was black?

"Lord Dalton." The countess inclined her head. "Where is His Grace?"

"Feeling a touch indisposed at the moment, nothing to worry about, he'll be fine this evening."

"What a shame," said the countess. "Do tell him we are so pleased to be here on this auspicious occasion."

"Oh, I will." Lord Dalton grinned, his deep blue eyes full of devilry.

A dignified steward with a shiny bald patch at the back of his head ushered them into a cavernous entrance hall. Warbury Park was a blur of dark wood paneling, bloodthirsty hunting tapestries, and white plastered ceilings too high for mere mortals. This was the coliseum where four girls would fight to the death—their prize, a duke.

The mythological beasts worked in gold and crimson on the carpeting covering the stairs to the next floor jeered at her.

*Imposter. Fraud.*

How had she ever thought this could work? One glance and a footman could tell she was no lady.

The steward announced that Lady Desmond and Lady Dorothea would occupy the Jonquil Suite.

More oak-paneled walls, faraway white ceiling, and patterned canary-yellow silk stretched above a carved wood bed. The countess and Charlene had adjoining rooms separated by a large dressing room. Manon and the countess's dour lady's maid, Kincaid, were already here supervising the unpacking.

Charlene unhooked her velvet spencer and removed her bonnet. She'd only be in the way while the countess and her troops of maids and footmen ensured none of the fragile gowns had been damaged in transit.

She stared out of the narrow, diamond-mullioned windows at the emerald lawns flowing into thick oak woods bordered by skirts of bluebells and violets. Such peaceful vistas weren't meant for girls accustomed to the bustle and grit of Covent Garden.

What was she doing here? This was a Lady Dorothea room. A room for a girl who sipped chocolate for breakfast and had a new pair of slippers for every ball gown.

If the footman hadn't already voiced his suspicions, she might have a chance at bribing him. What would be the price for a footman's silence?

A low, husky voice startled her. "There you are. Thought you could escape from me? Not likely."

Charlene ran damp palms down the unfamiliar fine muslin of her skirts and turned around. The rude footman stood in her doorway, his arms and ankles crossed, a mocking grin quirking up one side of his finely molded lips.

*Remember, it's his word against yours. And you're Lady Dorothea.* She raised her chin and fixed him with a haughty stare. "Are you addressing me?"

He strode toward her.

No doubt those passionate, hooded green eyes turned the parlor maids to jelly, but they did nothing to her. She'd been towered over before. Propositioned. Assaulted. She was a fortified stronghold, immune to broad shoulders.

No romantic preambles for this one. He cupped her chin in his large hands and dragged a thumb across her lower lip. "The artist didn't do you justice." He stared into her eyes. "There's far more stormy gray than placid blue in your eyes."

Anger bloomed in her mind, strong and swift.

She jerked her head back, but he held her firmly. She met his gaze. "Kindly remove your hands or I'll—"

"Shhh . . . don't speak." He pressed his thumb against her lips, silencing her. "You're not going to stand on ceremony, are you? Pretend you don't know me?"

Charlene's heart thumped. "I *don't* know you. We've never met before."

He grinned. "Yes we have."

"You're mistaken. Now let me go."

"We've met," he insisted.

She shook her head. "That's impossible." *Please, please don't say you met me at the Pink Feather.*

He brushed a curl away from her cheek. "I meet you every night, angel face . . ."

Every night?

" . . . in my dreams," he finished.

Relief washed through her. He was only another man who saw her petite figure, yellow curls, and blue eyes and assumed she was a porcelain doll fashioned for his pleasure.

Looks could be deceiving.

His lips descended and hot breath fanned her cheek.

He was so huge, so male. She collected herself and straightened to her full height, which only brought her in eye contact with his angular jaw.

Charlene adopted the clipped, autocratic tones of the countess. "This is unacceptable. The duke will hear of this outrage. Now leave this instant."

"Ordering me about on my own estate?"

His estate? Now that was one liberty too far.

Charlene flexed on the balls of her heels, tensing for what came next. "If you don't leave this instant, I'll make you sorry."

He raised one brow. "And how would you do that? Step on my toes? Rap my knuckles?"

*That's it. This footman needs a lesson.* Charlene angled toward him and tilted her head, smiling coyly. "I have my ways. All that is required is a bit of this." She lifted onto her tiptoes and leaned forward.

He blinked. The men who tried to kiss her always did.

"And some of this." She ran a finger along the edge of his starched collar and found a strong grip.

"And then *this*." She turned her right hip into his thighs and stepped in, catching him off balance with a sweeping throw. *Harai Goshi*. The easiest way to incapacitate someone much bigger and stronger than oneself.

When they landed together on the carpet, she swiftly wrapped her arms around his neck, applying a basic collar choke, with enough pressure to reduce his air supply without cutting it off, crushing his face against her chest.

Unfortunately, he'd made quite a lot of noise crashing to the floor.

The countess appeared in the doorway, followed by Manon, who squeaked and clasped her hands to her heart.

The balding steward rushed into the room and

dropped to his knees. "Speak to me! Are you injured, Your Grace?"

Had he just said . . . ?

"Your Grace?" Charlene echoed.

"Guilty as charged," came the booming response, muffled by a mouthful of bosom and lace.

# Chapter 4

*Bugger and blast.*

Charlene leapt to her feet. A footman might be unusually tall, and possess piercing green eyes and the kind of angular jaw one could use to cut glass, but that bred-in-the-bone sense of entitlement? Pure duke. Why was he dressed as a servant? It was a dreadful trick to play on a girl.

Pretending to be someone else. Running about seducing people.

Exactly what *she* was doing.

*Blast it all to hell.*

The steward flapped his arms like an overwrought mother hen and helped the duke stand.

The countess was uncharacteristically rendered speechless.

"I do apologize, Your Grace. I had no idea. That is . . . I thought . . ." One probably didn't call attention to the fact that a duke was dressed as a footman.

She'd be lucky if he didn't clap her in prison. Rumpling a duke's collar and wrestling him to the floor had to be a capital offense.

"Well," Charlene said brightly, "we seem to

have commenced our acquaintance in rather an unconventional manner, Your Grace. Please allow me to apologize. I trust you have a whole room full of snowy linens? Excellent. Well then, we should keep unpacking, so lovely to have met—"

"Stop." His voice was deep and low and infused with such authority that she instinctively obeyed.

She'd been blathering. *Pull yourself together.* How would Lady Dorothea react in this situation?

Lady Dorothea would never have been in this situation.

"What the dickens *was* that, Lady Dorothea?" asked the duke.

"A . . . mistake?"

No one acknowledged her feeble attempt at humor.

Lady Desmond's eyes narrowed until they were icy blue slivers. However, like any seasoned military strategist, she recovered swiftly. "Gracious, the strange talents one learns abroad." She swatted Charlene's shoulder. "Lady Dorothea returned from a Roman tour mere days ago," she said, as if that explained everything.

The duke raised one perfectly arched, perfectly ducal eyebrow.

"Ah . . . yes." Charlene cleared her throat. "I was quite taken with the . . . ah . . . statues of ancient athletes." Think, *think.* "Some young ladies collect souvenirs or develop a taste for flavored ices, but I discovered a mad passion for . . ." She searched for a plausible explanation. " . . . Roman wrestling."

Not that plausible. She added several eyelash flutters and a nervous Lady Dorothea giggle for good measure.

"Roman wrestling?" The duke's eyebrow rose higher. But he hadn't ordered her head on a pike yet. That had to be a good sign.

"Roman wrestling." Charlene warmed to her fabrication. "All those ancient marble wrestlers locked in mortal combat. So thrilling! And I thought to myself, why, I would like to know how to do that. How useful such a talent could be if there were one perfect bonnet in a shop window and two ladies spied it at the same moment." She attempted to appear simultaneously crestfallen, contrite, and ready for combat.

"It's true," said the countess. "When she arrived back from Italy, Lady Dorothea nearly toppled *me* with her embrace. And the poor servants, they're positively black and blue. Isn't that right?" She turned to Manon.

The maid nodded enthusiastically. "Lady Dorothea tosses me around as if I were a sack of flour." She curtsied. "Your Grace."

The seams of the borrowed jacket strained and stretched as the duke crossed his arms. "I can understand how that might be possible, since you're of a height. But what I don't understand is how a tiny thing like you managed to overturn *me*."

"I'm sure it was pure luck, that's all."

The duke turned to his steward. "Bickford, kindly warn the other household staff about Lady Dorothea's *mad passion*."

"Of course."

"There's no need for that." The countess dug her fingernails into Charlene's forearm. "Lady Dorothea will be a perfect lamb from this moment forth."

Charlene nodded and mustered what she hoped was a suitably sheeplike expression.

The duke's lips twitched. "Somehow I very much doubt that's possible."

His gaze moved slowly from the tips of her white leather half boots, up her gown, to linger on her bodice, which was askew and showing far too much flesh.

Why wasn't he angry? The men she knew would have been furious. After all, she had thrown him to the floor. But no, he looked, well, *hungry*. There was no other word for it. Any moment now Bickford would tie a napkin around his master's neck and hand him a fork and knife to carve her up with.

As he continued his lazy perusal, warmth spread from her belly to her cheeks. She felt exposed, as if his large hands were exploring her instead of his gaze. This put the attempted kiss in an entirely new light. It was a hopeful sign, wasn't it?

So far she'd made a proper hash of being seductive. But now she knew he was the duke. She stared at him as well, her gaze boldly sweeping his frame.

Ink-black hair falling in waves above the nape of his neck. Shoulders like crossbeams. Strong and oak-hewn. Long, lean legs.

Wealth, privilege, and beauty. Life had to be so easy for him.

She wanted to flip him again and wipe that predatory smile off his face.

Instead she smiled and giggled softly, lowering her eyelashes. Charlene *never* giggled.

"Lady Dorothea, I trust you will refrain from assaulting my servants long enough to join me for dinner at half past seven," the duke said.

Charlene nodded in the graceful, demure way the countess had taught her, but the duke was already striding from the room with Bickford and the flock of footmen following in his wake.

When the door shut, there was an ominous silence.

Charlene prepared for the worst.

The countess advanced on her with fire-and-brimstone eyes. "That, my girl, was *the* most vulgar, the most *shocking* display I have ever witnessed." The countess punctuated each adjective with a menacing step. "It was crass, base, unseemly, and the only question now is . . ."

She stopped in front of Charlene and grasped her arms. "Can you do it again?"

"I'm terribly sorry, I . . ."

Wait. *What*? "Do it again?"

"Throw him to the floor. Reduce him to a helpless puddle. Can you repeat it? Or was it only a momentary talent?"

The rattling carriage wheels must have jarred something loose in the countess's head.

"Well?" The countess tapped one narrow, elegant foot.

"Yes, of course. But . . . why would I?"

"Because, my dear, this duke clearly prefers wolves to lambs. Blanchard, wouldn't you agree?"

Blanchard grinned. "Without a doubt, your ladyship. The duke, he is captivated. She has bowled him over." She smiled. "Quite literally."

"Indeed. A complete change of strategy is in order."

The two women exchanged glances, then nodded in military precision.

"The peach satin," said the countess. "But which jewels?"

"The topaz?"

"Too demure."

"The diamonds and seed pearls?"

"Pardon me." Charlene waved her hand in the air.

They ignored her and continued discussing jewelry options.

"Pardon me!"

They turned and stared as if they had completely forgotten her presence.

"You're not furious with me?"

The countess's brow wrinkled. "Furious? I should say not. I will admit there was a precarious moment or two, but I must say I underestimated you, my girl. The duke enjoys unconventionality to a degree I never suspected."

"It's just that he was dressed as a footman and made advances. I was defending myself."

"The duke was obviously taking advantage of the freedom the uniform afforded him to indulge his . . . baser instincts. I think this works to our advantage."

Charlene still didn't understand. "But *why* was he dressed as a footman?"

The countess waved her hand dismissively. "My girl, dukes may do whatever they please. If he told us to eat the paper hanging on these walls, we'd all start tearing off strips."

While the countess and Manon plotted, Charlene reflected that what could have been a disaster had transformed into a small victory. She'd catapulted a duke over her hip and placed him in a choke hold, and the countess had congratulated her.

How extraordinary.

Perhaps she could do this after all.

He hadn't seemed to mind her strength, and he'd stared, as if she was an intriguing challenge to unwrap and savor.

She was *intriguing*.

Charlene took smooth, lilting, future-duchess steps to the mahogany-framed oval mirror in the corner of the room and practiced smiling seductively.

She could captivate him.

It didn't matter if he made her heart sprint and her stomach somersault. She would never lose contact with the knowledge that she was Charlene.

Not the swooning type.

She would convince him that she was madly in love with him. It would only be an act.

She needed to find a quiet corner and practice her *katas*. The duke was an unusually large and heavily muscled man, not the portly peer she'd imagined. She needed to be in top form if she was required to throw him again.

Especially since he would no doubt be ready for her next time.

"**S**he tumbled me on my arse like a public house brawler," James said.

Dalton sprayed brandy on the library carpet. "We're speaking of Lady Dorothea? That diminutive thing?"

"The very one. Quite a grip on her. Arms like a sailor. Wouldn't be surprised if they were covered in ink tattoos." James rested his aching neck on the chair cushion. "You can stop laughing now."

"Can't. It's too droll. The great Goliath felled by a dainty David."

"I was trying to frighten her off. I thought since I was dressed as a footman, if I was unforgivably rude, she'd faint and be declared unwell and have to go back to London, or at least be confined to her chamber."

"And you did that, *why*?"

"I told you. I can't afford any distractions. I want a sensible wife, one that won't cause me any trouble. And Lady Dorothea is trouble. You can see the storm brewing in her eyes from twenty paces. One moment I was staring into those tempestuous eyes, and the next, *bam*! Flat on my back with her wrists locked around my neck and my feet kicking like I was hanging from a noose on Snow Hill."

It had been wholly unexpected, and inexplicably arousing.

"Clearly Lady Dorothea knows how to make an impression," drawled Dalton. "I've never noticed her before. Seems a quiet, nervous sort of girl."

"Said she'd developed a passion for Roman wrestling in Italy."

"Roman wrestling?"

"That's what she said. It's so implausible, it can only be true."

"D'you suppose we could persuade Lady Dorothea to wrestle Lady Augusta before she leaves? Just one round? I know gents who would pay a great deal to see that."

James reached over and punched Dalton's shoulder.

"Ouch. What was that for?" Dalton asked.

"This is a business arrangement. Not an erotic prizefight."

Land him on his arse. He'd teach her a lesson. Yes, that is exactly what he had to do. Charm and disarm her and then, *bam*! Flat on *her* back. See how *she* liked it.

Of course there would be a bed to catch them. And she'd be wearing a chemise and nothing more. Of the very thin, very transparent variety.

James clutched his forehead. *Absolutely not.* Business transaction. Rational. Bloodless.

Lady Dorothea was enigmatic, delectable, and completely distracting. More capable of inflicting further ruin than of salvaging his reputation. What if she went about pitching barristers?

Or wrestling matrons whose bonnets she disapproved of?

"Well, what of the other contenders?" Dalton asked. "What do you make of them?"

James checked the ladies off on his fingers. "Lady Augusta practically plastered herself to my chest."

"I saw that. She likes footmen, apparently."

"My future wife can't like footmen. Chaste. Biddable. That's what I need. Lady Vivienne sailed across the courtyard like the Queen of Sheba—she'd certainly silence the gossips. And Miss Tombs is quite promising." James drained his glass. "Those dimples are adorable."

But it wasn't Miss Tombs's dimples that plagued him.

He kept revisiting that oddly perfect moment as he drowned in Lady Dorothea's stormy gaze.

The moment right before she tumbled him arse over elbow.

*Get a hold of yourself.*

What kind of wife would she make? The dangerous kind. The kind that would never be content with a business arrangement. The kind that would want to change him, bend him to her purposes. He needed a pleasant wife, refined and subtle, attractive, but not outrageously so, someone to redeem his reputation and counterbalance his recklessness.

"Since I was unsuccessful in deterring Lady Dorothea, I'll ignore her the remainder of the visit," James announced.

Dalton smiled knowingly. "Hurt your pride, eh? Not every day a man is thrown by a little chit like that."

"My pride is *not* hurt. She's not the bride for me, that's all. I'll be living in the West Indies most of the time. I have to know my wife is living a staid, blameless existence."

He might not have been fit to be a duke, but he needed a wife fit to be a duchess. And duchesses did *not* practice Roman wrestling.

James swirled the brandy in his glass, remembering the feeling of being pressed against her soft bosom.

One gentle tug on that bodice and her breasts would have spilled into his mouth.

He groaned.

Lady Dorothea and her lush curves and lethal elbows had to go.

The sooner the better.

# Chapter 5

"Hold your breath," Manon urged.

Charlene sucked in her breath, and Manon attempted to button the back of the bodice again. Lucifer take Lady Dorothea and her sylph-like figure. Her gown wasn't going to fit Charlene. "I can't understand it, I've laced your stays as tightly as they will go," Manon said.

Charlene let out her breath. "It's not going to work. The bodice is too tight."

"No. It. Isn't." Manon shoved her knee into the small of Charlene's back. "Think slender thoughts. Imagine you are a dancer at the ballet, or a willow tree."

Willowy. She'd never been willowy. Even as a child.

"There," Manon crowed. "It is fastened."

"But I can't breathe."

"Good. Then maybe you will faint and the duke will have to carry you to your chamber." Manon turned her to face the mirror.

The evening gown was made of delicate peach silk with an embroidered lace net overlay. The puffed sleeves were caught up with ribbons and satin rosettes.

Charlene glanced down. Her breasts were pushed nearly to her chin. Lady Dorothea had to be considerably smaller on top.

Somehow this gown seemed more wanton than the red and purple silks the ladies at the Pink Feather flaunted. Something about the way the lace clung to the flesh-colored silk. As if she'd been naked underneath. Manon had liberally dampened Charlene's petticoats with rose-scented water so they clung to her, outlining her form.

Charlene always kept covered in serviceable gray cotton or worsted, discouraging the wrong attention from the wrong kind of men. Now here she was with her bosom spilling out and her limbs on display.

"Is this quite decent?" she asked.

The maid shrugged. "It is French. We know how to dress for men. The mounds on top, they will make the duke want to use you for his pillow."

*This is wrong.*

*No, no regrets.* A chance like this only came along once in a lifetime. If she had to mimic the girls at the Pink Feather, she would. She had to be alluring enough to win a marriage proposal from the duke.

*You are living on borrowed time, Charlene. Wearing borrowed dresses. Using a borrowed name.*

And a good thing, too. Despite the oil of roses and the fine silk, she was still Charlene.

Illegitimate. Raised in a bawdy house. Charlene.

No amount of expensive dusting powder could cover that.

Manon fastened a necklace of diamonds and seed pearls fashioned into a spray of flowers around Charlene's neck. It had to be worth a fortune.

"I'm liable to break this."

Manon laughed. "Don't worry, you won't. It's sturdier than it looks." She tucked peach tea roses and curling ostrich feathers into Charlene's upswept curls. A pair of exquisite, openwork gloves to cover hands that were far from milky white completed the transformation.

Charlene wasn't accustomed to wearing feathers. They drifted down and tickled her nose.

"The feathers are very suggestive, *non*?" asked Manon. "They sway and entice. They will draw the duke's eyes to you."

Charlene stared at the expensive lady in the mirror. "That's not me," she whispered.

"It is. You're ready to hunt a duke. Come." Manon drew her toward Lady Desmond's room.

The countess clutched both chair arms. "Astonishing. You could be Lady Dorothea."

For one brief moment, Charlene glimpsed a doting mother, soft with pride, but then the countess's face hardened into its habitual expression of untouchable grandeur. "She will do nicely. Well done, Blanchard."

Manon curtsied. "Thank you, your ladyship."

The countess turned to Charlene. "Remember, one hint of commoner and all is lost. Stay as silent as possible. Say nothing to Lady Augusta. She will try to bait you. She's a foolish, vindictive girl. Remain intent on the duke. Do not, on any account, eat anything. You need to reduce if you are to fit into the blush velvet tomorrow."

The countess floated from the room, still lecturing, and Charlene had to rush to keep up. She wasn't accustomed to satin slippers that laced around her ankles.

How was she supposed to seduce the duke if she couldn't speak, eat, or even walk?

It promised to be a wonderful evening.

They descended the stairs and crossed into the drawing room.

It was a foreign country. Great swathes of green and blue carpet spread before her like an uncharted sea. On the other side, the inhabitants perched on velvet sofas and sipped something amber out of slender glasses.

"The gilt ceiling was commissioned for King James I," whispered the countess in Charlene's ear, continuing her lessons as they approached the ladies. There was no sign of the duke or Lord Dalton.

All eyes turned to Charlene. They knew she was a stranger in their land. She couldn't do this. It would never work.

*Run away. Before they throw you in prison for trespassing.*

"Lady Dorothea, darling," cooed a gorgeous blonde whose smile didn't ascend to her frosty blue eyes. "I haven't seen you in simply *ages*. I hear you've been in Italy? Come, sit by me." She patted the sofa next to her.

"Careful, that's Lady Augusta," the countess whispered urgently in Charlene's ear, giving her a shove forward.

*Lady Augusta. Reigning beauty of the* ton *but unmarried after three seasons. Family's becoming desperate.* Charlene recited the countess's lessons in her mind. *She's Lady Dorothea's rival. Use extreme caution.*

"My heavens." Lady Augusta stared at Charlene's bosom as she sat down. "How the sea air agreed with you. Why, you are positively *bursting* with health. Isn't that so, Mama?"

Lady Gloucester, Lady Augusta's overly feathered and bejeweled mama, used a quizzing glass to stare at Charlene's bounteous cleavage. She sniffed disapprovingly.

*Silly woman. Former opera singer. Married scandalously above her station.*

Lady Augusta put her arm around Charlene's waist. "Do tell us about your Roman tour. It appears you sampled much of the cuisine."

Charlene added *spiteful witch* to Lady Augusta's description.

"Do tell us all about it," said a girl with deep dimples, unusual, pale blue-green eyes, and light brown hair. "I long to travel."

"Hush, Miss Tombs. Better to stay by hearth and home, I always say," said Lady Tombs.

What had the countess said about Lady Tombs? *A grasping social climber who married a wealthy baronet.*

Miss Tombs smiled, and the genuine warmth in her eyes bolstered Charlene's courage.

"If I couldn't visit Paris at least once a year, I'd simply die," yawned a willowy brunette, who had to be Lady Vivienne. She'd certainly never had to think a thin thought in her life. "Thank goodness that silly war is over."

"I couldn't agree more, Lady Vivienne," said her mother, the Marchioness of Selby, who was equally brunette and willowy. "One simply cannot find the same quality here in England. No, it is Paris for modistes, and Switzerland for spas. You really should try a spa, Lady Tombs. I know a charming one in Baden. It would *vastly* improve your complexion."

"Well," huffed Lady Tombs.

Thinly veiled insults volleyed back and forth, requiring nothing more than a nod from Charlene.

They weren't so different from the girls she knew. Measuring themselves against one another, vying to be purchased, protected. How did the sanctity of marriage make it any less objectionable? The lady the duke purchased would be owned just as fully and cast aside just as easily if he tired of her or if she didn't produce an heir.

Charlene would never give herself to a man— for money or for a marriage contract—because it was the same the world over, on the most respectable streets or in the worst hellhole. Men rutting to make themselves feel powerful. Girls pretending to smile, pretending to laugh, feeding egos that craved dominion and control.

She would never be owned. She was here to earn freedom for herself, her sister, and her friends at the Pink Feather.

She mustn't relax her guard for even one moment.

She glanced longingly at a tray heaped with frosted biscuits. Lady Desmond's eyes flashed the *don't you dare* warning. She hadn't said anything about not drinking, though. Charlene accepted one of the dainty glasses from a servant. The drink was sweet and left an almond taste in her mouth.

She could only take shallow breaths in the constricting bodice, which made her feel light-headed.

Kyuzo's training had prepared her to throw men twice her size and maintain mental serenity during a physical attack.

It had done nothing to steel her against the dangers of an empty stomach and an overly constrictive bodice.


Lady Dorothea's clothing was as provoking as her wrestling maneuvers.

Her peach silk gown was covered in lace that cleverly suggested she was wreathed in clinging cobwebs and all James had to do was brush them away to reach warm, naked flesh.

She was seated halfway down the sixteen-foot-long dining room table.

Not far enough.

James turned to his left to avoid the cobwebs and was nearly blinded by one of Lady Augusta's floating feathers. Had it really been his idea to invite eight females to dine? There was enough waving plumage to stuff a feather bed.

Lady Selby, seated at the far end of the table as the ranking female in the absence of relatives, stared down her severe nose.

"I must say, Your Grace, I'm surprised to find there are no other gentlemen here this evening." Her cultured tones cut across the room like a knife. "I've always said that one must have an equal number of ladies and gentlemen so that the conversation may be sufficiently varied."

"I provided Lord Dalton. He should serve as well as a dozen."

Dalton turned to the marchioness, employing the full force of his dark blue eyes and cleft chin. "Is that a new brooch, Lady Selby? So fetching. It sets off your eyes to perfection."

"Humph," said the marchioness, but her expression softened and a spark appeared in her eye.

"I know several eminent gentlemen with nearby estates," offered Lady Gloucester. "Lord Grant, for example."

Lady Dorothea made a strangled noise.

"He's only recently returned from his estate in Scotland," continued Lady Gloucester. "Yesterday he made a sizable donation to the Gloucester Female Asylum, my charitable institution for the maintenance and education of indigent young girls, after Lady Augusta and I conducted a tour of the premises."

Lady Dorothea coughed into her napkin.

"Do you know Lord Grant, Lady Dorothea?" asked Lady Gloucester.

"I wouldn't let him near a young g—" Lady Dorothea winced and sucked in her breath as if someone had kicked her under the table. Someone wearing purple velvet and answering to the title Lady Desmond. "That is . . ." She pasted a smile on her face. "Only in passing. I only know him in passing."

What had she been about to say?

Lady Augusta caught the duke's eye and smiled. "Are you a patron of charitable concerns, Your Grace?"

"Not in England."

"Then you'll have to visit our asylum. Your heart will be moved to generosity like so many before you. The girls are models of pious docility."

When she said the word *heart,* she clasped both hands to her bosom, no doubt with the hope of drawing his gaze. Her ivory gown was nearly as revealing as Lady Dorothea's. There was no denying she was pretty, but her cornflower blue eyes and ample curves left him unmoved.

He nodded noncommittally and continued attacking his stewed pigeon, avoiding the enticing fare displayed farther down the table. Lady Dorothea's bodice appeared entirely too small to contain her sumptuous breasts.

In fact, she appeared to be one deep breath away from disaster.

He could only hope the fabric held, or he might be forced to throw her over his shoulder and carry her to the nearest bed, which wouldn't lead to a prudent and passionless marriage.

"I do find the country so charming this time of year," said Lady Vivienne. "The leaves will turn soon, so picturesque." She was wearing a cool silver silk that set off her sophisticated beauty. Her bodice was quite reserved by comparison with the others. Quite duchess-like.

"The oaks are splendid at our estate in Somerset," commented Miss Tombs. "They march along as far as the eye can see, cloaked in vermillion and gold." She stared at the wall, clearly far away from the dining room.

The ladies moved from oak trees, to pheasant hunting, to the possibility of an unseasonable frost, while James grew ever more uncomfortable.

The walls seemed to be closing in on him, and the ladies' mingled floral scents were giving him a headache. How many excruciating dinners had he endured in this room when he'd been old enough to dine with his parents? The old duke had loved to hear himself talk. They'd been expected to endure his rants in silence.

When James was older, meals became full-scale wars, James playing the provocateur, the rebel, to anger his father, and William caught in the cross fire.

"I've no idea how you could have stayed away from England so long, Your Grace," the marchioness said. "The society can't have been as congenial in the West Indies. Was there even a season?"

"I loathe the season."

The shock and dismay on their faces was comical.

They began talking over each other.

"Loathe the season, why, how can that be?"

"What could you possibly find objectionable about such a venerable tradition?"

"The exhibitions, the races, the balls . . ."

Dalton grinned, clearly enjoying the spectacle. "Really, old boy," he added his voice to the mix. "Never say you don't like the *season*. That's positively unpatriotic."

James nodded at the sideboard, and Robert leapt to attention. He had several bottles of aged French claret decanting on the sideboard.

Once James had a fortifying glass of wine in his hand, he interrupted the still-dithering ladies. "I detest it because of the preening, the prancing, the fatuous courtship rituals. Men hopping about in peacock-colored waistcoats. Debutantes displaying themselves for the highest bidder."

Lady Dorothea tossed her head. "I see. You'd rather lure prospective mates to your home and audition us like a theatrical chorus. Why not simply hire an auctioneer? Put us on display? Dispense with any pretense of civility?"

She winced again.

"Precisely, Lady Dorothea. Why prevaricate?" he answered. "I'm dispensing with the hypocrisy. Everyone knows why young ladies attend balls. This occasion is no different."

"It is *vastly* different," sputtered Lady Tombs. "My daughter would never be in a theatrical chorus."

She stared around the table challengingly, daring someone to contradict her.

Dalton chuckled. If James had been able to reach him, he would have kicked *him* under the table. He wasn't helping matters.

"Tell us about the improvements you've made to Warbury Park, Your Grace." Lady Desmond made an attempt to steer the conversation along safer lines. "I hear you've modernized the kitchens?"

"Yes, tell us about the kitchens!" enthused dimpled Miss Tombs. "One must be ever so careful these days. I hope your housekeeper supervises the preparation of your breads? Especially the rye? I never eat bread myself, not after reading the fascinating writing of the learned Dr. Thuillier. You see, the grains could be simply riddled with *Claviceps purpurea*. I have no wish to see my skin peeling off in a slow, loathsome rot. Well, would you?"

There really was no answer to that.

He was saved by the arrival of Josefa carrying a gleaming silver tray heaped with the beginning of the second course—beef prepared with his favorite fragrant brown sauce. She glared at poor Robert, who had rushed to take the tray, and wasn't satisfied until she had safely placed her masterpiece in front of James.

He smiled and reached for her weathered hand. "Allow me to present Mrs. Mendoza, my cook." Instead of curtsying, she merely nodded, openly appraising the ladies one by one.

There was a scandalized silence.

"Pleased to meet you, Mrs. Mendoza," Lady Dorothea finally said.

Josefa studied Lady Dorothea. "Such a beauty," she said in her thick Spanish accent. She turned to James. "*Hermosa*, no?"

Dalton winked at Josefa. "Señora, you are the most charming of all."

Josefa wagged her finger at Dalton. "You naughty boy." She turned back to Lady Dorothea. "Your father, he is a very important man?"

Lady Dorothea's brow puckered. "Ah . . . yes."

Josefa gave an approving nod. "Good. I like this one. She has manners."

"Good gracious," exclaimed Lady Desmond, not bothering to hide her astonishment.

James choked back a guffaw. If they knew the truth there would be a true uproar.

Josefa was only posing as his cook. In reality she was his business associate, and she had a vested interest in James finding a well-connected bride.

"I hope you enjoy the beef, ladies," Josefa said. She inclined her head toward the footmen. "*Bueno*, you may serve." She walked out of the room, the dark brown chignon of hair twisted on top of her head held as regally high as the marchioness's feathers.

Dalton caught James's eye, a wide grin on his face.

"My goodness," said Lady Gloucester. "What a *singular* person."

James could envision the ladies recounting the

ordeal of Dinner with His Disgrace over tea with their friends when they returned to London.

*Oh la, you'll never believe what he did next. He introduced his cook to us at the table. And she didn't even curtsy. I could have just died. . .*

"I've never in all my life been introduced to a cook while dining," said the marchioness. "And what on earth is this sauce? It's quite pungent."

The ladies pushed the beef around on their plates.

Lady Vivienne took a small bite and immediately brought her napkin to her lips to camouflage a bout of coughing. "Whatever is this flavored with?"

"I believe it has red chili peppers, anise, some coriander. And powdered cocoa beans. Rumor has it the Aztec people served a similar dish to Cortez when he arrived to conquer them, thinking he was a god."

"Cocoa? You mean the cocoa we drink?" Lady Augusta eyed her plate with more interest. "I never thought it could be used in a sauce."

"Some contend that one ounce of cocoa contains as much nourishment as one pound of beef. Man could subsist on chocolate alone if he had to," James said.

"You have opened a cocoa manufactory, as I understand." Lady Vivienne smiled smugly. She'd prepared.

"A small one. Not far from here, near Guildford. I'm modifying Banbury Hall."

The marchioness raised an eyebrow. "Surely you have no need to engage in trade."

"Need, no, but passion. I dream of Parliament lowering import duty taxes on cocoa beans grown on farms that use no slave labor."

Josefa's family owned just such a farm in the remote coastal village of Chuao, in the country of Venezuela and James was her primary investor.

Lady Dorothea smiled approvingly. "That's a wonderful idea."

"If import taxes are lowered, and better production methods discovered, everyone will be able to afford the nourishment and pleasure of drinking chocolate." He waved a hand through the air. "Chocolate for the masses."

"Admirable, I'm sure." It was evident that Lady Vivienne thought it was anything but admirable that he advocated for something as plebeian-sounding as *chocolate for the masses*.

Lady Dorothea took a small taste of sauce. A blissful smile tilted up the edges of her delectable mouth.

The other ladies fanned themselves with their napkins.

"Have a sip of wine, ladies. I know it's not customary for you to drink, but you'll find it perfectly complements the sauce and takes some of the spice away."

"Our family never partakes of spirits," announced Lady Tombs. " 'For he shall separate himself from wine and strong drink,' " she intoned. " 'And shall drink no vinegar of wine, or vinegar of strong drink, neither shall he drink any liquor of grapes, nor eat moist grapes, or dried.' "

Miss Tombs winced. "I've always wanted to see

Italy, but really, have you heard how they make wine there? They step on it with their feet." She smiled brightly. "Their *feet*. Do you know what manner of deformities may be contracted from feet? Why, only *Verruca vulgaris,* that's what!"

At their blank looks she added, "That's Latin for 'warts.' My cousin Adeline has one on the side of her nose, poor thing."

"Alice," her mother hissed.

*Lord. Save him from this dinner.*

Lady Dorothea raised her glass to the Tombs ladies. " 'Come, come, good wine is a good familiar creature, if it be well used: exclaim no more against it.' " She took a healthy swallow. "Mr. Shakespeare."

Dalton clapped. "Bravo, Lady Dorothea. Well said."

James had to agree. Hell, she had more wit and fire than all the other ladies combined.

She lifted her wineglass to Dalton, and when she lowered it, her bodice slipped even lower. James held his breath, mesmerized by the swell of her creamy breasts.

The thin scrap of silk held.

His control was wearing dangerously thin.

# Chapter 6

The duke stared at her with intense, forbidding green eyes.

Charlene hoped he wasn't playing *one-of-these-ladies-is-not-like-the-others*. She was trying to blend in with the others, but every time she opened her mouth, the countess kicked her under the table.

Between ankle jabs from the countess and being forced to forego a mountain of mouthwatering delicacies, Charlene was in her own private hell. The gown was too tight only in the bodice. Couldn't she eat just a bit?

She sighed as the deliciously spiced beef was removed from the table only half finished.

What a crime.

It had been a very near thing with Grant. If the duke had invited his neighbor to dine, it would have been disastrous. Fooling an empty-headed ninny like Lady Augusta was one thing. Outwitting a treacherous adversary who knew her as Charlene would have been nearly impossible.

She drained her wine, remembering the feel of the baron's hand clamped around her neck, the gleam of lust in his hard eyes.

Her glass was immediately refilled, despite the countess's frantic signals. None of the other girls drank their wine, but Charlene didn't care. It made her feel reckless and daring. Perfectly capable of entrancing a whole army of dukes.

"I'm fond of wine mulled with lemon and nutmeg," said Lady Augusta in her breathy, little-girl voice. "Mama is forever telling me to pace myself." She fluttered thick, curled lashes. "Sometimes I just can't say no, I'm afraid."

That silky wheat-colored hair, those pouty berry-red lips and enormous lake-blue eyes. It really wasn't fair. Lady Augusta was too gorgeous, and well aware of the fact. She narrowed her eyes at Charlene in the polite equivalent of a tigress unsheathing her claws.

"Lady Dorothea, dear," she simpered. "Remember when you drank too much ratafia at your coming out? Lud, I thought you would die of mortification when you cast your accounts all over Lady Beckinsale's gold silk in the lady's retiring room."

Had that truly happened to Lady Dorothea? Poor thing. Charlene gripped her fork and contemplated sinking it straight between Lady Augusta's perfectly proportioned breasts.

Instead, she smiled sweetly. "How could I forget? But wasn't that also the night you were found on the balcony with a *certain someone*? You'd lost a button as I recall? Had it gone down your bodice?"

Lady Augusta's cheeks flamed scarlet. "I never!"

she exclaimed. "I declare, what has come over you? You never used to put more than two words together."

"Ladies, please," warned the marchioness. "This is most unbecoming." She fixed each of them with a censorious stare.

The duke stared as well. His hot gaze made Charlene conscious of every movement she made, every breath she took.

"Lord Dalton, I hear you plan to race in the Gold Cup next June," said Lady Vivienne. "Will it be Anticipation or Sir Marmalade?"

The conversation turned to racehorses, a subject of which Charlene knew nothing, thereby leaving her to her thoughts.

The duke didn't seem to be swallowing Lady Augusta's half-naïve, half-temptress bait. And Miss Doom and Gloom Tombs didn't appear to be employing any strategy whatsoever. It was strange how she sounded quite normal until she said anything to the duke, and then words like *warts* and *loathsome rot* erupted.

Maybe she had nervous attacks, like Lady Dorothea.

Lady Vivienne played her cards to her chest, gambling on the appeal of the alluring lady of mystery.

None of these girls needed him the way she did. They battled for prestige, glory, the thrill of being called "Her Grace." Charlene was fighting for freedom, her sister's innocence, her mother's health. She couldn't fail.

Before tonight, she'd thought there was only one kind of nobleman. The domineering, imperious kind, who made the whole world dance to his whims with a firm hand on the reins.

But this duke was far more complicated.

His hands were large, with ragged nails and visible calluses on the fingertips and palms, as if he gripped his reins without gloves. She pictured those hands gripping *her*. Urging *her* to a gallop.

Now where had *that* thought come from?

It had to be the wine. She wasn't accustomed to drinking anything stronger than an occasional sip of watered-down cordial.

He was unconventional. He didn't follow any of the rules the countess had enumerated. He had his elbows on the table, and he'd introduced a servant to them at dinner.

That had been rather sweet, actually.

Although *sweet* wasn't the word that usually came to mind when she thought of him.

Formidable.

Elemental.

The outdoors followed him inside in the pine-needle green of his eyes, the strong oak of his shoulders.

He was ill at ease crammed into a chair in a dining hall. He kept drumming his fingers on the tabletop and tapping his foot on the carpet, restless and ready to be in motion again.

So different from his languid friend, Lord Dalton, who exuded the allure of a choirboy gone astray, with his golden hair, classical profile, and wolfish grin.

Lord Dalton didn't make her think about being *gripped*, though.

The duke slid his wineglass slowly over the sharp contours of his jaw and stared at Charlene with feral intensity.

She lifted her chin, held his gaze, and wriggled her shoulders the tiniest little bit. Her bodice shifted dangerously lower.

A muscle twitched in his jaw.

Kyuzo had taught her that all adversaries had weaknesses. He'd also taught her not to let fear control her mind.

Feminine voices rose and fell, exclaimed and giggled.

Charlene tilted her head, imagining how she would seduce this duke when they were finally alone.

Unknot the cravat, undo the buttons, slide off the coat. Taut flesh beneath her questing fingers. Tightly leashed power. A man in complete control of his body, so aware of his own appeal he expected women to fight over him.

Her breath quickened.

She lifted her wineglass, took a small sip, and deliberately missed her mouth.

Ruby droplets slid down her chin and between her breasts. She dabbed with her napkin, quickly catching the drops before they stained the expensive gown, the soft pressure making her breasts strain against the thin silk.

The duke's hand tightened around his glass until she thought the stem would break.

He rose in a clatter of tableware and scraping

chair legs. "This meal is finished," he announced, and strode out of the room.

Servants rushed forward to clear plates, and ladies exchanged shocked glances.

"His Disgrace has spoken, ladies." Lord Dalton gave them a crooked smile. "You'll have to forgive him. He's grown unaccustomed to polite company." He rose and offered his arm to Lady Selby. "Allow me to escort you to the drawing room."

**D**amn these cutaway tailcoats and skintight pantaloons.

A man couldn't have a cockstand without becoming a circus attraction. James had sat at the table, waiting for his *situation* to subside before he called an end to the interminable meal.

A woman hadn't affected him this way in . . . ever. Certainly never a young, inexperienced one.

He preferred his bedmates older and more experienced. During his travels there had been a very inventive widow in France. An opera singer with magnificent . . . *lungs* . . . in Florence. A lovely actress in Trinidad. Women who understood the rules of the game and played for their own pleasure. For the heated glances, the chase, the sublime moment of consummation. Maidens were too much trouble. They didn't understand the rules of the game.

But something about Lady Dorothea obliterated his control and changed all the rules. The way she wreaked havoc with his sangfroid screamed of peril.

He should stay away from her. Choose Lady Vivienne or Miss Tombs and be done with this nonsense. Then he could head straight to London and into the arms of some luscious little feather-head of an actress whose only mystery was how she ever managed to memorize her lines.

Lady Dorothea was too much of an enigma—throwing him to the floor one moment, playing the brazen coquette the next. He didn't need a complicated maze that ended in hazardous distraction.

He should go chop some wood. Drink a bottle of brandy.

Anything to take his mind off blue-gray eyes tinged with the threat of stormy seas.

Dalton poked his head in the study door. "You're being unforgivably rude, you know. Come back and apologize. Their feathers are all ruffled."

James sighed. "I'm too accustomed to living in the forest. I've lost the taste for inane chatter. I should choose Miss Tombs and be done with it. At least she'd keep my home spotlessly clean. What was I thinking? I should have had Cumberford choose me a bride. There are far too many females in this house. I can't think."

It had been wrong to invite them here to compete for him. As Lady Dorothea had so helpfully pointed out to the entire table.

James ripped the cork out of a bottle of cognac with his teeth and took a swallow.

"Four ladies. Three days. How bad can it be?" Dalton mimicked James's deep voice.

"Very funny."

"Why not Lady Vivienne?"

"If I listen to my head, I choose her. But other parts . . ."

"Prefer Lady Dorothea."

"Is it that obvious?"

Dalton lit a cigar with a stick from the fire. "Afraid so."

"Hellfire." James sighed again. "How did this happen? This is supposed to be rational. Bloodless."

"Got her hooks into you, does she?"

"These are innocent debutantes, Dalton, not courtesans."

"You'd be surprised. The last lady standing becomes a duchess. I'd wager they're willing to fight dirty. You'd better keep your door locked at night, or you might have a debutante bent on ruin slipping into your bed. Trust me on this one." He paused and tilted his head. "Come to think of it, can we secretly exchange bedchambers? I would be delighted to sacrifice myself in your stead."

"You really think they would sink to that?"

"Absolutely. They're out for blood. You heard Lady Dorothea and Lady Augusta bickering at dinner."

"You might have your erotic prizefight after all."

Dalton grabbed the bottle. "Why don't you send them all home and round up a new batch next year?"

"I have to see this through. If you hadn't noticed, I brought a child with me from Trinidad. Flor's had a difficult life. I had hoped I might find a wife willing to accept my bastard and provide her some guidance and protection."

"Isn't that what the governess is for?"

"Governesses are a tedious lot. Flor's dispatched two already. She needs a mother. Someone to smooth her way in society. When I return to Trinidad, I'll stay for at least a year." He had no idea how to raise a young girl. Especially a rebellious one who reminded him so much of himself at her age.

They passed the bottle back and forth.

"What about you?" James asked. "Doesn't your family want you to marry?"

"Of course. My mother would like nothing better, but I can't. I have my reasons." His face darkened. "I prefer the faro tables at Brooks's. Blissfully free of husband-hunting females."

"Are you happy?" James asked. "Playing the indolent rake?"

Dalton put his chin on his fist and stared into the flames, his blue eyes filled with shadows. "I'm on a leash with a narrow circumference, old friend. The club, the tailor, the occasional accommodating widow, back to the club. You're doing the right thing leaving it all behind." Dalton shook his head, as if to clear his thoughts. "Enough about me. You have a salon full of females to entertain."

"Wouldn't want to disappoint them. I'll have to do something even more shocking. Give them a titillating tale to tell."

"That's the spirit! You do know they're placing wagers at the club?"

"On what?"

"*This.* His Disgrace's Bride Hunt. Odds are favoring Lady Augusta, since she's the only famous beauty. I sent a note placing my wager today. I have intimate information, you know."

"And?" James prompted. "Who did you choose?"

"I've got three hundred on Lady Dorothea."

James swallowed too quickly and coughed. "You're going to lose that wager."

Dalton smiled slyly. "I don't think so."

# Chapter 7

"**W**hat do you think he'll do next?" Miss Tombs whispered to Charlene. "He's dressed as a footman, served us outlandish food, and curtailed the meal in a wonderfully unconventional manner." Her dimples deepened. "Isn't this fun?"

Charlene smiled and nodded, only to be polite. This wasn't fun. This was war.

And she was an armored citadel.

The duke was playing games, trying to shock them, catch them off guard. Or maybe he was sending them a warning. That was more plausible. He was taking pains to prove unequivocally that he would never be a solicitous husband, that the ladies could only hope for abandonment at worst and eccentricity at best.

Miss Tombs settled onto the couch beside Charlene. "You were superb at dinner. What a performance!"

What did she mean by performance? Charlene searched her face, but her smile was open, friendly, with no malice.

People saw what they expected to see, just like the countess kept telling her. "Thank you, Miss Tombs. And you were . . . charming."

"Oh, please call me Alice! And there's no need to lie," she said cheerfully. "I know I'm hopeless. Nothing to be done. That's just me."

Sighing heavily, deep in conversation with Lady Gloucester, Lady Tombs surveyed her daughter from across the room. The mothers had gravitated to one side of the room, while Lady Vivienne and Lady Augusta were talking to each other nearby.

"Drives poor Mama absolutely insane," Alice whispered in Charlene's ear.

Charlene couldn't decide when Alice was being serious. She seemed so intelligent but obviously had no idea how to attract a male. She had light brown hair and lithe curves, but her pale, aquamarine eyes that danced between green and blue made her truly alluring. It was lucky she didn't seem interested in landing the duke.

"You might try speaking of more . . . ordinary topics," Charlene said.

"Oh, you mean like the weather? Or horses?"

"Exactly."

Alice smiled. "It's very magnanimous of you to help me. I'll try, I promise."

Why had Charlene emptied so many glasses of wine? Her head was fuzzy.

As if on cue, a footman offered her a glass of something orange colored that smelled like Christmas pudding. Alice declined, but Charlene took a glass.

"I thought you were delightfully saucy. I'm sure I saw the duke gazing at you admiringly," Alice said.

Lady Vivienne sank back against the sofa cushions, one elegant, long-fingered hand sweeping through the air. "He does seem rather unhinged," Charlene heard her say.

"Uncivilized," agreed Lady Augusta. "Those arms. So unfashionably muscled. Like a dockworker. I'll wager he could lift me with only one of them. I hear he's a heartless rake. Do you know, Lady Caroline told me . . ." She dipped her head, speaking too low for Charlene to catch the words.

The subject of their conversation entered the room, followed by Lord Dalton. The duke positioned himself on a velvet-cushioned stool in the very center of the drawing room, as if he'd been posing for an art class and they'd been meant to sketch him.

He shrugged out of his tailcoat and flung it to a footman.

There was an audible ripple of interest from the girls, and protest from the mothers.

Then he began unfastening his cuffs.

First one.

Then the other.

Alice caught Charlene's eye and leaned in to whisper. "See? What did I tell you?"

He rolled up his sleeves, deliberately flouting all drawing room conventions. One's host wasn't supposed to strip himself after dinner, exposing heavily muscled and sun-darkened forearms.

You could have heard a pin drop across the room.

He sat on the stool with legs akimbo, spine

straight, shoulders firm, so commanding and in control. Everything female and inebriated in Charlene awoke. But she wasn't the swooning type. And her heart never palpitated or even fluttered.

Except right now she couldn't catch her breath, and her heart galloped against her rib cage.

*Brace yourself, Charlene. You have strong defenses. You are no man's doxy.*

"Ladies," said the duke, "I pray you will forgive my incivility. I have been too long in the company of rough men. Allow me to play for you."

He cradled the guitar against his body, his fingers traveled over the strings and teased the tuning pegs into alignment.

"I give you a Spanish fandango. A courtship dance I learned to play during my travels through Andalusia."

There was a dizzy crescendo of notes and then the rhythm began, slow and steady. A foreign cadence, highlighted by lilting, tremulous grace notes. He drilled the strings for emphasis, slapping the heel of his hand against the guitar, making it sing and click like the sound of heels striking a polished floor.

With rolled-up shirtsleeves and that thick, dark hair falling into his eyes, the duke was unlike any other nobleman she'd met. There was nothing smooth or polished about him. He sat with his legs spread wide, bracing the guitar on one bent knee.

*This must be how he got his calluses and ragged fin-*

*gernails*, Charlene reflected as she watched him striking the strings. He played with abandon, not caring what they thought. His fingers shook the guitar neck, then gently caressed the strings.

The rhythm grew faster, more frenzied, he attacked the strings, his hair falling into his eyes. The visibility of his emotions startled her. He grimaced and sighed, lost in the music. The melody vibrated into her. Invaded her. It was sad and euphoric all at once.

For this one moment she forgot why she was here and simply let herself feel the music.

*I am a man and you are a woman,* the strings sang. *This is our dance. There is no shame. No sin. Follow my lead, let me guide you. Here are the steps, move with me.*

The other ladies were rapt, leaning forward in their seats, lips parted.

The music was fierce and demanding one moment, heart-achingly melancholy the next.

Charlene imagined his fingers caressing her, coaxing sighs from her lips.

The song came crashing to an end, and a wooden clicking sound drew their eyes to the drawing room doorway.

A child stood, framed for effect, her hands raised to one side. The duke raised his head, nodded at the girl, and began a new song.

She couldn't have been more than six or seven years old. Her abundant black hair was caught into a graceful chignon at the side of her neck and decorated with a red rose. Her skin was a soft shade of brown. She was wrapped in a red silk scarf with a long fringe that brushed the carpet.

She swayed in time to the music, her little red slippers tapping the floor as she twirled into the room, a bright smile on her face as she wove between the furniture and reached the duke.

She raised her arms into the air, and Charlene saw she held hollow wooden discs in her fingers, tied to her thumbs with red silk cords. She rapped them together in time to the music, and their clattering served as a sharp counterpoint to the duke's strumming.

The pair moved in perfect synchronicity, her feet and his fingers performing an intricate conversation of taps and runs. She flung her hands up into the air and twirled her wrists gracefully, whirling and clicking.

Who was this child, and why was he playing for her so sweetly?

As the dance ended, the little girl plucked the red rose from her hair and offered it to Lady Augusta with a pretty curtsy.

Lady Augusta giggled. Her mother stared piercingly at the duke, as if by sheer dint of will she could transform him from a guitar-playing, shirt-sleeve-rolling disgrace into a cricket-playing, properly buttoned peer of the realm.

Lady Augusta patted the girl's cheek.

Lady Selby raised her quizzing glass. "My, what an enchanting child. Whose is she, Your Grace?"

"I am Flor Maria," the girl lisped with a heavy foreign accent. "Who are *you*?"

"Flor," the duke said warningly.

Charlene suppressed a smile.

"Gracious." The marchioness lowered her glass. "Such manners."

"Flor is a very nice name," Charlene said.

The girl nodded. "My mama named me Flor. She is with the *ángeles* now. Do angels dance, do you think? They must dance. For if they do not, Mama will not be happy in heaven."

"You're a wonderful dancer," said Charlene.

"I can teach you how to dance, and how to use the *castañuelas*." Flor held the wooden discs toward Charlene.

The duke winked at Charlene. "Lady Dorothea may not be able to learn a fandango."

Flor stared intently. "She is quite fair haired, but I think I could teach her."

Lord Dalton grinned. "What about Lady Vivienne?" He gestured to the brunette.

Flor turned to Lady Vivienne. "Certainly. You shall begin your lessons tomorrow," she said to Lady Vivienne and Charlene. "You may begin by practicing your toe taps. Toe first, heel second. Like this." She demonstrated. "Toe then heel."

Lady Vivienne was obviously unaccustomed to taking orders from six-year-olds and didn't know how to respond.

Charlene nodded solemnly. "I promise to practice."

"Really, whose child is she?" persisted the marchioness. "One of your servants, perhaps?"

The duke placed a hand on Flor's head. "She's mine."

The marchioness dropped her quizzing glass

and it swung from a chain around her neck. "Yours?"

Lady Desmond gaped at the duke. "You were married abroad?"

The duke gripped the neck of the guitar. "I was not."

There were gasps and murmurs from the ladies.

Now that he said it, Charlene saw the resemblance. The clear green of the girl's eyes, the determined lines of her jaw.

He acknowledged his foreign, illegitimate daughter. The unwanted, unacknowledged child inside Charlene wanted to stand up and shout, *Hurrah!*

"This is not a suitable topic for the young ladies. Please remove the child from our presence, Your Grace." Lady Selby lifted her chin in the air haughtily.

Flor looked up at her father with questioning eyes, sensing the wave of disapproval rolling toward her.

She tugged on the duke's sleeve. "Why don't these ladies like me, Papa?" She shivered. "No one ever tells me I'm pretty here, and it's so cold. I want to go home."

The duke pointed to the door. "Off to bed now. Where's Miss Pratt?"

"I want to stay here with you." The girl's plump lower lip trembled, and Charlene's heart melted.

"I think you're very pretty," Charlene said.

Flor raised dark green eyes that shimmered with tears. "Thank you," she sniffed.

"You've made a friend, Lady Dorothea." There was a mean edge to Lady Augusta's voice.

The duke handed his guitar to a footman and rose. "Miss Pratt!" he bellowed.

A thin woman in a severe gray dress and white cap hurried into the room. "I am mortified, Your Grace." She dropped a hasty curtsy. "My ladies." She curtsied again, this time to the marchioness. "I had no idea she had escaped. I thought she was asleep." She grasped her charge by the shoulder and tried to pry the wooden discs out of her fingers.

"Don't touch my *castañuelas*. They were Mama's." Flor glared challengingly at the ladies. "No one touches my *castañuelas*."

"Flor! You must apologize. Do you want the fine ladies to think you a savage?"

Flor stuck her chin in the air. "I'm not a savage."

"Good gracious." The marchioness tilted her regal head. "Such an unfortunate temperament."

"I do apologize," the governess said, her lips pinched, as if she'd been eating lemons. "Come along, child." She pulled Flor from the room.

"Who was her mother, Your Grace?" the marchioness asked.

"A . . . friend."

"I trust you don't make a habit of exhibiting the child in public."

Both countesses nodded.

The duke fastened his cuffs and accepted his coat from a footman.

"I have a foreign child who was born out of

wedlock," he said. "If that is a fatal flaw, you are quite welcome to take your daughters and leave."

Charlene sensed that he was barely containing his fury.

"Oh." The marchioness blinked. "Well." She seemed to be seriously thinking about gathering Lady Vivienne and departing.

Charlene imagined the dialogue happening in the marchioness's mind.

*The duke has one of those daughters.*

*Yes, but he's a duke. And Lady Vivienne will be a duchess!*

*But the child is foreign. How repugnant.*

*Yes, but one could keep the child hidden away, dower her heavily, and marry her off at fifteen to some minor Spanish nobility.*

Lady Tombs's plumes quivered. "Such an indelicate topic. Miss Tombs, perhaps you had better start humming something. I don't think this conversation is quite the thing."

Alice pursed her pink lips. "The child said she was cold. It must be much warmer in the West Indies. The poor little thing."

Charlene nodded. "I'm sure she's lonely as well. Children of her age need companionship." She addressed the duke. "Are there no neighbor children for her to play with?"

Heads swiveled. Lady Selby stared at her as if she had sprouted horns and cloven hooves, and Lady Desmond's foot tapped a warning.

Apparently ladies did not suggest that a duke's bastard play with neighbor children.

"One does not allow children of *that kind* to fraternize in public, Lady Dorothea," said the marchioness with great displeasure.

"I don't believe Flor should be penalized for the circumstances of her birth," Charlene said. "How can one hold a child responsible for—?"

"What my daughter means to say," Lady Desmond broke in smoothly, "is that the governess should maintain control over her charge."

The ladies nodded.

That's not at all what she'd meant to say.

*Breathe. Gentle flowing river. You are Lady Dorothea. Not illegitimate Charlene.*

"I entreat you to change the subject." Lady Tombs wrung her hands. "These innocent darlings should never be subjected to such an indecorous topic."

Charlene barely suppressed a biting retort. These ladies were so wrong in their presumed superiority.

"I gather none of you are leaving?" the duke asked with a sardonic twist to his lips, as if he was rather hoping to thin the herd.

The ladies contemplated the carpet.

"Shall we play vingt-et-un?" Lady Tombs suggested, breaking the uncomfortable silence.

"As you wish," the duke said.

*Drat.* The countess hadn't had time to teach Charlene any parlor games. She'd have to invent a reason to excuse herself from the game.

Charlene wondered if Lady Dorothea would be ashamed of Flor and want to hide her from society. The duke already left his daughter to the care of that pinch-faced governess, when the child was clearly in need of love and companionship.

Still, he did acknowledge her, and presumably he would dower her. Charlene respected that, but it didn't change the fact that he was a *duke*. She knew that his title and inherited wealth bred corruption.

If Lady Augusta's whispers were to be believed, he was a rogue who'd left a trail of broken hearts across several continents. He had brought his daughter home with him, but that didn't mean he hadn't left a legion of unacknowledged children to rot in obscurity.

Watching him play guitar for his daughter had made her want to like him.

Which was completely out of the question.

As footmen brought card tables and rearranged chairs, James studied Lady Dorothea. He hadn't meant to reveal his daughter until after he chose a bride, because he knew the tempest Flor would provoke. He'd never thought one of the ladies would leap to her defense. Dukes often acknowledged illegitimate children, but they seldom invited them into their homes.

He sat down next to Dalton at one of the tables, still mulling over Lady Dorothea's surprising unconventionality.

"Will you join us, Lady Dorothea?" asked Dalton, angling to have her placed next to James, since he had those three hundred pounds riding on her.

"I'm afraid I have a slight headache," she responded. "I'll sit here by the fire and watch the fun."

Dalton's eyes danced with mischief. "Then His Grace will keep you company. I've often heard him say he much prefers watching cards to playing them."

James frowned. He'd never said that. Oh, of course. Three hundred pounds.

"Well played, sir," he murmured, rising to join Lady Dorothea.

"The rules of fair play don't apply to love and gentlemen's wagers" was the irritating response.

The mothers jostled their daughters into position around the card tables, displaying the wares to best advantage.

James could sit near Lady Dorothea. He didn't have to talk to her, or gaze at her, or wonder what it would be like to feel those decadent curves filling his hands. His lips. He certainly didn't have to imagine what it would feel like if *he* was filling—

"What are you thinking about?" Lady Dorothea's smoky contralto caressed his senses. Why had she sounded so different at dinner? More affected, higher pitched.

He cleared his throat. "I . . . was wondering why you were so kind to my daughter."

"It must be difficult for her to be here in an unfamiliar land, with no other children to play with. She's very lonely."

"I hadn't really thought about that. You must have grown up in a large family?"

She paused for a moment. "I have . . . two brothers. And you, Your Grace?"

"I had one brother."

She lifted her hand to her mouth. "Oh, I'm terribly sorry, I forgot your loss."

He waited for her to say more—the usual trite phrases about how he would learn to bear the loss in time, or that he was the duke now for a greater purpose—but she didn't.

She sat so still that even the feathers in her hair stopped swaying.

The flames in the enormous white chalk fireplace licked at logs from his oak trees. The ancient wood burned hot and long.

The ladies played cards, placing bets and laughing shrilly. Lady Augusta tossed her head, sending plumes and pearls quivering, staring at him boldly.

Lady Dorothea remained silent.

An image sprang to mind unbidden. Standing next to her on the deck of a ship, with salt wind whipping her curls against his mouth. She wouldn't care if her hair was mussed or the tea service jittered about on the table.

Despite her delicate features and small frame, she was strong.

She was someone he could lean on.

What an unexpected thought. One didn't lean on society misses. One protected them, shielded their eyes to the harsh truths of the world, cosseted and spoiled them.

To shake his thoughts away, he began talking again. "William was a good man. Steady and conventional. He'd been groomed to assume the title his whole life and would have made an excellent duke. Sober and just."

He couldn't stop the bitterness from creeping into his voice. "While I am thoroughly unfit for the title . . . and for fatherhood."

"We can't always choose our path. Sometimes we are given a task . . . an opportunity . . . and we rise to the occasion, or stagger under life's blows."

He remained silent this time, contemplating her words. She spoke with conviction, as if she'd experienced hardship. Maybe there was something in her past, some hidden pain that he knew nothing about. It made him curious.

"You speak as if you have some experience of life's blows, Lady Dorothea."

"I? How could I? I've led a very sheltered life, Your Grace." She took a sip from her glass of cordial. "How did you come to bring Flor to England with you?"

"She was given to me unexpectedly. I sired her. And I accept the responsibility for her well-being," he said. "I didn't even know she existed until her mother brought her to me, two weeks before we sailed for England."

"Was she very sad to give up her child?"

"She died of yellow fever four days after she left Flor with me. I couldn't abandon my child to die of a fever . . . or be captured by slavers. I apologize for speaking plainly, Lady Dorothea, but it's the truth. The only safe place for her is here.

I certainly could never take her with me on my travels."

Lady Dorothea sighed. "So much loss. It's clear she misses her mother terribly, and to lose her father will be heartbreaking. Was her mother a very good friend of yours, Your Grace?"

"We were barely acquainted." This conversation was veering into extremely unexpected territory. Flor's mother, Maria, had been a Trinidadian actress of Spanish, European, and African heritage. They'd shared several nights. He'd been careful. There never should have been a child. But when Maria had brought Flor to him, so many years later, he'd seen the child's green eyes and known, somehow, that she was his.

He swirled the brandy in his glass. Now Lady Dorothea knew more about him than all but a handful of people. Something about the fathomless depths in her eyes seemed to free his tongue. "She's an intelligent child, lively and curious. But she has a rebellious streak and can be a holy terror when crossed. She's made short work of two governesses already, and Miss Pratt is exhibiting signs of defeat. She has that permanent wrinkle between her brows that signifies she's about to pack her valise and depart on the next mail coach."

"Let her go," Lady Dorothea said, leaning in earnestly. "She's too stern. Find a governess with a gentler touch."

"Flor needs a strict routine."

"She needs compassion."

"She needs to learn to be strong and emotionless. She has screaming fits. She'll have to learn control if she is to enter society."

"Have you ever thought that maybe she screams because she's lonely and she wants your attention?"

"I don't expect the daughter of an earl to recognize how cruel society can be. You've never had to endure scorn or ridicule. In England's eyes, Flor will have too many existing counts against her already—her birth, her foreignness. . . . Can you see that I only wish to protect her?"

"What I see is a young girl who thinks no one loves her. You should spend more time with her."

"If I spend time with her now, it will be even more difficult for her when I return to Trinidad and leave her here. She has to become accustomed to my absence. She will have a new mother soon, someone to protect her and use her influence to better her lot in life."

"Your Grace," said the marchioness, raising her voice to be heard over the conversation. "Will you join us? We're about to start another round."

Lady Augusta flashed an unpleasant smile. "Before we play again, I hear Lady Dorothea has a talent to share. Do give us a demonstration of *Roman wrestling*, dear."

Lady Vivienne frowned. "Whatever can you mean by 'wrestling'?"

"I'm quite sure I don't wish to know. Miss Tombs, we should retire," said Lady Tombs.

"Indeed," said Lady Desmond, "I find myself

overcome by fatigue. Come along, Lady Dorothea. No one can possibly be interested in the *outré* skills you acquired on your travels."

"Come now, if she has a new skill, we'd all like to see it." Lady Augusta rose and walked to the fire. She snatched a jeweled pin from Lady Dorothea's hair and held it aloft. "Pretend I'm a jewel thief. What would you do?"

"Give it back." Lady Dorothea's voice was low and even.

"Oh *that* wouldn't do any good," goaded Lady Augusta. "I'd be halfway down the piazza by now."

"Give me the pin."

"You'll have to take it from me." Lady Augusta tossed her head challengingly.

Lady Dorothea's hands balled into fists.

"Ladies, please," Lady Gloucester said sternly. "We've had a long evening. It's time to retire."

Lady Augusta's eyes narrowed. "What if I were attacking you, what would you do?" She stared into Lady Dorothea's eyes, deliberately raising her hand as if she was going to strike her.

Lady Desmond gasped.

James jumped to his feet, his protective urge awakened, but he needn't have bothered.

Lady Dorothea blocked Lady Augusta's blow, and then, in a blur of sudden movement, Lady Augusta stumbled backward onto a sofa. On the way down, her hand clawed at the back of Lady Dorothea's gown.

There was a loud ripping noise.

A button flew through the air.

And Lady Dorothea's dress ripped open down the back like a peach splitting in half.

She retrieved the bodice before it fell, but not before he caught a glimpse of lush curves and even one rosy-tipped nipple.

From the pandemonium that ensued, one would have thought a murderer was on the loose.

Girls shrieked, at least one mama fainted, Dalton gaped, and Lady Dorothea stood like a stunned deer facing an arrow.

James rushed to her side.

"Here, take this." He shrugged out of his coat and draped it around her shoulders, pulling it closed.

Her eyes were as glassy as a frozen winter lake.

"I'm sorry," she whispered. "I can't do this."

# Chapter 8

James had half a mind to send Lady Dorothea back to London on the basis of clear unsuitability. A duchess never burst her seams in public.

*Peach silk splitting to reveal lush, rounded breasts and a glimpse, just one tantalizing glimpse, of a pert, rosy nipple that he wanted to. . .*

*Stop thinking about it, James.*

Thankfully, the shock of Lady Dorothea's unveiling had supplanted the scandal of his illegitimate child.

James climbed the stairs to the nursery. Lady Dorothea had said he should spend more time with his daughter. He'd never even been to the nursery. He eased the door open.

Flor was in bed, her little fists clenched tightly, her knees touching her thin chest. He reached down. Stopped shy of touching her hair.

She slept in a ball of fierce concentration. Eyes screwed shut, her thick lashes casting shadows on her cheeks. Long black hair twining with the bedclothes. Even on the long ship ride to London she had slept through the lurching of the boat on the waves.

The voyage to England had been difficult for her. She'd sobbed and sobbed, mourning her mother, bewildered by the sudden change of circumstances.

Truth be told, he'd been glad of her company on the long voyage. After several weeks, she had emerged from her misery, wide-eyed and curious, and her wonder had distracted him from thinking about what lay ahead. How he was the last of his line and would have to face the memories he'd buried for so long. Her presence had given him a purpose, a new goal. Protect her, bring her safely to England to a new life and provide her with a new mother.

She'd made friends with the first mate, who'd fashioned her little dolls out of scraps of broadcloth and rope. James had thought that if she could befriend a grizzled sailor, perhaps she could conquer even the frigid hearts of the British aristocracy.

Life would never be easy for a girl like her.

Lady Dorothea was wrong about how to handle her. If he coddled Flor, it would only make her more dependent and easily hurt. She would only have the last laugh if she beat them at their own game. Developed an even stiffer backbone than the marchioness and distanced herself from her disgraceful reprobate of a father.

She was too quick to rage and tears. Just as he'd been. Before his father beat that out of him. James was going to do her the best service he could: leave her alone. Give her a mother instead, someone with a firm, yet gentle hand. It was best for him to maintain distance from Flor. She would have more of chance to flourish with a mother to guide her.

Lady Dorothea thought he should love his daughter.

She used the word far too liberally.

After his mother had died, James had realized that love bored a hole straight through your chest, like a worm burrowing through an apple. And when you took your shirt off, you saw right through to the walls.

Love was a dangerous word. The precursor to Loss and Loneliness.

Better for his daughter to learn constraint.

Coolness. Control.


*Never lose control, Charlene.* How many times had Kyozu told her that? *You're too quick to temper. Your opponent will make mistakes when you are calm.*

Charlene burrowed beneath the covers, drawing them over the ruined gown she still wore. The countess had warned her about Lady Augusta, yet Charlene had allowed herself to be needled into losing her temper. Tears pricked her eyes.

She'd failed. Embarrassed Lady Dorothea beyond repair.

The other ladies had to be laughing about it right now, recounting the incident in a scandalized hush. There had been pity, not desire, in the duke's eyes as he'd handed her his coat. Charlene supposed her true nature would always burst free, marking her as an intruder in their restrictive, superficial world.

Defending herself against the amorous advances of a duke masquerading as a footman was pardonable. Tumbling her rival onto the sofa, even if she jolly well deserved it, in front of a group whose listings in *Debrett's* were longer than her arm was too far beyond the pale.

Not to mention the mortifying matter of splitting her seams. When the countess had told her the duke preferred wolves, she certainly hadn't meant for something as uncivilized as *this* to happen.

Charlene groaned, her cheeks burning. She shouldn't care about offending officious patricians, but the truth was she did care. She wanted to be good at this. Part of her yearned to prove she was the equal of the beauties of the *ton* and just as capable of winning a duke.

The door opened.

"Are you hiding, Miss Beckett?" It was the countess's stern voice.

Charlene pushed the covers off her head and swiped a hand across her eyes. "I do apologize. I lost control. I'll pay for the gown."

Lady Desmond brushed a hand through the air. "The gown served its purpose. It won't be needed again."

"I did inform Blanchard it was precariously tight."

The ghost of a smile flitted across Lady Desmond's face. "You should have seen their expressions. The duke stared after you as if every speck of light had fled the room. And the other ladies." The countess's lips twitched again. "Equal parts outrage and envy. Their maids are probably snipping bodice stitching as we speak in hopes of provoking a similar unveiling. You are very . . . well favored."

Charlene sat up further. Where was the wailing and wringing of hands?

"I was not displeased to see Lady Augusta receive her comeuppance, either," the countess said. "Of all the rude things, mentioning Dorothea's coming out accident."

"Did she truly . . . vomit?"

The countess looked away. "We don't speak of that evening." She turned back. "As much as I am loath to admit such a thing," the countess continued, "your bizarre outbursts appear to be working to our advantage."

Charlene pushed damp curls out of her eyes. "Then you think we are still in the race?"

"I should say we're very close to the finish line indeed. We need only find a way for you to be alone with the duke. Leave it to me, my girl, I'll find a way. He only needs a bit more encouragement, and he'll be mine."

The countess headed for the dressing room.

How odd. It seemed Charlene could do no wrong.

Throw a duke to the floor?

*Charming.*

Expose herself in public?

*Too perfect.*

She would never understand the nobility.

Manon entered to help her undress. "I hear you put on a performance for the duke," she said, her dark eyes sparkling with laughter.

"I suppose that's one way of putting it." Charlene still couldn't believe the countess wasn't angry.

Manon helped Charlene out of the ruined gown and plucked the pins and crushed roses from her hair. Charlene's stomach growled, loud enough for Manon to hear.

The maid glanced toward the dressing room. "I saved a plate for you, in the larder, below stairs. I daren't bring it here, her ladyship might catch me. You should eat. It won't do any good to starve."

"You mean I should go to the kitchens?"

"Why not? Everyone will be asleep soon, and you need your strength. Besides," she smiled, "I have a feeling the duke prefers curves."

Charlene returned her smile. "I suppose no one would stop an earl's daughter from raiding the larder if she had a midnight craving."

Manon nodded and plaited Charlene's hair into a loose braid, tying the end with a silk ribbon.

"What a strange situation, don't you think?" Charlene asked the maid. "Thank you for helping me."

Manon giggled. "So theatrical, *non*? Hidden identities, handsome dukes, gowns that give way on cue . . ."

"I truly thought my time before the curtain was

over. Seems I've been given one more chance. I mustn't fail."

Manon folded the torn lace-covered dress over her arm. "Don't worry, *chérie*. The duke is halfway in love with you, he just doesn't know it yet." She left, shutting the door between the rooms behind her.

She was wrong, of course. Men like the duke didn't know how to love. They only knew how to possess. He was a man who took what he wanted, when he wanted it, and brooked no arguments. What would have happened if she hadn't been able to defend herself when he'd accosted her that afternoon, when he'd been dressed as a footman?

Had she been the woman who'd caught his eye, or would he have done the same to any of them and she'd merely been the most convenient?

She had to try to understand what he desired, what would bring him to the point of offering marriage. Play the coquette, or continue provoking him with unconventional behavior? It was difficult to tell which approach would succeed.

Charlene flopped onto the bed and spread his black tailcoat over her chest. It smelled of freshly cut pine boughs, masculine and woodsy. There was a hint of smoke from the fireplace. The apple tang of expensive spirits.

She slid a hand down the smooth cotton of her nightgown, under the coat.

Her fingers moved down her abdomen and lower, between her thighs.

There'd been a thread tied *here*. Stretched between her body and the duke's fingers while he'd played his guitar. She'd experienced every forceful strum and stroke on the strings as if he'd been playing *her*.

The wool of his coat scratched her cheeks and lips. His scent surrounded her. His fingers strummed, coaxing sighs from her lips. Her breathing quickened.

She thrust the coat aside and swung upright.

*She* was the one being seduced, damn him. It wouldn't do.

She had to remember the secrets a handsome, charming exterior could hide. She'd seen it too many times before. There were girls bearing the mark of Lord Grant's branding iron on every street in Covent Garden. Charlene had nearly become one of them.

A man who treated women like livestock.

Was the duke any different? Assembling a harem to compete for his favor.

Charlene had to stop thinking he was somehow better. He was an aristocrat, arrogant and controlling. Women were pawns, to be manipulated for his purposes and discarded if they failed to please.

She must remain strong and in control.

He had a weakness, and she would find it.

Tomorrow, Charlene would don her disguise and be the most cultured, alluring debutante the duke had ever met. She would simper, and bat her eyelashes, and reel him in.

Tonight, in plain cotton with her hair braided,

she was simply Charlene. Defensive, ill-mannered Charlene, who cared nothing for maintaining a slender figure.

She wrapped one of Lady Dorothea's soft ivory-colored pashminas around her shoulders and slipped out of her room and down the stairs. She tiptoed through the cavernous dining hall with its mahogany and bronze sideboards, and out the back door she had seen the servants entering from. She followed a long hallway with multiple doors, taking a few wrong turns before she found the narrow servant's stairs leading down.

Charlene swung the kitchen door open and froze. Her candle flame danced over gleaming copper pots, cured meats hanging from wide ceiling beams, and a tall figure looming over the black iron kitchen range.

It was the duke.

# Chapter 9

Lady Dorothea stood in the kitchen doorway clad in a thin white cotton shift and ivory shawl, her hair loosely braided and cascading over her shoulder almost to her waist. The candlestick she held illuminated blue-gray eyes gone wide with surprise.

"Can't sleep, Lady Dorothea?" James asked.

"I . . . ah . . ." She looked like she was going to run away, but then the surprise melted and was replaced by a saucy glint. "I had a midnight craving." She entered the kitchen and set her candlestick on the table. "May I join you?"

She smiled. A slow-blooming smile that unfurled large enough to fill the kitchen and powerful enough to heat the entire estate.

He couldn't see anything else.

He wanted to hold his hands out, warm himself in the heat of that smile.

It was his turn to stammer. "Of course . . . if you like . . ." He turned back to his pot of chocolate, whisking furiously. He should leave. She was too tempting. Too dangerous.

One mug of chocolate, some polite conversation, then off to bed.

*Separate* beds.

"What are you mixing?" She stood beside him.

"My custom cocoa blend."

She closed her eyes and inhaled. "It smells heavenly."

James stopped stirring. He could see the round swell of her breasts through the thin cotton and wool. Breasts he now knew were the perfect size to fit in his palm. Her long braid was tied with a scrap of blue silk. If he tugged on the ribbon, her hair would come unraveled and spill around her like sunlight tumbling down a well.

The smell of scorching milk dragged his attention back to the range. He stirred the mixture. *Careful, James. You might get burned.*

He cleared his throat, marshaling his thoughts. Yes, they were alone. Yes, she was wearing a cotton shift. Of the thin, transparent variety. But that didn't mean he had to transform into a lusting beast.

"Some nights I can't sleep," he said. "Drinking cocoa with sweetened milk helps calm me."

An understatement. He hadn't slept more than a few unbroken hours at a time since he'd arrived in England. Always the same nightmare. Mud walls. Smell of damp earth and burial shrouds. Bread. Sour ale.

"I was too hungry to sleep," she said. "Mama has me on a strict reducing program. I gained nearly a stone in Italy."

*You're absolutely luscious,* he wanted to say. *Don't lose an inch.*

"Of course everyone knows that now," she said with a rueful smile. "After what happened with Lady Augusta."

He suppressed a smile, remembering the scandalized reactions of the other ladies. "Indeed. It was difficult to miss."

"I'm afraid I ruined the evening."

"Ruined? I would say enlivened. Lady Augusta landing on the sofa and then your . . . your—"

"My bodice. Ripping." There was a sardonic edge to her voice. "I'm glad it was so entertaining for everyone. I daresay they'll be recounting the story of my bodice ripping at Almack's for all eternity. I shall never be invited back."

"Not likely." He smothered another smile.

"Oh, go on. Laugh. It *was* humorous, I suppose."

He grinned.

She smiled back. The intimate, just-for-him smile that made him long to do irreparably wicked things.

No, she was an innocent. There would be no wickedness tonight.

He crumbled another dark, pressed cake of cocoa into the pot.

She ran a finger over the spices he'd assembled on the countertop, lingering over orange cinnamon sticks, vanilla and cardamom pods, dried red chili peppers. "I had no idea it required so many ingredients."

"On my travels I observed many ways to prepare drinking chocolate. The ancient Aztecs believed the gods granted them chocolate. They forbade women and children to drink it. Priests mixed their own blood with the chocolate and left it as an offering in the tombs of their dead."

"Gracious." She stared at the frothing mixture.

"No blood in this," he assured her. "Only cardamom and vanilla. Some honey. A touch of chili pepper."

She was dreamy-eyed in the wavering candlelight.

He reached out, dipped his finger into her braid, coming away with a few stray rose petals. "We might try these." He crushed the petals and flung them into the pot. "For sweetness."

Damn his treacherous body. One touch of her soft hair and he had another *situation*. At least this time the dressing gown knotted over his clothing provided more coverage. "Fetch those mugs, if you please," he said, his voice sounding gruff and strained.

She found two earthenware mugs on a shelf and set them on the countertop.

He poured the chocolate mixture into the mugs and set them on the kitchen table.

She reached for a mug.

"Have a care." He held out his hand, stopping short of touching her arm. "It's very hot. Wait a moment."

Turning away from the temptation of her bold eyes, he threw more wood on the range, fanning the glowing embers until they licked to flame.

When he rose, she was sitting on the bench, cradling the mug in her hands. One side of her shawl had slipped off her shoulder, revealing, through the thin cotton of her nightgown, more than she could know. Full, round breasts with impertinent nipples that begged to be kissed. Even a tantalizing triangle of darkness between her thighs.

*Remember what happened the last time you wanted to kiss her?*

*Bam! Flat on your back.*

He wanted to do more than kiss her. Wanted it more than he'd wanted anything in a long time. He couldn't act on those urges, of course. He sat on the opposite side of the table, putting three feet of sturdy oak between them.

She blew on her chocolate and took a tiny sip. "Oh," she said as she stared at him. "How delicious. I wish my . . . mama could taste this."

"We'll visit my cocoa manufactory tomorrow. She can sample some there."

"Is it a large manufactory?"

"The hall is still under construction. I have only a handful of workers at the moment."

"But you'll employ many more in the future."

"Several more."

"Children?"

"I believe the minimum age in the contract is sixteen."

She nodded and the tip of her long braid brushed against her breasts.

He took a gulp of chocolate and nearly cursed when he burned the roof of his mouth. Served him right. "Why do you ask?"

"The plight of children in our factories here in

England is a sad one. I hear their ears are some-times nailed to the workbench if they dare to run away." She shuddered. "If young girls do manage to escape, they are sold and broken like china, and the pieces are swept into the gutter."

What did she know of gutters? "Are you in-volved in charity work, Lady Dorothea?"

She glanced up sharply, her eyes clouding. "I've visited the rookeries. With guards, of course. Such young girls turning to sin . . . it breaks my heart."

He regarded her for a moment. She looked im-possibly beautiful with her cheeks flushed from emotion and the heated drink. "You're not at all what I expected. An earl's daughter, society's dar-ling, and yet you are so forthright, compassionate, and . . ."

*Fresh* was the word that came to mind.

Fresh like clear river water after a mountain ramble. Like bread still warm from the range.

Or the scent of newly roasted cocoa beans.


The duke reached over and tucked a stray curl behind her ear. "You're a thoroughly surprising woman, you know that?"

The countess would be overjoyed. This was sufficient ammunition to thoroughly compromise Lady Dorothea. Alone with the duke. Wearing nothing but thin cotton and a shawl.

Shivering more from the touch of his fingers on her cheek than from the chill in the air.

Charlene had thought he would kiss her when

he'd reached over to pluck the rose petals from her hair.

The candle flame cast striped shadows along his angular jaw and smudged his eyes with darkness as he drank his chocolate.

Charlene blew on the grainy liquid and took a small sip. There was the semi-bitterness of the chocolate tempered by sweet honey and creamy milk. The rich red flavor of cinnamon and cardamom and a hint of pepper that half-burned her throat.

He watched her reaction intently. "What do you think?"

"Truthfully? It's sinful. Absolutely sinful." She smiled in the seductive way she'd been practicing in the mirror.

He took a gulp of chocolate without blowing on it beforehand and bit back an oath when it burned his tongue.

Charlene had rarely tried drinking chocolate, because it was far too expensive. She tasted the promise of his kiss with every sultry sip. He bided his time. But he was also gripping his mug so hard his knuckles had turned white.

He was going to kiss her. He *had* to kiss her. It didn't matter what he was saying. She heard the desire in his ragged breathing.

"Tell me about your travels." Charlene was surprised to find herself genuinely interested. She'd never considered traveling. It wasn't an option for girls raised in bawdy houses with piles of debt, and vulnerable sisters to protect.

"I'm always searching for the highest-quality cocoa beans. Like these." He ripped open a paper parcel that was sitting on the table, and a stream of dark brown, almond-shaped beans spilled out.

The duke inhaled, and the harsh lines of his mouth eased. "Venezuelan cocoa. You can't find that aroma anywhere else in England. It grows on my farm in Trinidad."

He ran his fingers through the beans. Shaped them into mounds. "They smell of dense forest. Sunlight filtering through striated leaves."

Charlene inhaled the earthy scent and took one of the beans in her fingers. "They grow like this? On trees?"

The duke shook his head. "No, they grow in crimson-colored pods longer than my hand. When you crack one open, the thick white pulp is sweet and clean." He stared into the shadowy corners of the kitchen, his voice going dreamy and low. "Popinjays scold overhead. There is the smell of wet, decaying vegetation and the tart green of new life."

As she listened, Charlene could see it clearly.

"Later, the beans are heaped on banana leaves," he continued. "Covered with more leaves. They're roasted in the sun until they ferment and turn this orange-brown color."

He rubbed one of the beans between his thumb and forefinger. A thin husk fell off in flakes. "The inside of the bean is crushed to make cocoa."

He held out a small, dark fragment. "Taste."

She opened her mouth and rolled the bean on her tongue before chewing. More bitter than the drink, with a smokier flavor.

"Your description of Trinidad is surpassingly lovely," she said.

"Yes. But there is so much evil as well. Even though the slave trade itself has been abolished, the horrors continue on Spanish and British sugar and cocoa plantations. Enslaved Africans labor over eighteen hours a day, eating only charred bananas and rice. Most are forced to sleep on wooden planks, twenty to a small room."

"This happens on your farms?"

"No." He shook his head vehemently. "The farms I invest in are run by free men and women, working for good wages and an equal share of the profits."

A duke with a conscience? Was there such an animal? "I'm extremely glad to hear it," Charlene said.

"I've been writing a monthly report to Parliament enumerating the atrocities I've witnessed," the duke said.

His fingers splayed on the tabletop. "Some gains have been made. The Vienna Congress. But it's only a spattering of ink on paper. The inhumanity continues."

He was silent for several moments, staring into the candle flame, his melancholy like a gust of winter wind entering through a crack in a windowsill.

She wanted to comfort him, tell him things would be fine. But that would be another lie to add to her collection.

"I'm sorry, you can have no interest in these grim topics," he said.

"On the contrary, I follow the cause of abolition with great passion."

"Really? That's quite surprising."

"Why should it be surprising? I can read. I have a mind. We're not all featherbrains, you know. We think about more than china patterns and ball gowns." She stared into the candle flame. "I believe every soul is born free. I'm willing to fight for freedom, no matter the cost."

He held up his hands. "I meant no offense. It's only that men like my late father, and all the other complacent peers, molder in their clubs, carving up the world like they carve a roast. Turning a blind eye to the barbarity being carried out in their names."

"Will you take your seat and argue your views in person?"

He shook his head. "I can't stay in England, where life is preordained. I'll only be here long enough to take a wife, produce an heir. Ally myself with a powerful political force like your father who can help lower import duty taxes on cocoa that is produced with no slave labor."

So that was why he had chosen this particular group of ladies. For their fathers. It all started to make more sense.

"You'll leave Flor behind?"

He paused. "She will be better off here without me. With a mother to shape her development into a young lady. I've no idea what to do with a young child."

Death lurked in his eyes, shadowed his smile. He was the last of his line.

She reached across the table and placed her hand on his arm. He was so in need of comfort. Maybe he didn't realize it, but she could see the hurt in his eyes, feel his need for connection.

"Your cocoa is growing cold," he said.

She raised her mug and took another sip. Her chemise hitched up over her breasts. When she lowered her arm, she dislodged the fabric a bit more and it slipped down, exposing more shoulder and the curve of her breast.

He gulped his own cocoa. Set his mug down.

*Now* he would kiss her.

But he didn't.

If Lulu painted his portrait, she'd have to show how his hair caught the candlelight and glowed almost blue. Like ink spreading over parchment. Like night spreading over a sky.

*Careful, Charlene. You're not given to poetry.*

"You have a bit of chocolate." He stood and reached across the table to brush his thumb across her full lower lip. *"Here."*

Her eyes closed and her breath hitched.

There was the sound of a bench scraping across the floor.

She kept her eyes tightly closed. Now. Now he would kiss her.

Footsteps.

Still no kiss. She quieted her breathing, tilted her lips up. Waiting. Ready.

"I'm going to kiss you," he breathed in her ear. "You have exactly three seconds to leave. I advise you to leave."

He waited for a moment. "Please leave."

Her eyes flew open. "I can stop you at any time and throw you to the floorboards, remember?"

"Is that a challenge?" His green eyes grew smoky and intense. "I've never been able to resist a dare."

"Maybe," she said archly.

He sat down on the bench next to her, deliberately close.

She lifted her chin. "I'm not afraid."

A wicked smile played over his lips. "You should be."

Oh, he was arrogant. He thought his kiss would overwhelm her. He had no idea. She'd been kissed before. But looking into his glittering eyes, she did feel a small wedge of fear. Not fear of him, fear of *herself*.

She wanted him to kiss her. Not only because of the reward but because the restless feeling in the pit of her stomach that had begun when he'd played his guitar was worse than ever, driving her to seek an answer to the sweet ache.

Maybe he was unconventional, and had a conscience, but he still assumed women should be falling over themselves to fight over him.

"One," he said.

The countess would be thrilled.

*The countess.*

She'd completely forgotten there was no use being compromised if the countess wasn't there to burst in upon them.

*Blast.*

"Two." He tugged on her shawl until it slipped off her shoulders and pooled on the floor.

She forgot all about the countess.

But no three came.

One small, unspoken word echoed in the space between their lips. He ran one finger lightly down her cheek, his eyes lingering on her mouth. Then he parted her lips with his thumb and tilted her head back. His thumb stroked her lips and slipped inside her mouth, the tip touching her tongue.

She tasted cinnamon from the chocolate and salt from his skin. Her neck was fragile and slim resting in his large hand.

This wasn't the right time.

She should wait until the countess could interrupt them.

This would be madness.

"Three," she whispered.

# Chapter 10

**B**efore the word ended he wrapped an arm around her waist and crushed her against his solid frame. His kiss was soft at first, a series of light touches along the contours of her lower lip.

His hand cupped her face, his fingers splayed across her cheek, gently guiding her head back to give him more access. When his tongue slid along her lips, she tasted chocolate and a warning hint of red chili. The slow, teasing kiss made it difficult to remember why she would ever want to stop him. Instead, she wanted more.

She opened her lips and he answered the invitation, his tongue slipping deeper. Strong fingers tugged at the ribbon tying her braid, loosening the tangles until her hair fell around her shoulders and heat swept through her body.

Gathering her curls in his fists and pulling her head back, he stared into her eyes. "God help me, I want you," he groaned.

His lips moved over hers, his tongue coaxing her lips wider. His kiss was a blatant invitation to sin. It told her that he knew all her secret desires and would fulfill every one.

Minutes . . . years passed as he kissed her and kissed her. There was no thought of anything except the heated need that only his lips could quench. He stroked her shoulders soothingly, shifting the angle of their mouths to delve deeper.

His tongue flicked over hers, demanding an answer. She buried her fingers in his thick hair, pressing against him so thoroughly that she lost all sense of where her curves ended and his hard edges began.

She ran her hands down his back and strong muscles, knotted and bunched beneath her touch. He was so big. So overwhelming. His heat and strength surrounded her, intoxicated her.

"Yes," he murmured in her ear. "Touch me, too." *She didn't want him to stop.*

She'd lived for so long so tightly protected. So closed to the possibility that a man could give, as well as take, pleasure.

His fingers caressed across her throat, and his thumb traced the sensitive hollow at the base of her neck. What had happened to all her fine resolutions about maintaining control and curbing her emotions? There was nothing tidy or controlled about this moment.

She turned her head and rubbed against his cheek, the faint stubble scraping her skin. This small pain brought the pleasure into stark focus. So much pleasure. Radiating up from the ache between her thighs, rippling up her belly, spreading to her breasts, and suffusing her cheeks with warmth.

Another slight movement and her lips brushed his. Tentatively, she kissed his lower lip. He remained still under her exploration. She grew bolder, darting her tongue into his mouth. He closed his eyes and moaned softly.

The sound made her feel powerful. This was the Duke of Harland, His Disgrace, an uncivilized brute . . . and she could make him *moan*.

She trailed kisses along his jaw, slipping one hand inside the front of his dressing gown. His heart beat, wild and erratic.

He slid his hands down her back until they settled around her bum. With a firm grip, he pulled her against the evidence of his arousal. Hard and insistent. Pushing through the thin cotton of her nightgown.

He tugged at her earlobe with his lips. "Aren't you going to stop me, Lady Dorothea?" he whispered. "I thought you said you could incapacitate me at any moment."

Rattled, she pushed her hand against his chest, setting him at arm's length. "I was going to stop you momentarily."

"Really? It didn't feel that way to me." His breathing was ragged, his voice rough with emotion. She saw him make a conscious effort to slow his breathing. There was that mocking arched eyebrow again.

He ran a hand through his hair. Retied his dressing gown.

"I was merely being polite," Charlene said, the melting feeling swiftly evaporating.

He gave a short laugh. "Run off to bed now, before you tell more lies."

This had been a challenge to him. Nothing more. Nothing earthshaking or life-changing or any of the other daft ideas that had flitted through her mind.

He'd confirmed her initial assessment. He was laughing at her desire.

Two could play this game.

"Well? How did I score?" she asked.

"What?"

"I assume you're testing all of us? Isn't that what you're doing? Running us through our paces like candidates for your stables? I want to know my score."

He turned away from her.

"One to ten. My score on the kissing scale. Out with it," she persisted.

"Go to bed." He clenched his jaw.

She raised her chin. "I'd hate to think I scored less than Lady Augusta. Although she is quite lovely. If you like the desperate type."

"Go to bed. *Now.*"

"Did Lady Vivienne learn any new kissing techniques in France?"

"We're not having this discussion."

"Six," Charlene said.

He looked at her blankly.

"I give you a six. It started in seven territory, but then you ruined it by talking at the end. Definitely a six."

*Liar.* There was no scale for the magnitude of

that kiss. But if it had meant so little to him, she wasn't about to admit that it had been monumental for her.

"A six? *Please.* I'll have you know that I've never had any . . . oh no. I see what you're doing, goading me into talking. It won't work. This conversation is over. I'll not say another word."

The duke drummed his fingers against the tabletop.

He was full of bravado. He'd said he didn't need a wife, only an heir. But his hands told a different story, finding a musical rhythm on the wooden tabletop, as if it had been his guitar. His hands told Charlene that he wanted to touch her, take comfort in her.

And the duke's eyes belied his words as well. The loss and darkness beneath the clear green surface called to her. Told her that he only pushed her away because he didn't know how to be a duke, or how to be a father. Or a husband.

She had to resist the invitation in his eyes, his hands. An invitation to open to him, to heal him, give him the warmth he craved.

That wasn't what she'd been employed for. She was here to seduce him into a compromising situation and extract a marriage proposal.

Nothing more.

She couldn't give him anything, except lies.

"Kindly go to bed, Lady Dorothea," he said through gritted teeth. "And leave me in peace."

"Thank you for the chocolate, Your Grace." She paused in the doorway. "Though I sincerely doubt it will help either of us sleep."

# Chapter 11

There were dark shadows under the duke's eyes that told of a sleepless night. Not that Charlene had met his gaze this morning. He was steadfastly avoiding her, giving all his attention to Lady Vivienne.

He stepped into the rowboat and stood with legs widespread, offering his hand to the willowy brunette.

"Are you sure she's seaworthy?" Lady Vivienne asked, lifting her hem away from the muddy riverbank and eyeing the peeling paint on the duke's rowboat.

"Slightly disreputable but perfectly seaworthy. Froggy's carried me down the river Wey for twenty-eight summers now. Nothing to fear."

When he'd offered to take them for a ride on the river, Charlene had expected something more ducal than a humble rowboat with the name *Froggy* emblazoned in fading green paint on the side. The boat was conveniently too small to accommodate the mothers—he'd left them to their own devices. They hadn't even protested the idea of their precious daughters in a boat with His Disgrace without a chaperone. Charlene was surprised by how willing they were to flout the rules of propriety in pursuit of their prize.

He positioned Lady Vivienne and Lady Augusta in the stern and Charlene and Alice in the bow. Untying the mooring with an expert flick of his fingers, he used an oar to push off from the shore.

He settled on the middle bench and dipped the oar in the water.

That's when Charlene's suspicions were confirmed.

The duke was ignoring her.

Charlene and Alice had a splendid view . . . of his back.

Once again, he'd discarded his coat and rolled up his shirtsleeves. Was the man ever fully clothed? She didn't care a whit that his powerful back muscles strained against the thin silk of his fawn-colored waistcoat as he pulled the oars through the water. Or that his forearms were corded with muscle and had to be as thick around as her calves.

What manner of man kissed a girl with such passion, then turned his back on her? Charlene had relived every spine-tingling moment of their encounter over and over, unable to sleep. But for him, she was only another girl who succumbed to his charm. She'd been a momentarily interesting challenge. Nothing more.

"Perfect. Just perfect," Charlene muttered under her breath.

"Don't be discouraged," Alice whispered. "After last night, the duke will *have* to choose you."

Charlene stared. "What do you mean?" Surely she hadn't seen them kissing.

"You know." Alice glanced at Charlene's chest, her cheeks turning pink. "Your *display*. I saw the way he stared."

"Oh, yes. Of course. My display. How could I have forgotten?"

Alice squeezed her hand. When she wasn't talking to the duke, she was surprisingly normal.

"I feel you and I could be friends, Lady Dorothea, if we weren't . . . that is to say . . ."

"Competitors?"

Alice nodded. Charlene hadn't expected to like any of the ladies.

Alice stared wistfully into Charlene's eyes. "I don't have many friends in London. We're not exactly an illustrious family," she whispered. "My great-grandfather was a millworker, for all papa's a baronet now. I don't suppose you can imagine what that feels like."

*You'd be surprised*, Charlene thought. She squeezed Alice's hand. "Now who's discouraged? You're absolutely charming. If they can't see that, then you don't need them."

Alice smiled. "That's exceedingly nice of you. Perhaps you might come to tea some afternoon?"

"I'd like that." Tea with Miss Tombs. Charlene added that to the growing list of things she'd have to tell Lady Dorothea when this was over.

"I hope we shan't capsize, Your Grace," Lady Augusta fluttered, clasping her hands to the pale green silk spencer stretched across her ample bosom. "I don't know how to swim. You'd have to save me from drowning."

"No danger of that, we are only going for a quick jaunt down a river that's barely over four feet at its deepest."

Charlene didn't know how to swim. She'd never been on a boat before. She liked the feeling of the breeze on her cheeks and the sparkle of sunlight on the water. This was the sort of day that was entirely wasted on a city. A glorious English countryside day with a cloudless azure sky. Not a hint of coal smoke in the air, only the sweet smell of new-mown hay.

A pity she couldn't enjoy the scenery. She was far too tense for that.

Charlene glared at the duke's back, hoping the oars would leave splinters.

And she wanted to pitch Lady Augusta and her baby voice overboard.

She had to do something to regain his attention.

She couldn't seduce him if he pretended she didn't exist.

It was time for desperate measures.

It was impossible to ignore Lady Dorothea.

James could feel her behind him, glowing with sensuality. He had to turn around to steer, so he knew she was the only lady who hadn't opened a silk parasol. He might also have noticed that the sun was teasing her curls to flame, her eyes reflected the turquoise sky, and her yellow bonnet was trimmed with glossy red cherries the exact color of her sweetly curved lips.

Those lips.

He hadn't slept last night thinking of their extraordinary kiss. Imagining what could have happened on the sturdy kitchen table if he'd thrown his scruples to the wind.

She'd been willing.

And so very tempting, with her golden hair unbound and the taste of his chocolate on her tongue.

He rowed harder, seeking to lose himself in the exertion of the pull and sway of the oars. Sweat trickled between his shoulder blades as he watched the river roll by. If he was staring at the churning oars, he wasn't staring at *her*.

She'd left her shawl on the kitchen floor. Damned if he hadn't buried his face in its soft folds, inhaling the lingering scent of crushed rose petals and warm woman.

What the devil had he been thinking? Making her chocolate. Telling her about Trinidad. He never *conversed* with females. Except Josefa. Amend that. He never conversed with females he wanted to bed.

Those situations only required practiced words.

*Your hair smells nice.*

*Do you need help with those stockings?*

*Yes, just like that. Keep doing that.*

He never unburdened his soul.

And another thing. A *six*. He was *not* a six. That kiss had definitely been in the way-beyond-ten range.

He'd asked Dalton to stay another day and entertain the mothers, because James wanted to observe the ladies without their overbearing chaperones. See which one exhibited the good sense and innate grace necessary for the role of the perfect duchess.

Lady Vivienne would be a prudent choice. Her bonnet was trimmed with dead pheasants that didn't bobble like those sly cherries. She was equally inert, staring serenely at the scenery, not a hair or thread disarranged.

If the conversation strayed away from the topic of stables, she tended to yawn, but that wasn't a bad quality for a wife. She truly was a thoroughbred—tall, slender, with the unmistakable stamp of good breeding on every lineament.

Lady Augusta, on the other hand, was openly ogling him. She leaned in, and the sharp edges of her parasol nearly blinded him. "Have you been to Gentleman Jackson's?" She leered at his arms. "You are quite well developed."

"I've never enjoyed pugilism. I prefer to make myself useful. I chop my own firewood. Row my own boats."

He turned around to steer and caught Lady Dorothea rolling her eyes. He rowed even harder.

"Oh," Lady Augusta exclaimed as they flew through the water. "Must we go so swiftly?" Her face began to take on the green of her jacket, and she clapped a hand to her mouth.

Miss Tombs seemed to be delivering a treatise on vegetables to Lady Dorothea, from the snatches of conversation he overheard. He wanted to like Miss Tombs. She was quite stunning and seemed a good-natured girl. But she was so . . . odd.

He turned his head slightly. "What are you speaking of, Miss Tombs?" he inquired, intrigued.

"Frugivorousness. Are you acquainted with the topic, Your Grace?"

"I can't say I—"

"Oh, then I shall lend you my copy of *A Vindication of Natural Diet* by Mr. Percy Bysshe Shelley. I have it in my valise. I have not eaten animal flesh since I read it, and I have reduced by fully one stone. Man is not meant to be carnivorous. Rather, we are frugivorous."

Miss Tombs nodded, sending her long, pink bonnet ribbons fluttering in the breeze. "Mr. Shelley recommends a dinner of potatoes, beans, peas, turnips, lettuce, with a dessert of apples, gooseberries, strawberries, currants, raspberries, and in winter, oranges, apples, and pears. I was telling Lady Dorothea that if she would only convert and become a devotee of fruits and vegetables, her life would vastly improve."

"A devotee. Of vegetables," he repeated. Apparently, Miss Tombs was deadly in earnest about this vegetable stuff.

Lady Vivienne yawned.

"Precisely." Miss Tombs's startling blue-green eyes widened. "You must never, never under any circumstance take into yourself anything that Once Had Life. Promise me you will try."

James pictured a thick slice of ham. "I'm afraid I

cannot promise that," he said gravely. "Think about ham, Miss Tombs. Or a succulent cut of lamb."

Lady Dorothea smothered a giggle in her hand.

"You must also give up wine, and any other spirits," Miss Tombs continued.

"That's where I must draw the line, Miss Tombs. I can't live without wine."

"But wine has no healthful properties! It is polluted. You must only drink purified water and nothing else. Mr. Shelley is very clear on the point. I shall write you out a list of fruits and vegetables that are particularly healthful."

"That won't be necessary—"

"No, no, I insist. Once you read Mr. Shelley's pamphlet, you will see the light and join me in banishing animal flesh from your diet."

Miss Tombs continued enumerating the delights of frugivorousness.

James caught Lady Dorothea's eye. There was that smile again, the one that made the sun shine brighter and the birds begin to sing.

He wanted to kiss her again.

They could have a very nice time in a rowboat. If it were only the two of them. And if she climbed on top of him while he rowed.

Her shapely legs wrapped around his waist. Her softness sliding down around him, until she took all of him inside her.

Riding him. Rocking the boat until he had to stop rowing, had to stow the oars and steer *her* instead. Up and down. A tidal wave of passion big enough to envelop an entire village.

"Your Grace?" Lady Vivienne regarded him quizzically.

It was a good thing he'd flung his coat across his breeches flap, or he'd really have given Lady Augusta something to ogle.

"Pardon?"

"How many foals do you expect this year?"

He made some acceptable reply, but talk of stables was difficult to concentrate on when those cherries winked behind him above a butter-colored gown that hugged lavish curves.

The next time he turned around, Lady Dorothea's bonnet had fallen down her back. She'd tilted her head and offered her face to the sun, leaving the slender column of her throat bare and exposed.

James nearly groaned aloud. What he wouldn't give to see her naked and glowing in the morning sun.

"Is that a black-headed bunting?" Lady Dorothea pointed toward the shore.

"A what?" asked Lady Vivienne.

"There, in those trees. I saw a flash of yellow and a black head. Might I have a closer viewing?"

The duke angled toward shore.

"It *is* a black-headed bunting. They are so rare. I've never seen one except in books." Lady Dorothea leaned out of the boat, scanning the tree line.

"Where?" asked Miss Tombs. "I don't see anything at all."

"Have a care, Lady Dorothea," James said.

Too late. She leaned out too far. She tottered for a moment, then lost her balance.

James instinctively jumped up to catch hold of her skirts.

Not a good idea. His bulk suddenly shifting to the side of the boat tilted the whole thing.

The girls screamed and panicked, clutching for him, and that decided it.

Lady Dorothea crashed into the water, James followed, and the rest of them slid down the benches into the cold, muddy river

White and red silk parasols spun down the river like kites soaring in the sky.

"Keep calm, ladies. There's no danger. The water is shallow!"

Utter bedlam punctuated by terrified shrieks and gurgles.

Ladies flapping and sputtering like angry waterfowl.

Good Lord, if any of them were injured, he would never hear the end of it.

He sighed and began scooping up wet debutantes.

# Chapter 12

This had *not* been the plan.

Charlene had envisioned sliding gracefully into the water and reemerging into the duke's strong arms. He was supposed to stare at her with that heated gaze, overcome by the impossible-to-be-unaffected-by sight of her wet gown hugging her body.

Now there were wet gowns outlining *four* curvaceous ladies, and he was rescuing them before her. Of course. Because he was *ignoring* her.

It would serve him right if she drowned.

Fighting back rising panic, she flailed her arms in the chest-high water. Her boots stuck in the muddy riverbed. She tried to walk forward, but her hem was caught on something. She wrenched at the fabric, to no avail.

The duke carried a clinging Lady Augusta out of the river.

Lady Vivienne calmly swam to shore and walked up the bank on her own.

Charlene would try to do the same if her skirts came loose, but she only sank deeper into the mud. *Panic* wasn't the right word anymore. Abject terror, more like.

It galled her to admit it, but she needed rescuing.

*No.* She did *not* need rescuing. She would free herself and find the shore, no thanks to the duke. She yanked with all her strength.

Nothing. Still trapped.

Now the duke carried Alice out of the water and set her beside Lady Augusta.

If Charlene perished in a watery grave a few feet from land, it would be his fault. Some gallant knight, leaving her trapped in the muck so long.

He dove into the river and swam toward her with long, sure strokes.

She redoubled her efforts, but the gown remained trapped.

He emerged, shaking his head, sending drops splattering against her cheeks. Water dripped from his black hair in rivulets over his shoulders. He'd lost his cravat. His shirt and waistcoat were stuck to his formidable chest.

For one breathless moment all she could see was him—solid, warm, and safe.

Large hands shaped her waist. He tried to pull her out of the water.

"What's this?" he asked, puzzled by his inability to lift her.

"My blasted gown is caught on something."

"My, such language," he teased.

"Are you going to rescue me or not?"

He chuckled, wrapped his arms around her waist, and reached behind to pull at her gown. "Must have snagged on a rock or a tree root. Don't worry, I'll cut you loose."

He reached into the water and came up wielding an ivory-handled knife.

She tried to twist away from his embrace. She did *not* need to be rescued.

"Hold still for a moment," he commanded.

Charlene tried one more time to break free but only succeeded in swallowing water. She clutched the duke's neck, sputtering and coughing.

"Lady Dorothea, if you don't stop thrashing about, I'll cut *you* instead of the gown. Now hold still!"

He wedged the knife between his teeth and immobilized her against his chest. With the blade between his teeth, he looked like a pirate about to scale the hull and plunder a ship.

Plunder her.

He transferred the knife to one hand. "Keep your arms around my neck." He sawed at the fabric of her gown. "A bit more. And . . . there. You're free as a black-throated bunwing, or whatever it was you saw in the trees."

The sudden relief of being freed nearly made her cry. She bit her lip. She would not cry. "*Bunting.* Black-headed bunting. They're extraordinarily rare."

"Not worth a dunking, in my opinion." He grinned and flipped his knife back to wherever it had come from.

She was still holding on to his neck. She had to keep her chin out of the water, didn't she? He was solid and warm, and holding her far too close, his arms wrapped around her waist, his green eyes shifting from amusement to something far more intimate.

He tightened his grip, crushing her against his chest. "You could have drowned," he said, his voice low and fierce.

And then he swept her into his arms.

They said that in novels, didn't they? He swept her away, swept her into his arms. But that's really exactly what it was like. One moment she was mired in mud, trapped by tree roots, and the next moment his arms were around her and she was held tightly against his chest, above the waterline.

She buried her face in his neck.

She had the silliest desire to kiss his neck.

Or maybe lick the droplets of water off his chest.

And her heart might have been palpitating. Only faintly. But still.

Charlene didn't need a man to rescue her. She didn't need a man at all. Her new boardinghouse would be female only—except for Kyuzo. He would be the defense instructor and teach the girls to believe in their own strength.

So why did it feel so blissful to be held in the duke's arms? To be rescued? It had to be the fright of nearly drowning. It couldn't be anything else.

She rested her head against his chest as he strode through the water, carrying her weight easily.

"Thank you," she whispered, too soft for him to hear.

"Poor old Froggy." The duke glanced back, and

Charlene followed his gaze. The rowboat was stuck in the mud, only its prow visible.

"Can he be repaired?"

"Not likely. He's had his day." The duke's voice softened. "He used to be my favorite escape."

Charlene glanced up but could only see his square jaw from her current position against his chest. "Escape?"

"After my mother died, Warbury Park was a prison for me. When I came home on school holidays I spent entire days drifting down the river with some apples and a pile of books, hiding from my tyrant of a father. Even now, I don't like sleeping in that moldering pile of bricks. Too many ghosts."

His mother died when he was young. His father was a tyrant. He liked to read. What did he like to read?

*Not relevant, Charlene.*

He set her on the grass next to Alice.

"What an adventure!" he said in a jovial, booming voice. "Won't you ladies have a tale to tell."

Four shivering, soggy girls stared back.

"What will we d-do now?" Lady Augusta asked, her teeth chattering.

"We'll find a grassy patch and dry in the sun before we walk home."

"*Walk* home?" Lady Vivienne tilted her head quizzically, her ruined bonnet shedding water.

"Unless you want to wait here alone while I go back to fetch another boat. There's no easy passage through these woods for a carriage. I don't want to leave you alone. I think we should walk back together. Come along." He motioned for them to stand. "There's an orchard nearby. The apples ripened early this year because of the warm spring."

Charlene and the ladies straggled after him in their sodden gowns and mud-caked boots. It was slow going.

"This is all your fault," hissed Lady Augusta to Charlene. "You're always causing trouble— ruining gowns, wrestling people to the floor. You should go home. He'll never choose a walking disaster like you."

Alice took Charlene's arm. "I should think Lady Dorothea is the *least* of your worries, Lady Augusta."

Lady Augusta narrowed her eyes. "What do you mean by that comment?"

"One of your ringlets is dangling most precariously. I shouldn't wonder if you're in imminent danger of losing it altogether."

"Oh!" Lady Augusta's hand flew to her hair. One of the long blonde curls hanging from the side of her bonnet came off in her fingers. "Why you . . ." she sputtered. "You're as bad as Lady Dorothea!" She dropped behind them to adjust her hair.

Charlene grinned at Alice. "Thank you."

Alice smiled back. "My mother wears false curls. I can spot them every time. Normally I wouldn't call attention to it, but she's so very unpleasant."

The two girls walked arm in arm, wet boots

squelching and sodden muslin impeding their progress.

The duke walked in front of them, toward a meadow of grasses and ferns dotted with dainty purple flowers.

"Goodness, do you think his breeches are becoming tighter?" Alice whispered.

"I was wondering the same thing," Charlene breathed.

The duke's soaked buckskin breeches clung to his physique, outlining every well-defined muscle in his posterior and thighs. Heat flooded Charlene's cheeks, keeping her warm despite the cold, wet gown.

He was a front-page scandal, the picture of sin itself.

His Disgrace, in skintight breeches and transparent linen, leading his flock of debutantes into the woods.

"It's really too bad," Alice sighed. "He's making this far too difficult. My last marital prospect was nigh on sixty, and his breath smelled like cod liver oil."

Charlene glanced at Alice. Understanding dawned. "You don't *want* to marry." Suddenly it all made perfect sense. The loathsome rot, the vegetable treatise. No one was that addlepated. "You're *trying* to be disqualified."

Alice's blue-green eyes sparkled. "You've guessed my secret. Papa ordered me to make an advantageous match, but I want to have at least one adventure first."

Charlene smiled. "That's understandable."

"It is? No one else seems to think so. They all think I should be pining for a husband and a family . . . as if those were the only laudable goals for a girl."

"I think it's natural to want to experience a little bit of life first before settling down and becoming a wife."

"You're the first person I've told," Alice said. "For some reason I feel I can trust you. So you see, we're not competitors at all." She smiled wistfully. "I hope we will be friends."

They could never be friends. Alice was brilliant and entertaining, but if she knew Charlene's secret, there would be no more talk of friendship. Not between a genteel young lady and a courtesan's daughter.

A cloud drifted over the sun. Charlene shivered. She had to remain intent on her mission. Nothing could distract her.

"Now then." The duke stopped in the middle of the meadow. "There's nothing for it. All of you. Out of those soaked gowns."

"What did you say?" exclaimed Lady Vivienne.

"You'll catch your deaths if you don't dry those wet gowns," he said.

"But we couldn't possibly disrobe . . . could we?" Lady Augusta licked her full pink lips. "You'll *see* us."

"I assure you, I've seen females in their undergarments before."

Lady Vivienne's graceful hand flew to her cheeks. "We'd rather die."

"His Grace is right," Charlene said. "We'll all catch our deaths if we don't dry at least one layer. I will be happy to remove my gown."

The duke nodded. "Thank you, Lady Dorothea. Very sensible of you."

Lady Vivienne and Lady Augusta glanced at each other doubtfully.

"Well . . . I don't want to catch a chill." Lady Augusta batted her eyelashes at the duke.

The duke cleared his throat. "I'm off to fetch some apples. When I return, your gowns will be spread out on the grasses. That's a ducal order."

A purely feminine thrill eddied through Charlene's body as she watched him marching away to gather food. No wonder he'd been so ill at ease in the dining room. This was his natural habitat. Wide expanses of earth. Sunlight glinting on his hair.

Alice and Charlene helped each other remove dripping bonnets and muddy half boots. Charlene's yellow straw hat was squashed, and the once-jaunty cherries looked sad and bedraggled. They undid each other's gowns and spread them atop the meadow grass to dry.

The ladies attempted to remain as proper as possible, repinning their hair and tucking their stocking feet demurely under themselves. They still had layers of over-petticoats, sturdy cotton corsets, and shifts to protect them from the duke's eyes.

Charlene's stockings were in shreds from her riverbed ordeal, so she untied her garters and shed her stockings. She buried her bare toes in the warm, fragrant meadow grass and unbound her wet hair, ignoring the censorious look from Lady Vivienne and the murderous one from Lady Augusta.

Charlene held the advantage here, having been raised in a house full of scantily clad women. In fact, the situation was ideal for her seductive purposes.

The duke returned. He'd removed his waistcoat and was using it as an apple basket. "This isn't so bad, is it?" he asked, setting his harvest down on the grass, averting his eyes from the ladies. "We'll be dry and back at the house before you know it."

"If you thought the vegetables were good, watch this," Alice whispered in Charlene's ear. She jumped to her feet and shook her head, unraveling her chignon until her hair whipped around her shoulders. "I have an eel in my hair! I can feel it slithering. Help me, Your Grace!"

She shook her petticoats, performing a bizarre hopping eel-and-duke-dispelling shimmy. "I'm simply covered in eels. I can feel them wriggling. Ohh . . ."

The duke caught her by the shoulders. "Miss Tombs, there are no eels in your hair or anywhere else on your person." He plucked a twig out of her hair. "It's nothing but a bit of bracken."

"Gracious heavens! Is it wriggling?"

Charlene smothered a laugh. Alice should be on the stage with that natural comedic talent.

The duke pulled a slender silver flask out of the pocket of his discarded waistcoat and unscrewed the cap. He grabbed Alice's hair, tilted her head back, and poured something down her throat. She struggled and coughed, but he held her motionless, pinioned with one large arm.

"This will calm you." He poured more down her throat. Then he took a large drink himself. "All of you. Have a swallow. It will warm you."

Lady Augusta held out her hand with a flirtatious smile, and the duke handed her the flask. She took a long swallow and didn't even cough. She gazed challengingly at Charlene.

Charlene took the flask and drank. It burned down her throat and set her empty stomach ablaze, leaving a pleasant aftertaste of peaches. She handed the flask to Lady Vivienne.

The duke sat down and removed his boots, emptying a brackish stream of water from each. "My valet won't be happy about these." He reached into the top of one of the boots and pulled the knife out of what had to be an internal holster. He began carving the peel off an apple with one long, continuous stroke.

Charlene couldn't help staring.

All the girls stared.

His white linen shirt was still wet and transparent and did more to emphasize than hide the powerful muscles of his chest and his flat, ridged abdomen. There was black hair under his armpits, and his skin glowed dark bronze in the sunlight. She even saw a faint line of dark hair leading into his pale, fawn-colored buckskin trousers.

He was a prize specimen.

They should lock him in a cage at Edward

Cross's menagerie on King Street with the lions and tigers and let all the young ladies have a gawk.

WILD DUKE IN HIS PRIME, the sign would read. PREFERS CHOCOLATE AND VIRGINS. STAY BEHIND ROPES.

*He's beautiful*, she thought. And then, *I want him*.

The longing came from some elemental, undiscovered corner of her mind. She wasn't accustomed to wanting men. *They* wanted *her*. And she'd always vowed never to be owned, never to relinquish her freedom.

Yet here she was. *Wanting*.

It wouldn't matter what she wanted two days from now, she reminded herself. She would never see the duke again. She had to rein in her emotions. Remember this was a task. A role. Nothing more.

Seduce a duke.

Exit stage left.

She studied her rivals. Lady Vivienne had made a bed of grass into a throne and somehow managed to stay elegant and unruffled even with a mud-encrusted hem, damn her. Lady Augusta was the type of girl who needed all the male attention for herself. Even now she was wringing the edge of her petticoat, deliberately pulling it higher than necessary to reveal shapely ankles and trim calves, glancing coyly at the duke to see if he was watching.

He was watching, out of the corner of his eye, with an indulgent smile, like some Ottoman pasha surrounded by his harem. Women must have thrown themselves at his feet and lifted their petticoats all the time. It was his due.

Charlene narrowed her eyes.

Wealth, privilege, and beauty. Once again she dearly wanted to wipe that smug smile off his face. With her elbow.

Alice sat down beside Charlene and leaned in to whisper in her ear. "What did you think of my eel dance?"

"You're a wonder," Charlene whispered back.

Alice smiled modestly. "I do try."

The duke finished peeling the apple and held it out to Charlene with a wicked glint in his eyes, like the serpent tempting Eve. "Try a Golden Pippin, Lady Dorothea."

Her breath caught.

She reached for the apple. His fingers brushed hers, and she felt his touch all the way to her toes.

He held her gaze as she took a bite. The crisp tartness burst in her mouth, followed by a mellow honey flavor. The other ladies faded away. Without warning, she was back in the kitchen with her neck arched and her breasts crushed against his chest, tasting chocolate and spices on his tongue.

His lips curved in a lazy smile that said he knew exactly what she was thinking about.

She lowered the apple from her lips.

This Eve already knew about sin.

And *she'd* do the tempting, thank you very much.

# Chapter 13

How was James supposed to make a rational choice when every shadowy recess of his mind was flooded with the blinding need to ravish Lady Dorothea?

In a meadow of purple flowers with her sunshine curls tumbling around bare shoulders.

That wet shift of hers wasn't hiding much. He could see her corset through the white cotton, and the swell of her breasts. He didn't have to imagine what color her nipples were. In the brief glimpse he'd had last night, he'd seen rosy, up-tilted perfection.

He wanted to lay her down in the meadow grass and flowers. Tug the shift over her breasts, unlace the corset. Watch her nipples stiffen in the late summer breeze. Close his mouth around one peak and listen to her gasp.

She took another bite of apple.

A bee buzzed past his ear. He needed to taste her, the tartness on her tongue, the honey between her thighs.

She smiled. A new variety of smile. A knowing, seductive, Cupid's arrow of a smile aimed firmly below the waist.

It hit the mark.

He shifted in the grass, crossing his legs. He couldn't recline in the center of a group of innocent debutantes and treat them to an anatomy lesson on the aroused male of the species.

Think about wriggling eels. Latin verbs. Family crypts.

There. That last one had worked. He was only recently out of his mourning blacks. His father would have expected him to be a failure at this. To be ruled by his passions instead of rationality. He had to prove the old despot wrong.

He wasn't here to find an enthusiastic bedmate. He was here because he urgently required a suitable duchess and an heir. He was no longer the devil-may-care spare. He had obligations. A factory to complete. Import taxes to lower. A rebellious daughter who needed a mother's care.

He had to find a suitable wife and fulfill his obligations as swiftly as possible so he could return to Trinidad. Back to the life he'd built for himself. Not with the tainted, corrupt Harland family wealth but by his own sweat and hard work.

There was absolutely no place in his plans for bucolic frolicking with golden-haired sirens who couldn't keep their opinions to themselves and probably would scandalize the *ton* more than appease it.

He held out an apple to Lady Vivienne.

"Are you fond of the hunt, Your Grace?" she said in her cultured accents, taking a few ladylike nips from the apple. She nodded at the woodlands in the distance. "You must have a splendid fox season."

She perched in her petticoat and shift, elegant and unflappable as ever. Staying with the approved topics. Stables and hunting. Was there something in the duchess manual about that? *When all else fails, a man will always be happy to expound upon hunting.*

"I'll be here for a few more months," he said. "Do you enjoy riding to hounds, Lady Vivienne?"

"Certainly." She smiled. "I hope that's not terribly shocking. I was raised on horses, you see, and, if my flattering brothers are to be believed, I'm the equal of any equestrian."

Lady Augusta pouted. He wasn't paying her enough attention, apparently. "And what pastimes do you enjoy, Lady Augusta?" he dutifully asked.

"Who, me?" She fluttered her eyelashes, speaking in the breathy, little-girl voice that was probably supposed to make him feel protective but only made him want to cringe.

"I'm the picture of domesticity," she said. "I enjoy embroidering table linens. And . . . baby dresses." She twirled a blonde curl around her finger. "I want *heaps* of children. Simply heaps."

Well. This certainly wasn't a conversation they'd be having if the mamas were here. As if she could read his mind, Lady Augusta continued. "My heavens, if our mamas could see us right now. Why, I would fear for your safety."

"Oh yes," Miss Tombs said. "My mama wouldn't approve. Not one bit." She retrieved the flask from the grass and took several more swallows. "Especially if she saw me drinking this . . . what is this?"

"French brandy. I have a whole cellar full."

"Oh dear. Mr. Shelley would be so dismayed. You know I've never touched a drop in my life." She swallowed more. "I find I quite like it!"

"Steady on—I think you've had enough." James grabbed the flask. "We haven't heard from you, Miss Tombs," James said, to distract her. "What about you?"

"I'd like to see the . . ." Miss Tombs stopped speaking. She lifted her finger. "I'd like to take a bath," she pronounced. "A nice, long, hot bath to wash all this mud away." She giggled. "Really, that's all I want from life."

She was slurring her words. Was she . . . *drunk*? He was beginning to think there was something a bit off about poor Miss Tombs.

Lady Dorothea was silent for once. She plucked one of the lacy purple flowers.

"And you, Lady Dorothea," he prompted.

"If I could have anything in this life, it would be for females to have the same rights and freedoms afforded to males," she said softly.

"Gracious, Lady Dorothea," said Lady Augusta. "Are you a bluestocking?"

"But I'll take smaller victories," Lady Dorothea continued, disregarding Lady Augusta. "The good health of my family. Rain drumming against a window while I laugh and cry over a book."

James stared, entranced.

Miss Tombs recaptured the flask. "Brandy!" She licked the last drops. "I like brandy!"

James wrestled the flask away. "It's time I escorted you home. I'll wait beyond those trees while you dress."

Who knew bride hunting would turn out to be so disastrous for one's clothing . . . and sanity? There would be hell to pay back at the manor when the mamas saw the bedraggled state of their dear daughters.

They were met an hour later in the great hall by a pack of furious mothers. James would have preferred to face Napoleon's battalions.

"We've been worried half to death!"

"What happened to your boots?"

"Lady Augusta, where is your bonnet? Your cheeks are as red as a tomato!"

Dalton stood behind the buzzing swarm. He shrugged and mimed, "*Sorry,*" then jerked his head toward the hallway and made a motion like he was tipping back a bottle.

James lifted his arms, and the tide of distraught voices quieted. "Ladies, please. All will be explained. We had a small mishap, but all is well—"

"We were capsized!" Miss Tombs appeared under his outstretched arm. Her hair stuck out at odd angles, and she swayed back and forth. He had to place an arm around her waist to steady her.

"And then there was an eel in my hair with horrid little eyes and sharp teeth, but the duke routed him." She did a brief recap of the eel-dispelling dance. "And then"—she paused for effect—"he ordered us to remove our gowns!"

*Oh, dear Lord.*

There was the ominous silence of troops readying their rifles for a volley.

Dalton made a choking sound and clapped his hand over his mouth.

A sly smile played over Lady Dorothea's lips. She was clearly enjoying his time in front of the firing squad.

The mothers clamored for an explanation, all speaking at the same time.

"Surely that can't be true."

"Remove your gowns? Preposterous."

"You must be mistaken."

"What is the meaning of this?"

"It was a preventive measure, you understand," James said. "Your daughters were cold and wet. The walk home in sodden gowns would have exposed them to a chill."

There was a moment of stunned silence. Then the squawking started again.

"You *walked* home?" asked Lady Gloucester, her voice rising above the others. "What happened to the boat?"

"Froggy drowned," said Lady Augusta. "And I nearly did as well. His Grace rescued me. He plucked me out of the water with only one arm. Imagine that!"

Her mother raised her eyebrows. "I am imagining it."

"Miss Tombs, come here this instant," Lady Tombs demanded.

Miss Tombs wove forward on unsteady legs.

Her mother grabbed her chin and sniffed her breath. "You would not, by chance, have given my daughter spirits?"

"Brandy!" pronounced Miss Tombs gleefully.

Her mother's jowls quivered. "This is the limit. The absolute limit. Is life one colossal joke to you, Your Grace? How dare you smile when my daughter was nearly drowned! And then to corrupt her with the Devil's water. Come, Miss Tombs. We are leaving this instant!"

Miss Tombs glanced from her mother to the duke and then back to her mother. "We are?"

Was that a triumphant gleam in her eye? It almost seemed as if she had staged the scene somehow.

"There's no need for that," he said. "It was only a few drops to warm them."

"My mind is quite made up. We ride for London." Lady Tombs grabbed her daughter's wrist and dragged her across the room.

Miss Tombs waved to Lady Dorothea. "I do hope we meet again."

Funny, she didn't sound drunk now.

"Come away immediately, Miss Tombs. I just know you've caught a chill."

"Lady Tombs, if I have given offense, I'm heartily sorry," James said to their departing backs, not really meaning his words.

He rounded on the remaining ladies. "Anyone else wish to leave?" He swept a hand toward the entrance. "The door is there."

Mothers froze.

No one said anything.

Lady Dorothea smoothed a hand down her waist, pulling the fabric of her ruined gown tight against the swell of her hip. Which made him recall the way her generous curves had appeared to advantage in her wet, clinging petticoats. And how she'd nestled against him when he'd carried her out of the river as though she'd been fashioned expressly to fit into his arms. And the wit and fire in her eyes as she'd advocated for the freedoms of females.

He needed a damned drink.

"Right, then," he said briskly. "Despite our detour into the river, we will follow the schedule and visit my new manufactory. I suggest everyone take a brief rest. We depart promptly after luncheon."

He cut a swathe through enemy lines, avoiding Lady Dorothea's amused gaze, avoiding her *everything*, and retreated to the manly haven of the library, where Dalton was waiting with more brandy.

James didn't usually drink this much, but these were desperate times.

"I want her gone," James said to Dalton after he'd dulled the keenest edge of his frustration.

"Which one?"

"Dorothea."

"Oh, so now she's *Dorothea*."

"What? Did I say Dorothea? I meant *Lady* Dorothea. Although if she's a proper lady, I'm a damned milkmaid."

James paced across the library carpet. "She's more of a menace. A destructive force of nature. She should come with a warning printed on her forehead: DANGER! MAYHEM! RENDING CLOTH AHEAD!"

"That bad, eh?" chuckled Dalton. "What did she do this time?"

James warmed his hands in front of the fire. He should probably change into clean clothes, but all he wanted to do right now was have a drink, blessedly free from all things feminine.

"She capsized my rowboat searching for some rare bird she saw in the trees," James said. "Then she caught her skirts on a rock and nearly drowned, and I had to cut her loose with my knife."

Dalton grinned widely. "Splendid. At this rate I'll win the wager before sundown."

"What? Are you mad?"

"I'll even increase the stakes. Five hundred pounds."

"You *are* mad." James dropped into a chair. "You see what she did to my cuffs?" He held up his muddied sleeves. "And just look at my boots."

"Since when do you care? Always been unfashionably rough-clad."

"Yes, but the boots are only the start. Imagine what she would do to my heart."

Dalton shook his head in mock sympathy. "So. Tell me, old friend. You saw them all in their wet petticoats. Who has the most shapely . . . you know." Dalton made a round grabbing motion in the direction of James's chest.

James raised his eyebrows. "Really? You're going to ask me that? Find out for yourself," he said irritably.

"I might do, at that." Dalton kicked his heels out and crossed his legs. "Lady Augusta's been making eyes at me while your back is turned."

"What a hell of a morning. A few sips of brandy and Miss Tombs acted as if I'd poured a whole bottle down her throat. I should have listened to you. This was a terrible idea."

"I hate to say I told you so . . ."

"Then don't. I'll get through this. We'll follow the schedule. Visit the manufactory so my new fiancée will give a glowing report to her papa on my business concerns. Then a trot through the woods, one more dinner, and it will all be over."

"Quite right. Follow the schedule. Choose someone suitable such as Lady Vivienne. Nothing simpler."

James raised his eyebrows.

"What are you looking at me like that for?" Dalton asked. "It's probably a very good plan."

"Only?"

"Five hundred pounds says it's not going to work."

# Chapter 14

Two hours later, near the entrance to the duke's cocoa manufactory outside the nearby town of Guildford, Charlene was wondering how she could find a way to be alone with him with all these people around.

He was a true duke this afternoon, buttoned and gloved, tall and commanding in his black beaver hat and black wool greatcoat.

Men hurried about with soot-blackened faces, feeding coal and wood furnaces. Bricklayers constructed walls for new outbuildings. There was a bustle of activity and noise.

"What is that enormous hammer protruding from the building?" shouted Lady Augusta over the chaos. "It almost seems alive, as though it could break free and crush us all."

The gigantic black iron hammer surged upward and then descended, pausing for a moment at the bottom with a sigh and a groan before continuing upward again.

"A Watt steam engine," replied the duke. "Fry of Bristol was the first to install one more than ten years ago. It harnesses steam power to grind the cocoa and will take the place of twenty men."

"All that power." Lady Augusta shuddered. "Are you sure you can control it?"

"Men built it, men control it."

Lady Vivienne lifted her hem to step over a pile of horse dung, wrinkling her nose, while Lady Augusta eyed one of the strapping young bricklayers working nearby.

"How many acres do you have here, Your Grace?" asked the countess, coming to stand next to Charlene.

"Fourteen hundred or so. Banbury Hall was the only existing structure."

Charlene wasn't concerned that he wouldn't meet her eye. She understood now that it was a promising sign when he avoided her. She'd seen the longing in his eyes when he'd handed her the apple, and again after Alice's precipitous departure.

The flare of heat, the desperation.

He wanted her. As much as she wanted him.

Charlene had been sorry to see Alice go. She'd grown fond of her bizarre pronouncements and marriage-avoiding machinations. Too bad Lady Vivienne hadn't left instead. She was the biggest threat to Charlene's success.

Charlene surveyed the scene with interest. So many of the working girls in Covent Garden started as child laborers, then turned to selling themselves because of paltry wages and appalling conditions. She was glad to have the chance to view the inside of a manufactory and see the conditions firsthand.

An elderly man with a shock of white hair that matched his white coat bustled to meet them.

"Ladies, my chemist, Mr. Van Veen," said the duke. "He came all the way from Amsterdam to help me find a method for taking away some of the natural bitterness of cocoa to produce a milder, sweeter drink."

Mr. Van Veen's watery blue eyes crinkled, and he bowed over and over, like a windmill. "My ladies, such an honor. Such an honor."

"Will you give us the tour?" the duke asked.

"With pleasure. This way, please, ladies." Van Veen led the way through the doorway and up a flight of stairs.

Lord Dalton settled into step beside Charlene at the back of the group. He leaned down to speak in her ear so the countess wouldn't hear them. "I must say, Lady Dorothea, you have hidden depths."

She searched his face as they continued down a long corridor. Best to remain silent until he explained himself.

"All those nights hovering on the edges of ballrooms with the wallflowers. I hardly noticed you at all. And now *this*." He winked. "Hidden depths."

Charlene smiled, relieved that he still believed her ruse. "Thank you, Lord Dalton."

"My money's on you," he said. "Don't disappoint me now."

"What do you mean?"

"All of London is placing wagers, waiting with bated breath to see which one of you Harland chooses."

Drat. The countess wouldn't like the notoriety. "How do you know?"

"I had a letter from a friend at the club. Seems the bets are flying fast and furious." He patted her arm. "You're not going to become faint-hearted, are you? When you're so close to winning your duke? I'll do what I can to help. You can rely on me."

He winked again.

He was handsome, with those mischievous, deep blue eyes and that thick, burnished hair, and his shoulders were nearly as broad as the duke's, but Lord Dalton's hand on her arm didn't make her feel anything. No mad urge to lick his chest. No palpitating.

The duke's wide shoulders led them into a room at the far end of the corridor. It was quieter here.

"This is the winnowing room," he said. "Here the roasted cocoa beans are shelled and readied for grinding. We only have a small operation now, as you can see, but soon there will be room for more winnowers in the new hall."

It was a large, open room, obviously the old hall's kitchens, with ten young girls seated at low wooden tables.

The duke nodded to a tall, heavyset man with a bulbous nose, who was overseeing the winnowers. The man swept off his brown hat and bowed.

The winnowers were young girls dressed in white pinafore aprons and white frilled caps, industriously cracking and rolling what Charlene recognized as the same beans the duke had shown her last night.

She tried smiling at one of them, a thin girl with long brown hair plaited in braids, but she only ducked her head back to her work. She couldn't be more than fifteen.

Charlene took an instant dislike to the foreman with the bulbous, pockmarked nose when she caught him staring at her chest. She'd seen that appraising stare too many times at the Pink Feather.

The duke ran his hand through the beans on one of the tables, bending down to breathe in the aroma. "I'm eager to bring some of our new drinking chocolate formula back to Trinidad so the cocoa farmers can taste it. They will be so pleased."

He wasn't doing all of this for the money, that was certain. So why was he doing it?

She remembered the reverent quality in his voice when he'd described the dense forest where the cocoa beans grew. She could picture him on his farm in the West Indies. He'd be in shirtsleeves and breeches, the sun bronzing his skin and taking some of the shadows out of his eyes.

He helped nurture the trees, growing the finest cocoa, his dream to make drinking chocolate affordable for the masses. It was his way of being useful, and different from his father.

Affordable chocolate was certainly something Charlene could approve of, since she'd never been able to indulge in the expensive luxury.

"And here we have the experimentation chamber, where Van Veen reigns supreme," the duke said, placing his hand on Mr. Van Veen's shoulder as they entered the next room.

Van Veen rubbed his hands together. "These vats are full of our new formula, ladies."

The copper vats steamed and hissed, giving off a rich chocolate smell. It made Charlene remember the duke's kiss in the kitchens.

Her heart simmered like the cocoa solution bubbling in the vats. She stole a glance at the duke. Their eyes met and he quickly turned away.

A frisson of anticipation loped down her spine. Tonight she would taste him again.

"What will you call your drinking chocolate?" Lady Vivienne asked.

"I haven't found a suitable name yet."

"Perhaps Van Veen's Cocoa? You wouldn't want your family name associated with commerce, I'm sure."

The duke frowned. He was about to answer, when Lady Augusta interrupted. "This frothing stuff is cocoa?" She bent to peer into a copper vat. "May I have a taste? I take a cup of Fry and Hunt's cocoa every morning."

"Please have a care, my lady," exclaimed Mr. Van Veen. "You mustn't touch! You'll be scalded."

The duke took one of the round cakes of dried cocoa stacked on a table and broke off a small piece. "You may sample this if you like, Lady Augusta, even though it would be much better when dissolved with milk and sugar and heated."

Lady Augusta nibbled on the grainy bit of chocolate. Her tongue snaked out to capture a stray fleck. She placed a hand on her cheek, as if quite overcome. "Oh my. How delightful. May I take some home with me?"

"Of course," the duke said. "You'll all leave with a supply of my cocoa."

How magnanimous. A cold comfort for the girls he didn't choose. Charlene planned to leave with a duke.

Well, Lady Dorothea would leave with a duke.

And Charlene would have to save up her money and buy a tin of his chocolate if she wanted to taste his lips again.

The party moved to the next room to view the steam-powered cocoa press. Charlene took the opportunity to duck back into the winnowing room, just for one minute. She wanted to talk to the girls, ask them about their lives. Then she'd rejoin the group.

She lingered outside the winnowing room door, watching, unseen. The overseer bent down and whispered into the ear of the girl with the long brown plaits. She shrank away, shaking her head. He grabbed one of her braids, bending her small head backward in his powerful grip, reaching down her bodice with his other hand.

Hot rage gripped Charlene.

"Take your hands off her!" she shouted, striding into the room.

The overseer snatched his hand away and snapped upright. "You should stay with the duke, milady." He leered at her. "Wouldn't want to get lost now. All by yourself. You could trip on something."

Was that a threat? Charlene took a deep breath. This was probably going to become ugly. "You have no business touching these girls, sir. They are under your trust and care."

His large nose advanced. "Go back to your friends now, milady. This isn't your concern."

Charlene stood her ground. "*You* are my concern. Any man who abuses his power is *my concern*. Now apologize to . . . what's your name, dear?" she asked the brown-haired girl.

The girl shook her head and continued winnowing, mute and unresponsive.

The overseer glared down at Charlene, every individual crater on his nose visible.

All the tension of the past days stoked the fire of her fury. "You'll apologize to this girl, sir, or I'll use your bollocks for bells until you beg for mercy."

His eyes bulged. He only stopped himself from an angry retort because she was dressed as a fine lady. "You'd best leave now, milady."

Charlene was accustomed to bullies. Men who thought of girls as nothing but property and playthings. Her stomach churned.

The girls watched, stealing surreptitious glances at the scene unfolding in their workplace. Charlene had to be strong for them, and show them that females could defend themselves. She craned her neck back and shoved down her revulsion.

"You're such a big, strong man." She made her voice soft and suggestive. She ran her gloved finger lightly down his cheek.

He hesitated, unaccustomed to ladies in fine muslin touching him. "Er . . ."

"A strapping fellow such as yourself . . ." She smiled and skimmed the grayish edge of his neck cloth, searching for the right grip. " . . . do you really need to show your power over these small little girls?"

"Smith!" The duke's deep voice boomed into the room like a cannon blast.

The overseer jerked away from Charlene, staring with dismay at the duke. "Your Grace."

"I've been in the exact situation you find yourself in now, Smith, and whatever you have done to incur this lady's wrath, I assure you it's not worth the punishment she will inflict."

Smith stared at the duke, then at Charlene.

The duke strode into the center of the room, tall and menacing.

"Is there a problem here?" he asked Charlene.

Charlene glanced at the brown-haired girl, who was still feverishly working, her thin hands dexterously shedding husks, not daring to lift her eyes. Charlene pulled the duke aside, out of hearing of the girls. "I caught Smith with his hand down one of their bodices."

The duke's eyes darkened. "Smith," he roared. "Come here."

Smith skulked toward them, crushing the felt hat he held in his hands. "Yes, Your Grace?"

"I hear you were handling one of my employees."

Smith swallowed. "I was only teaching her how to winnow."

"Wrong."

Smith took a step backward. "But she's an indolent girl, she needed me to teach her."

"Wrong again." The duke's voice was as cold as a January wind and sent shivers down Charlene's spine.

Smith's face went white. Even his ruddy nose turned as pale as the inside of a radish. "Now see here, I wasn't doing anything wrong. She's a lazy girl. She needed a lesson."

The duke flicked a finger toward the door. "You're discharged. Gather your things and leave."

The winnowers stared, mouths agape. Charlene caught the brown-haired girl's eye and gave her an encouraging smile.

Smith clenched his huge hands into fists. "Now let's not be hasty, Your Grace. Let's talk this through like gentlemen."

As tall and big as Smith was, the duke was taller. And he had the advantage of intellect.

Before Charlene took another breath, the duke caught Smith by the collar and lifted him a full inch off the floor. The overseer scrabbled at the duke's fingers, attempting to loosen his hold but encountering nothing but unyielding granite.

"You're no gentleman." The duke shook Smith by the neck like a fox toying with a field mouse. Smith's eyes bulged and his feet kicked the floor.

"If I ever hear of you entering these premises again, I'll have you arrested," the duke said. "Or I'll kill you. Probably I'll kill you."

Now Charlene understood how he'd come by

the title of His Disgrace. He didn't look anything like a proper peer right now, with his muscles straining and murder in his eyes.

She wouldn't have been surprised to see his image on a tavern wall, stripped to the waist and advertised as England's reigning bare knuckle heavyweight champion.

Smith's mouth opened but no words emerged.

"What was that?" the duke asked, shaking him again.

"I-I'm leaving," Smith squeaked.

The duke thrust him away, and Smith caught the edge of a table to keep from falling. He lurched toward the door.

The duke approached the brown-haired girl. "You there, what's your name?"

The girl's brown eyes widened. "R-Rosie, Your E-eminence."

"Has Smith bothered you before?"

The girl's eyes scrunched up and a tear slid down her cheek.

"You're frightening her," Charlene whispered. "She won't talk to you. Let me try."

"Rosie?" Charlene asked.

"Yes, your ladyship?"

An older girl with the same brown hair and eyes nudged Rosie. "Curtsy to 'er ladyship," she whispered.

Rosie stood and dropped a clumsy curtsy.

"Don't be frightened," Charlene said. This would work better if she could exchange her fine lavender muslin for plain worsted. They would trust her more then.

The other girls at the table watched closely as she stood next to Rosie and bent to examine the cocoa beans heaped on the table. "How old are you?"

"Fifteen, your ladyship."

"And how many hours do you work every day?"

"Fourteen I reckon, your ladyship."

"And your pay?"

"Three bob a week, milady."

Charlene squeezed a cocoa bean until the husk crumbled into dust between her fingers.

Another tear slid down the girl's cheek. "Please don't send us away. We need the work, milady."

Charlene raised her head and spoke loud enough for all the girls to hear. "None of you will lose your place. There's no fear of that." She took Rosie's hand. "You can talk to me. Don't be afraid. Did Mr. Smith touch you often?"

She looked around at the other girls. The older girl nodded at Rosie. "You can tell the truth."

Rosie's lower lip trembled, and her gaze found the pile of beans in front of her. "Yes, milady, 'e touched us. But nothing more . . . so far."

Charlene's stomach sank into her boots, and she bit her lip so hard she tasted blood.

" 'E's rotten to the core, that one," the older girl said.

"I'm so sorry," said Charlene. What an inadequate thing to say.

There was nothing to say that would make the situation any less heartbreaking. She squeezed Rosie's hand. "We have to leave now, but please don't worry. Smith will never be back." She turned to the duke, who'd been watching the exchange with thunderclouds in his eyes.

The duke nodded grimly. "I'll find a female overseer and conduct an investigation. The salary they mentioned is lower than the one I authorized. Smith was probably pocketing the remainder. Back wages will be restored."

"Thank you, Your Grace," Rosie said, her eyes lighting with a happy spark. "That will be most welcome."

The duke was silent as they left the room. Charlene waited for him to say something, to apologize, but he only strode swiftly, so that she had to hurry to keep up, his back ramrod straight, his face set into harsh lines.

Outside in the corridor, he backed her against the wall. "What do you think you were doing sneaking off like that? Given your record, you could have fallen into a vat of cocoa and been scalded to death. I was worried."

So much for an apology. Charlene stuck out her chin. "I needed some air and tried to find my way outside."

"Don't lie to me." He flattened his hands against the wall, bracketing her face.

Charlene stayed motionless, listening to her own breathing. It made one's opponent commit errors.

"Admit it." He leaned in until his face was inches away. "You wanted to prove me wrong."

She smiled. Another effective technique. "And

it worked, didn't it? Three shillings a week? Do you call that a fair wage for skilled work?"

"I told you that wasn't the contract I approved."

"When was the last time you did an inspection to ascertain if your precious contract was being honored? I thought your manufactory would be more humane, yet I find these girls hunching over tables fourteen hours a day, subjected to harassment and low pay."

"Have a care, Lady Dorothea." A muscle clenched in his jaw. "You don't know the horrors I've witnessed in Trinidad and fought to put a stop to. Children dying of starvation. Pregnant women put to the lash. The tide of inhumanity is too strong. If one trickle is stopped, a flood of barbarism erupts somewhere else."

The pain etched on his face was so intense that she wanted to take him in her arms and comfort him.

She stared into his eyes. "I understand. But please don't neglect the abuses at your own doorstep. In my charity work I've seen girls like these forced into bawdy houses because of inadequate factory wages."

She was shaking. And she didn't care about being Lady Dorothea right now. In this moment she had the chance to do some good for these girls, to make the duke see his error.

"The reform societies seek to raise them up out of the mire of iniquity," she continued, "but tell me—who focuses on the root of the problem? Who educates them? Who gives them a fair wage?"

His hands moved from the wall to cup her chin. "I didn't think a privileged lady like you would care so deeply. What makes you care?"

*The resignation in a young girl's eyes after she sold her body for the first time.*

*The girls who worked the streets turning to cheap gin to dull the pain.*

*Red sores marring pretty faces, hair falling out in clumps when the pox took hold.*

"It's because I have so much," Charlene whispered. "And these girls have nothing. Nothing."

The duke wiped away her tears with his thumb, framing her face with his hands. "You never fail to surprise me."

"I have a dream, Your Grace. I want to start a boardinghouse for young girls. Not a prison masquerading as charity like Lady Gloucester's asylum, but a safe place for vulnerable girls to go when they have nowhere else to turn. I would provide for their education."

And she would teach them how to defend themselves. Give them confidence in their abilities.

Would Lady Dorothea say things like this? Would she even have cared enough to say something about Smith's treatment of the girls?

The duke smiled at her, and she forgot how to breathe.

"I like that idea immensely," he said.

She was suddenly aware of how close they were standing. How the wall pressed against her back and the duke hemmed her front, just as solid.

Where was the countess now? She should be here to catch them in a compromising position because Charlene was inches from being kissed again.

"You know?" said the duke. "I'm wondering if maybe my factory might serve a similar—"

She would never know what he'd been about to say because they were interrupted by a breathless Lady Gloucester, her plentiful bosom heaving with the exertion of running down the corridor.

The duke leapt away from Charlene, but Lady Gloucester didn't seem to have noticed their intimate position.

"Have you seen Lady Augusta? I can't think where she's gone."

The duke took Lady Gloucester's arm and ushered her down the hallway. "I'm sure she can't have gone far. When was the last time you saw her?"

"Only ten minutes ago. But that Van Veen fellow cornered me and was explaining all about cocoa solids or something, and I quite lost sight of her."

"There's a splendid view of the valley from an observation room upstairs. Perhaps she is enjoying the view."

"Do you think so? Oh, I hope so."

She was very distraught. What trouble did she think her daughter was in? Charlene recalled Lord Dalton's seductive smile and chiseled profile as he'd told her he'd help her win the duke.

All the storerooms along the corridor were empty or locked. They climbed upstairs. The duke opened a door.

And Lady Gloucester loosed an ear-piercing scream.

**D**alton stepped in front of Lady Augusta to shield her from view, but not before James registered her flushed cheeks, just-been-kissed lips, and disheveled hair.

"Why, Augusta, why?" Lady Gloucester wailed.

"Calm down, please," Dalton said. "I was only looking for something in her eye. I think she had a piece of dust caught in there."

James snorted.

"I feel faint." Lady Gloucester swayed. Charlene caught her and propped her up as best she could.

"Why must you always kiss the wrong ones, Augusta, you maddening girl?" Lady Gloucester moaned.

Lady Augusta tugged her bodice back into place. "I'm sorry, Mama. You know I try to be good." Her clear blue eyes brimmed with tears. "Only I'm simply not strong enough to resist. Only see his arms. And he *is* a marquess. Not exactly a footman like the . . ." She shut her mouth abruptly.

"You're far too beautiful to marry less than a d—" Lady Gloucester clamped her mouth closed as well, glancing around at the spectators, finally recalling she wasn't alone with her wayward daughter.

She supported her considerable bulk on Charlene's arm. "I don't suppose you would give Lady Augusta another chance, Your Grace? She comes from a family of eight." She glanced significantly at her daughter's hips. "Only think of the . . . possibilities."

James raised one eyebrow.

Lady Gloucester visibly quailed. "I didn't think so," she said, her double chin quivering.

Lady Augusta raced across the room and collapsed against her mother's bosom. "I'm sorry, Mother," she cried.

Charlene ushered the two sobbing women from the room. "Shall we find the other ladies?" James heard her say as they left.

He rounded on Dalton. "Just what was that?"

Dalton shrugged, attempting to look innocent. "What can I say? I never say no when a pretty girl wants a kiss. I can't help it if they are drawn to me like moths to a flame." His eyes danced. "And besides, this helps you narrow the field."

"So I'm supposed to thank you now?"

Dalton walked nonchalantly to the door, swinging an imaginary walking stick. "Now only two candidates remain. I know you'll make the right choice, old friend."

James bit back a choice retort and followed him out.

*Stick to the schedule, Harland,* he thought with grim determination.

Horse riding next. Something Lady Vivienne should excel at. Then dinner.

This would all be over soon.

Not soon enough.

# Chapter 15

**"I** refuse to pitch myself off a horse." Charlene folded her arms across her chest. She drew the line at bodily injury.

"You'll do whatever it takes," the countess said. "You don't know how to ride, but that doesn't mean you can't spoil Lady Vivienne's chances. Fetch Lady Dorothea's habit, Blanchard."

While Manon dressed Charlene in an olive green wool riding habit with military-inspired gold buttons and gold braid trim, the countess paced up and down the room, her shoulders rigid. "Think . . . *think*. What can we do?"

"Throw myself under his horse's hooves?" Charlene suggested sarcastically.

The countess looked thoughtful, as if she was considering the efficacy of being trampled in the pursuit of a duke. "No," she said, with some reluctance. "That might be too extreme. We'll have to send you down and create a diversion. Perhaps we could manufacture a small kitchen fire?"

Manon furrowed her brow. "Or perhaps Miss Beckett could twist her ankle while attempting to mount?"

"Feign an injury *before* she mounts that horse." The countess tapped her finger against her chin. "That might just work."

Wonderful. Charlene didn't relish the idea of making a spectacle of herself yet again. But attempting to actually ride the horse would be disastrous. That hadn't been a skill the countess could have taught her in a matter of hours.

Manon picked up a matching olive bonnet with a large curling plume mounted on the front, then fixed it atop Charlene's head.

"Oh," exclaimed the countess, looking out the window. "Lady Vivienne is already outside. You must hurry!"

Charlene raced down the stairs, nearly toppling a footman carrying a silver tray and tea service. Her boots slid across the endless expanse of marble, and she skidded to a stop at the doors. She burst outside, into the cool, late-afternoon air, and ran down the steps, stopping abruptly at the bottom.

They were trotting down the winding drive, Lady Vivienne perched elegantly on her sidesaddle in a gorgeous blue velvet riding habit that emphasized her slender curves, the duke astride a commanding black stallion.

Such a well-matched pair. Tall, sleek, patrician.

Charlene had to give Lady Vivienne credit—she'd underestimated her. Underneath all that ennui, there'd been a competitor, after all. What had she told the duke to make him leave without her?

Heedless of the fine wool of the riding habit,

Charlene plunked down on the bottom step and put her chin on her fist. If she knew how to ride a horse, she would gallop after them.

She hated feeling powerless.

Not willing to go back inside and face the countess's wrath yet, she rose and set off toward the wrought-iron gazebo in the center of the lawns, kicking the duke's glittering white pebbles along her path.

She should have kept her mouth closed in the factory. She'd criticized him too much. She'd never been able to suppress her opinion when she had something to say.

*Blast.*

If he proposed to Lady Vivienne, Charlene would be left with one hundred guineas, not enough to end their bondage to Grant or secure Lulu her apprenticeship.

Blast. Bugger. *Damn.* Pain sliced through her heart.

She might as well admit it. It hurt not only because of the money. It hurt because she wanted the duke to be fascinated and entranced, because she was beginning to like him.

As she neared the gazebo, Charlene heard the sound of sobbing. She walked up the steps. Flor was curled up in a ball on one of the iron benches, wrapped in her mother's red shawl, shaking with great, racking sobs that quaked through her whole body.

Charlene placed a hand on her back. "What's wrong, sweetheart?"

Flor peeked up at her with only one green eye. "I wanted to go riding with Papa, but he said no. I hate it here." She sobbed some more.

Charlene pushed her long, dark hair out of her eyes. "Sit up now, sweetheart."

Flor uncurled a little.

Charlene put an arm around her thin shoulders and produced a handkerchief. "You must miss your mother."

Flor nodded. "I try to be b-brave, Papa says I must try." Her face crumpled. "I don't feel brave."

She buried her face in Charlene's shoulder and cried. Charlene let her tears flow, stroking her hair and making soothing noises.

"Are you going to be my new mother?" Flor spoke into Charlene's chest.

Charlene worked on a snarl in Flor's loosely braided hair. She didn't want to lie.

"That's for your father to decide."

"I hope he chooses you." Flor's small voice quavered. "I'd like that."

"Oh darling, I'd like that, too."

Tears welled up in Charlene's eyes. She'd never thought this would become so complicated. She could only hope that Lady Dorothea would be kind to Flor and give her the love and care she so desperately needed.

"If you are my mother, will Miss Pratt have to go?" Flor asked, blowing her nose in the handkerchief.

"Don't you like her?"

"She doesn't like me. I heard her telling the

housekeeper that it was the Lord's test of her patience to teach an ungrateful brown child."

Outrage shot an arrow through Charlene's chest. She would have some choice words for Miss Pratt if she saw her again. "Dear heart, you mustn't pay her any heed. She's a bitter, unkind woman."

"But she's right. I never thought about it before I came to England. Here everyone has skin like milk." Flor lifted her hand to Charlene's cheek. "Like you. And Lady Vivienne." She started to sniffle again. "Miss Pratt makes me wear an itchy b-bonnet all day long." She narrowed her eyes at the discarded bonnet flung on the gazebo floor. "And she rubs lemon juice on my nose and cheeks and it stings, but she says it will improve my complexion."

Charlene's jaw clenched. Maybe she was here for a higher purpose than winning the duke for her half sister. And that higher purpose was sniffling in her arms, woebegone and unloved.

Charlene placed her hands on Flor's shoulders. "Now listen to me, Flor. Listen carefully."

Flor's eyes shimmered with tears. "Y-yes?"

"You are beautiful and strong and precious. Never let anyone tell you otherwise. Beauty comes in many different shades and shapes. Do you understand?"

Flor nodded.

"And another thing," Charlene said. "I hate bonnets, too."

Flor's eyes grew wide. "You do?"

Charlene ripped the bonnet from her head, scattering pins and feathers, and flung it onto the lawn. "Can't stand the horrid things."

Flor giggled.

Charlene hugged her. "That's better. You have such a nice laugh." She gestured to the pile of books sitting in disarray on the gazebo floor. "Were you reading?"

"These are Miss Pratt's books. I hate them."

Charlene had to smile at that. She lifted a slim volume and opened it at random. " 'Example Three. Of a little Girl that was wrought upon, when she was between Four and Five Years old, with some Account of her holy Life, and triumphant Death,' " she read aloud.

"All the children in that book die." Flor made a disgusted face. "They die and don't have any fun."

Charlene flipped the book closed. "Don't you have anything else? What about this one?" Charlene picked another book from the pile.

" 'The History of Little Goody Two-shoes,' " she read, " 'With the Means by which she acquired her Learning and Wisdom, and in Consequence thereof her Estate.' "

Flor stuck out her tongue. "That Goody Two-shoes never has any adventures."

Charlene laughed. "Don't you have any books you like?"

Flor leaned closer. "I have *Swiss Family Robinson*." She patted her pinafore pocket. "One of the sailors on the ship gave it to me. But Miss Pratt says I mustn't read it because it excites me too much."

Flor reminded Charlene of herself at that age. Chafing for fun, preferring to read tales about shipwrecked boys because they had all the adventures.

"Let's read it then, shall we?" Charlene asked.

Flor handed her the book and nestled against Charlene with a contented sigh.

"'For many days we had been tempest-tossed. Six times had the darkness closed over a wild and terrific scene . . .'" Charlene began. She read several chapters, stopping to answer Flor's animated questions about the strange flora and fauna the family encountered and their chances for survival on the island.

The sun was showing signs of setting when Charlene stopped reading. "We must go back inside." She hadn't seen the duke and Lady Vivienne return yet. Which was a very bad sign.

"Oh, let's not go yet," Flor protested. "Let's go out on the lawn and pretend we're the Swiss family." She dragged Charlene down the steps of the gazebo and on to the lawns. "You can be Fritz and I'll be Ernest!"

Charlene caught hold of Flor's arm. "Is that a wild boar I see?" she asked, pointing into the distance.

"I'll catch it!" Flor let loose a series of loud whoops and dashed across the lawn.

Charlene chased her, breathless and laughing. They rounded a hedge and ran straight into the duke and Lady Vivienne.

"Papa!" Flor launched herself at the duke and threw her arms around his legs.

Charlene dusted off her skirts. Lady Vivienne wasn't acting triumphant. In fact, she had rather a cross expression on her normally tranquil face.

Hope leapt in Charlene's heart.

"Shouldn't you be inside doing schoolwork?" the duke asked Flor in a steely voice. He turned to Charlene. "And you, Lady Dorothea. Aren't you supposed to be confined to your chamber with the megrims?"

Charlene glanced at Lady Vivienne. So that's what she'd told him. "I made a speedy recovery," she said sarcastically.

Lady Vivienne stared down her nose, exactly like the marchioness. "Where are your *bonnets*?"

Instantly, Charlene felt six years old again.

"Lady Dorothea *hates* bonnets." Flor looked at Charlene. "Tell her."

*Blast.* She cared more about championing Flor than pretending to be a proper lady right now. "Can't stand the horrid things," she said breezily.

"Well," huffed Lady Vivienne. "You'll both have *horrid* freckles tomorrow. See if you don't."

The duke held Flor at arm's length and surveyed her messy hair and grass-stained skirts. "You are supposed to be doing sums, and I find you racing about the lawn like a pair of colts." His lips turned down. "It won't do."

"Please, it was my fault. I thought she needed some fresh air," Charlene said.

"She needs to do her sums."

"We're not colts, Papa." Flor tugged on his hand. "We're the Swiss Family Robinson. Don't you want to play with us? You can be father Robinson." She eyed Lady Vivienne. "I don't suppose *you* want to play?"

Lady Vivienne sniffed again. "Certainly not. Mind your father and go inside immediately."

"Let's go in, dear," Charlene said. "We'll play more later."

Flor's eyes took on a mutinous expression. "Are you going to marry Lady Dorothea, Papa?"

There was a moment of uncomfortable silence.

Flor turned to Lady Vivienne. "I hope you don't marry *her*. She's no fun."

"Flor!" The duke rose and turned toward the house. "That's enough now. Go upstairs this instant."

Flor's lip trembled.

Lady Vivienne stared down her nose at Flor disdainfully.

Charlene took Flor's hand. "We'll walk back together, shall we?" she said softly. "Your father doesn't mean to speak in that tone, he's only tired from his long ride." She tossed him a look.

He narrowed his eyes.

Charlene tugged Flor back to the house, before she said something else she'd regret.

# Chapter 16

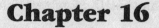

*Are you going to marry Lady Dorothea?*

How could he?

James positioned a log on the block and hefted an axe.

She'd just demonstrated why he couldn't marry her. She was actively encouraging Flor in her rebellious ways.

He slammed the blade into the wood.

*Crack.*

She was impulsive.

*Splinter.*

Irreverent.

*Thud.*

And worst of all? Impossible to ignore.

It was almost as if she was two people. One intent on meeting her exacting mother's standards, and, underneath the thin layer of propriety, someone fearless and outspoken, with passionate convictions and a decided disdain for social conventions.

He threw the newly split wood on the woodpile and paused, leaning on the axe.

The way they'd been tearing across the lawn, whooping and pretending to be shipwrecked boys.

The shock on Lady Vivienne's face. *Where are your bonnets?*

He smothered a smile. It had been undeniably amusing.

No. Not amusing. Deplorable. Highly inappropriate.

Flor had too much of James in her. She was restless. She couldn't sit still in the classroom when there were lawns to run across, rules to flout.

Probably Dorothea had been exactly the same at her age.

He wasn't here to find a sensual goddess with a razor-sharp intellect and a rebellious mind. He'd found that. And she was driving him insane.

He split wood until his arms ached and sweat dripped down his chest. He should go in and dress for dinner, but he wanted to exorcise Dorothea first.

He stood behind the old unused barns he'd converted into a workshop. He liked the large open space with no velvet draperies or ornamental plaster.

Most nights he slept in his workshop, on a pile of cushions. The nightmares were shorter out here. Less vivid. They seemed to fade the farther he was from his mother's chambers in the east wing. He hadn't visited that wing since he'd come back. Bickford had informed him that her chambers had been preserved exactly the way the duchess had left them. The household staff had loved his charming mother.

A shiver chased across James's shoulder blades.

He positioned more wood on the block.

He didn't want to revisit buried pain. He needed to follow the plan. Conclude things swiftly and return to Trinidad. But Dorothea did have a point. He'd had no idea there was corruption at the Banbury Hall manufactory. He couldn't be there to oversee every aspect of the business on two continents. Of course he would rectify it immediately, but it galled him that it had happened in the first place. He'd find a manager he could trust.

He was only one man. And he was being split along so many different fault lines.

He could still see the accusation in her blue-gray eyes. He'd disappointed her. Why did that sting so much?

"Hiding, Your Grace?"

Dorothea rounded the wall of the barn, her cheeks rosy, fists planted on her hips. The riding habit was gone and she was wearing something pale pink and virginal, but her hair was a wind-swept cascade of golden curls escaping from a bright red silk bandeau.

He placed another log on the block and raised his axe.

"Well?" she said.

"What? What do you want from me?"

*Crack.*

"Go apologize to your daughter."

*Splinter.*

"I can't do that."

*Thud.*

"Why not? She's your daughter. Don't you love her?"

"You don't understand."

"Try to explain."

He sighed and set the axe aside. He turned his back to her and stacked the fallen wood on top of the pile. "It doesn't matter if I love her. I have to keep my distance. She can't become too attached. I'll be leaving soon."

"You're very skilled at that, aren't you, *Your Grace*?"

Impressive how she made his title sound like a scurrilous oath. He rested his hands on the stack of wood. He knew her well enough by now to know that she wasn't finished giving her opinion, not by half.

"At what, Lady Dorothea?"

"You're so good at running away. At keeping your distance. Not letting anyone close to you." Her smoky voice was getting closer. Soon he would smell fresh, lemony tea roses. Feel her warmth and fire behind him.

He gripped the wood hard enough to drive a sliver into his palm. Still he didn't turn around. He couldn't. If he turned around, he'd want to take her in his arms, kiss those full lips. Make promises that were impossible to keep.

"Flor needs you. You've no idea how much," she said. "When was the last time you read her a story?" She didn't wait for him to respond. "And another thing. You need to send that governess away. Do you know what she makes Flor read?"

"I have a feeling you're going to tell me." He turned around.

And almost fell to his knees.

She was haloed by golden curls ablaze in the fading sun. So achingly sweet. He clenched his hand into a fist, and the sliver pierced deeper.

*That's what you get when you think about kissing her. Pain. Remember that.*

She extracted a slim volume from somewhere in her skirts and read the title aloud. *"A Token for Children: Being an Exact Account of the Conversion, Holy and Exemplary Lives and Joyful Deaths of Several Young Children, in Two Parts."*

She waved the book at him like a weapon. "Joyful deaths. Of *children.*"

"Doesn't sound very cheerful."

"And another thing." Dorothea advanced toward him. "Miss Pratt smears lemon juice on Flor's cheeks to make her skin lighter. It's abhorrent. I won't have it." She tossed the book onto the woodpile. "That's what I think of Miss Pratt." She wiped her hands on her skirts. *"Your Grace."*

"I didn't know about the lemon juice. I'll certainly command that to stop, but I did give her license to select the reading materials she thought best suited to teach my daughter to rein in her temper and become a proper young lady."

"A *proper young lady.*" She spat the words like an obscene oath, direct kin to *Your Grace.* *"Proper* is another word for prison, if you ask me."

"I don't recall asking you."

"A proper young lady shouldn't run on the lawn, or cry because she needs attention, or read adventure books. A proper young lady should walk sedately, keep her chin up, and read insipid morality tales. Is that it?"

This was definitely striking close to home. She must have hated her governess as a child. James pictured her plaguing a steady stream of governesses. Goading them into unbecoming fits of temper. Putting toads in their beds. Sending them screaming for the nearest mail coach.

"I don't want to take the joy out of her life," he said. "That's not my aim. I'm only trying to protect her, to guide her. I was sent down from school, disgraced forever because of one impetuous, *rebellious* decision."

"You will transform your vibrant, healthy, curious child into a model of silent, docile propriety. I say that's too bad." She narrowed her eyes. "Too *damn* bad. Do you think that if she speaks softly and never runs that the rest of England will let her forget who she is?"

"It will ultimately be for her own good."

Dorothea shook her head. The red bandeau slipped. She brushed curls away from her cheeks impatiently. "That's no excuse. She needs to be included in your life. Let her come downstairs tonight."

Any other young lady would have been begging him to keep his scandalous by-blow hidden. The marchioness's reaction had been typical of the reception he expected from the pious ladies of the *ton*. "It would antagonize my other guests."

"Only for a moment? She's so very lonely."

"Absolutely not."

"She needs love and acceptance. Don't abandon her."

"She needs to learn to control her emotions."

"Not every word that comes forth from your mouth is scripture, and not all your decisions are holy commandments."

"You're quite free with your criticism. You disapprove of the way I conduct my business and the way I educate my daughter. Tell me, Lady Dorothea, why you would possibly wish to continue your stay in my home a moment longer?"

There, that had silenced her. But only for a moment.

"Because you're sorely in need of reform." A glint appeared in her eyes. "And I've never been one to shirk a nearly impossible challenge."

Damn her for making him smile. "And I suppose you're precisely the irascible girl to attempt such a fool's mission?"

"I am."

She walked toward him. "You don't fool me. You cared about those girls at the factory. You hate the evil of enslavement. And you love your daughter. Somewhere deep inside that murky heart of yours, you want to do the right thing, but you're afraid of losing her, as you lost the rest of your family."

She went too far. So why did he want to kiss her so badly?

In his defense, the red ribbon tied around her curls was taunting him. It kept slipping down, threatening to loose a flood of silken temptation.

They stared at each other like a matador and

bull. He could almost feel steam rising from his nostrils.

Somewhere a crowd roared for blood.

Hang it all. He was His Disgrace. The exiled scoundrel.

He'd show her how badly in need of reform he was.

He closed the distance between them with one long stride and buried his fingers in her hair.

The silk bandeau finally lost the battle and slipped loose, sending honey and sunshine curls cascading around her shoulders.

Like a man who'd been wandering the desert for days, he found the wellspring of her lips, all the reasons he shouldn't kiss her disappearing like footprints in shifting sand.

Her soft, encouraging little moans destroyed his control.

"Dorothea," he groaned into her hair.

He took her mouth, crushing her hips against him, kissing her as if they'd been the last two humans on earth. As if the fate of civilization depended on this moment.

There was this.

Her heat burning through his linen. The urgency of her mouth moving beneath him, unconsciously mimicking the act of love. Opening for him, welcoming him inside.

He dipped his fingers into the edge of her bodice, skimming across the tops of her velvet-soft breasts. She shifted back in his arms, instinctively giving him better access.

If he slipped her bodice a few inches lower and lowered his head, he could feast on rosy nipples.

Instead, he buried his face in her curls, inhaling the fresh, innocent scent of tea roses.

He couldn't ravish a trusting debutante outside by the woodpile. No matter how saucily she goaded him to it.

He wrenched away, cursing himself for a lust-addled fool. "I'm sorry. We shouldn't . . ."

She looked up at him, breathing heavily, her blue eyes hazy. "That was . . . most definitely a ten." She smiled shakily, adjusting her skirts. "I knew you had it in you." She tossed her head but failed to sound truly flippant.

"Dorothea . . ." he began, not sure where he was going.

"I must return. Mother will be worried about me. You *will* apologize to Flor, won't you?"

"Of course. I was always going to."

She nodded. "Then we're even," she said, and left.

James watched her walk away, hips swaying, hair spilling down her back. He could chop down this entire forest and it wouldn't erase the memory of what had just happened.

Maybe she was right. Maybe he was scared of losing Flor. He'd chosen solitude over connection a long time ago, after his mother died and his father tried to beat the rebellion out of him and then banished him to the West Indies.

That wasn't something that would ever change. But he was going back to Trinidad and leaving his wife in England. He'd only return when it was absolutely necessary, for business, or to father more spares.

Dorothea was a female who would always follow an unpredictable path. He admired her mettle, but he wasn't looking for strength of spirit. He required a wife who would be his emissary of propriety and respectability, soothing gossips and investors while he remained overseas.

Lady Vivienne would never wrestle him to the floor.

Or throw his library books on the woodpile.

He needed to make a decision. Before he did something truly depraved with Dorothea and the choice was made for him.

# Chapter 17

There they were. His two remaining duchess candidates. Seated side by side in the salon after another interminable dinner, as different as two women could be. Fire and ice. Propriety and passion.

The mounded tops of Dorothea's breasts glowed above pale pink velvet, and diamonds gleamed in her hair, her ears, and at her throat, enough to finance an entire battalion.

He couldn't be in the same room with her without an overwhelming urge to throw her over his shoulder and claim her. He wanted her in his bed, wearing those diamonds and nothing more. He wanted to strip away the thin veneer of propriety and delve into the passion he'd glimpsed simmering beneath her genteel façade.

Her fire heated his blood, and her intelligence and wit dared him to imagine new possibilities.

"Perhaps Lady Vivienne might play the pianoforte, Your Grace?" the marchioness suggested.

James tore his gaze from Dorothea and nodded his assent. Lady Vivienne took a seat at the polished maple pianoforte. She wore a modest white gown and simple pearl jewelry that set off her dark hair and eyes. She was elegant, reserved, and the obvious, prudent choice.

She'd soothe the gossips and rehabilitate his reputation. Everyone knew his father had nearly disowned him. No doubt many questioned his fitness to assume the title. That last stunt at Cambridge had been the culmination of an illustrious career of transgressions, ranging from brandy binges to tupping a don's wife. And staying abroad for ten years hadn't won him any hearts.

He needed to prove them wrong, win them over, and Lady Vivienne would be an excellent weapon.

The Scarlatti sonata she chose had been written for harpsichord and lost something when played on the pianoforte, but it was a virtuoso piece and required an expert touch. Her nimble fingers flew over the keyboard, her left hand crossing over her right to perform the trills. It was a flawless performance, calculated to dazzle and impress.

The music she played was meant as a minor-keyed frenzy of frustrated longing. While she hit every note, it left him unmoved.

The thought of bedding her was uninspiring . . . but that had been his aim. He'd wanted a business arrangement, a marriage of convenience.

James imagined proposing to her.

"How do you feel about marriage, Lady Vivienne?" he'd ask.

"It's what one does, I suppose," she'd answer, yawning.

And on their wedding night.

"Shall we go to bed?" he'd ask.

"It's what one does, I suppose."

At the pianoforte, Lady Vivienne frowned slightly, completely focused on her task, ruthless in her single-mindedness. Was she *too* cold and detached? She had treated Flor with disdain when they caught his child running on the lawn. Would she learn to love Flor with time?

After her daughter finished playing, the marchioness turned to Dorothea. "Would you care for a turn on the pianoforte, Lady Dorothea?"

"I'm afraid Lady Dorothea can't play this evening," said Lady Desmond. "She . . . had an accident with her jewelry box this morning. Crushed her finger."

The marchioness raised her quizzing glass and trained it on Dorothea. "Is that so?"

"Only a slight injury. I might sing a song instead," Dorothea suggested.

The countess startled. "No, I'm sure the duke wishes to play his guitar again. Would you honor us?"

Interesting. The countess didn't want her daughter to perform. Now James's curiosity was piqued. Was she worried her daughter would do something outrageous? Sing a bawdy song and embarrass her?

"You've had enough of my guitar. I would rather hear Lady Dorothea sing," he said.

Dorothea smiled at him and his heart skipped a beat.

"I shall perform something current," she announced, rising from her seat. "From Mr. Bishop's *The Libertine*, which I . . . we . . . recently had the pleasure to see Miss Catharine Stephens perform at the Theatre Royal in Covent Garden."

Lady Desmond half-rose from her seat, as if she wanted to run and silence her daughter. She dug her nails into silk brocade.

The curve of Dorothea's hips settled into the deep arc of the pianoforte. Drawing a breath that made her bosom rise and fall over pink velvet, she knotted her hands in front of her waist.

One more breath like that and they'd be staring at her rosy-tipped breasts again.

*Please God, no more nipples,* he prayed. He wouldn't be responsible for the consequences. Not after he'd spent every second since their kiss this afternoon imagining what might have happened if his fingers had slipped two inches further into her bodice.

He might have to grab one of the footman's silver serving trays for cover.

Thankfully, everyone was looking at Dorothea as well, her mother with an anxious expression, the marchioness with a condescending half sneer, and Lady Vivienne . . . no, her gaze had wandered to the window and she was suppressing a yawn.

Dorothea began to sing. "Pretty lasses love's summer, remember, ever flies upon gossamer wing; Suffer not then, life's chilly December, to destroy Cupid's bow and his string."

Her voice wasn't opera quality, but it was strong

and true. The tune was simple, adapted from Mozart's *Don Giovanni*, if he wasn't mistaken, but it was the way she sang that arrested everyone's attention.

She slowed the melody, and, instead of warbling in a high soprano, drew the marrow from the notes in a husky contralto that tingled along his spine.

The simple song became fraught with poignancy—a young girl realizing her beauty would fade, her gossamer gowns no protection from winter's sting.

"Make haste, and be happy, like me," she sang. But instead of the blitheness of youth, every note was infused with heartache.

He studied her face. How had an untried debutante learned to sing with such subtlety and emotion?

The countess stopped clutching her chair arms and relaxed back into her seat, smiling with relief.

Dorothea caught his eye, singing directly to him now. "And ye lads, who are constantly changing, for a time though 'tis pleasant to run, from this beauty to that, ever ranging, yet, at last, pray, be constant to one."

The marchioness flapped a carved ivory fan. Lady Vivienne didn't yawn.

Dorothea was nearly whispering now, her eyes speaking of heartbreak and longing, almost as if she had a reason to doubt the constancy of men. His mind reverberated with questions. Had she been in love with someone else, and been jilted?

*Mine*, his traitorous mind declared with primitive possessiveness. She couldn't love anyone but him.

"Make haste, and be happy, like me . . ." she finished.

The room fell silent.

What had just happened? He'd been expecting something saucy and provocative, and instead she'd taken a standard drawing room ballad and made it ring with truth.

Where did these depths come from?

Dorothea resumed her seat, and Lady Desmond cleared her throat. "Lady Vivienne," she said with a hint of triumph in her cultured voice. "Will you honor us with another performance?"

"Certainly." Lady Vivienne settled onto the seat and launched into a Chopin sonata that was as serene and unflappable as she was.

James attempted to concentrate on the soothing technical expertise of her playing, but it was nearly impossible with all those enigmatic diamonds glittering in his peripheral vision.

Lady Vivienne played on, the notes flowing flawlessly. The duke stared at her, seemingly entranced. Charlene had to admit she was skilled, but there was something missing from her performance. It didn't make Charlene *feel* anything.

"Psst, Lady Dorothea." Flor's sleek head poked between a footman's legs.

Charlene shook her head. "Not now," she mouthed.

Flor held up the wooden discs she'd played the night before. What had she called them? Castanelas? She clicked them in her little fingers, a mischievous grin tilting up the side of her lips.

Charlene had seen that grin before. On the duke. Right before he bent to kiss her.

She glanced around the room. Everyone was watching Lady Vivienne, including the duke. She turned back to Flor and held up a finger. "One moment," she mouthed.

Flor's head disappeared.

Charlene leaned over to the countess. "I feel a bit faint," she whispered. "I'm going to slip outside for some air."

The countess nodded, and Charlene rose as silently as possible and tiptoed out of the salon. Flor was waiting on the balcony outside.

Charlene lifted her up and kissed her soft cheek. "You're going to land me in trouble, you little imp."

Flor wrapped her arms around Charlene's neck. "You don't want to listen to that, do you?" She wrinkled her nose in the direction of the salon.

"Chopin is exquisite, silly. What are you doing out here, anyway?"

"Practicing my *castañuelas*. Miss Pratt won't let me play them in the nursery." She held out the wooden discs. "Do you want me to teach you now?"

It was a warm evening, with the lingering smell of sunlight and bee pollen on the breeze. The piano music was faint out here, a tinkling accompaniment to the moonlight.

Charlene set Flor on her feet. She should go

back to the salon, but she felt such a kinship with this girl. It hurt dreadfully to think she'd never see her again.

She put her arm around Flor's shoulders and squeezed her slight frame. She hoped with all her heart that Lady Dorothea would feel the same way, that she would nurture Flor's independence instead of taming it in the name of propriety.

"No matter what happens, please remember that you are strong," Charlene said. "England can't change you unless you let it. There are some changes you might choose to make, and others that you can refuse."

Flor tilted her head to one side. "What do you mean?"

"Well, even if you don't like Miss Pratt, and she doesn't like you, it's important for you to listen and receive an education. Knowledge gives you power, Flor. I want you to promise to read as many books as possible, to never stop reading and thirsting for knowledge as long as you live."

Nodding solemnly, Flor crossed her heart with her finger. "I swear."

Charlene smiled. "I'd better have that lesson now."

Flor placed the two wooden discs in Charlene's hand and wrapped the red silk cord around her thumb. "Now open your hand, and then shut it again." She demonstrated the motion.

Charlene tried, but the wooden discs wouldn't cooperate. They flopped from her fingers, soundless.

"Here, watch me." Flor clicked the two pieces of hollow wood together, controlling the motion with her fingers.

This time Charlene managed to make a clicking sound. It wasn't so difficult. A few controlled flicks of her fingers. Soon she was lifting her arm and clicking along to Flor's delighted laughter.

"Wait," Flor said. "You need this." She unloosened her mother's red shawl from around her shoulders and draped it around Charlene's hips, tying it in a side knot. She ran to the balcony railing. "And this." She plucked a late summer rose from the vines twining through the iron railing.

Charlene bent down, and Flor tucked the rose behind her ear.

Flor stepped back to survey her handiwork. She nodded. "Now you are ready to dance."


**O**f course James found Dorothea dancing in the moonlight. She couldn't possibly sit demurely in the salon, and she'd obviously exceeded her quota of polite conversation during dinner. He'd pretended not to notice that she'd slipped away, and he'd waited a decent interval before following, on the pretext of hand-selecting a port from the cellars.

He couldn't help himself. He was the moth, and Dorothea was lit by a thousand dancing diamond flames as she twirled in Flor's red silk scarf, with a red rose tucked behind her ear.

If her red bandeau this afternoon had been maddening, the ember-colored silk knotted around her hips, hugging her tempting arse, was the equivalent of an army of matadors flourishing an entire line of capes.

Flor directed the dance, her dark hair absorbing the night, her small wedge of a face furrowed with concentration. She struck a pose, hip thrust to one side, back straight, neck held high, arm raised gracefully. "Follow me," she called.

Dorothea followed Flor across the balcony, easily imitating the steps and adding her own sensual flourishes into the dance.

James shut his eyes, but the enticing vision of Dorothea's full hips outlined in red silk continued rippling across the inside of his eyelids.

*Turn around. Return to the salon. Propose to calm and cultured Lady Vivienne.*

*None of this reckless dancing in the moonlight.*

Yet . . . Dorothea was so good with Flor. Even if she wasn't the most proper of young ladies, she obviously cared for Flor and would be kind to her.

He stood on the edge of the balcony, hovering between the two possibilities.

Damn it all. Moth. Flame.

He cleared his throat. Both females spun around with the same guilty expression on their faces.

Flor ran to him, but instead of flinging herself into his arms, as she normally would, she hesitated, stopping short, hands hanging by her sides.

*What had he done?*

He touched her hair, intensely aware of Dorothea glowing behind her. "You're supposed to be asleep, Flor." His voice was gruff and harsh to his ears.

"I know, Papa. I'm sorry." She took his hand, and the feeling of her soft little fingers brought back a memory. Standing on the deck of the ship back to England, Flor's small hand in his. Her sad eyes. The way the sea breeze whipped her hair around her face and she pushed it out of her eyes impatiently, not wanting to miss anything.

Flor pulled on his hand. "Papa? I taught Lady Dorothea how to use the *castañuelas*. Did you see?"

"I did see. You learn quickly, Lady Dorothea," he said, avoiding her gaze. She'd be quick to learn everything, he had no doubt. And there were so very many things he wanted to teach her.

"Fetch your guitar, Papa, and play for us," Flor suggested.

That was the last thing he needed—Dorothea's sumptuous hips undulating while he controlled the rhythm on his guitar.

Dorothea shook her head and unwrapped the silk cord from around her thumb. She handed the *castañuelas*, or castanets, as they were called in England, back to Flor. "It's late, dear, your father must return to his guests. Time for you to go back to bed."

"No." Flor stamped her foot. "I want Papa to play for us." Her lips pressed together in the mutinous expression he'd come to know so well in the last year. It signaled she was on the verge of erupting into one of her fits of temper.

Dorothea didn't scold his daughter; she only bent down until her eyes were at a level with Flor's and said, with careful patience, "Remember what I said to you earlier? We can't always have our way. Sometimes we have to bend, just a little bit. Sometimes we might even sway, like a tree in a storm, but we won't break. We only become stronger."

To his surprise, Flor nodded. "I understand," she said softly. "I'll go to bed."

James smiled. "Maybe just one dance before bed."

Flor's eyes sparked with excitement. "Really?" She brought his hand to Dorothea's hand. "Dance with Lady Dorothea, Papa."

He took Dorothea's hand. He couldn't stop himself. He wanted to touch her, in whatever way was available.

"May I have this dance, my lady?" He bowed over Dorothea's hand, brushing his lips across her knuckles, breathing in the scent of crushed rose petals.

For a moment, he had the strangest feeling that Dorothea was about to cry, but then she smiled and inclined her head, the polished debutante. "With pleasure, Your Grace."

Flor started humming a triple-meter waltz.

"I thought this was a Spanish dance?" James asked.

"No." Flor shook her head emphatically. "A waltz. You are in a fashionable ballroom, and everyone is watching you."

James laughed. "A waltz then." He clasped his

arm around Dorothea's waist. She stiffened for a moment, but relaxed as he guided her into the movement. They glided across the balcony, with Flor humming and giggling beside them.

There were shadows in the hollow of Dorothea's neck, in the cleft of her breasts, her eyes.

He leaned in to whisper in her ear. "The song you sang. It sounded as if you might have experienced a gentleman's inconstancy. Was there . . . is there . . . someone else?"

He tightened his grip around her waist. There'd better not be.

"No, there's no one."

Thank God. He believed her. She was a talented performer, that was all.

Dancing with her almost made him wish he'd been able to attend the season. To waltz with her in as many different ballrooms as possible.

She broke away from his grasp. "Dance with Flor now." There was a catch in her voice. Why did she sound so sad? He tilted her chin toward him.

"Please," she pleaded. "Dance with Flor."

James stepped away and bowed to his daughter. "May I have this dance, Lady Flor?"

She smiled shyly and curtsied. "Yes, Papa."

He lifted her into his arms, spinning her around the balcony. His daughter was full of light, and life, and laughter tonight. He realized he hadn't heard her laugh much. It was a lovely sound.

He glanced over Flor's head and met Dorothea's eyes. She smiled, but was that a tear glittering in her eye?

"You dance divinely, Lady Flor," he said with great gravity.

Flor wrapped her arms tighter around his neck. "Thank you ever so, Your Grace," she replied, with her best imitation of a society lady.

The murmur of voices from the salon grew louder. "Where is the duke?" he heard the marchioness ask loudly.

He set Flor down.

"Time for bed now," Dorothea said. She kissed Flor's cheek. "You'll remember what I told you?"

Flor nodded.

"I must go back," Dorothea said to James.

James carried Flor to the nursery and tucked her into bed. As she curled up and fell immediately into a deep sleep, the realization struck him like the flat of a heavy sword across his chest.

He was going to miss his fearless little Flor. Dearly.

And it had taken an equally outspoken woman with blue-gray eyes glowing brighter than diamonds in moonlight to make him see it.

# Chapter 18

**M**anon unfastened velvet buttons and removed diamonds.

Tomorrow, Charlene would never wear diamonds again, never be wrapped in the luxury that was Dorothea's birthright. Dorothea would perfect her trousseau of fine linens and silk in preparation for her wedding night while Charlene returned to gray worsted flannel nightgowns and a lonely, narrow bed.

In her mind, she'd dropped the "Lady" when she thought of her half sister. Didn't impersonating Dorothea entitle her to claim a more intimate acquaintance? It was probably silly, but Charlene was beginning to feel connected to her half sister. As if she was preparing her a gift.

*Here, take this duke. Be his perfect duchess. Be a good mother to Flor.*

The countess sailed into the room, still dressed in black silk and pearls. "Well, Miss Beckett?" she asked. "You were absent for quite some time, and the duke was as well. What happened?"

"We waltzed on the balcony in the moonlight."

"And?"

"He kissed me." Well, he hadn't actually kissed her, not this time. He'd been thoughtful. Pensive. But he'd wanted to kiss her. And he *had* kissed her, twice before.

"Splendid." The countess motioned to Manon. "Now for the coup de grâce. Run and fetch Madame Hélène's creation."

Manon curtsied and headed into the dressing room.

"You will go to him tonight," the countess said. "We have the location of his bedchamber on good intelligence. Blanchard will spirit you there, under cover of night. I will give you some time before I appear."

Charlene shook her head. "He won't be in his bedchamber."

"How can you possibly know that?"

"Don't worry, I know where he'll be."

The countess narrowed her eyes. "Where?"

"The kitchens."

"The kitchens? Why would he be there?"

"He has difficulty sleeping. His . . . cook told me he goes to the kitchens to prepare cocoa."

The countess removed her gold-embroidered wrap and compressed it into a small square with neat, precise folds. "Very well, then, I will meet you in the kitchens after a suitable interval. Need I remind you of the stakes here?"

Charlene met her calculating gaze. "I'm perfectly aware of the terms of our bargain."

The countess gave a curt nod. "Despite your unfortunate upbringing, you're a remarkably resourceful girl, with surprising backbone."

Charlene smiled. "Why, thank you, your lady-ship." It was as close to a compliment as she'd ever receive from the countess.

"I'm counting on you, Miss Beckett. Lady Doro-thea is counting on you. Don't fail us." The count-ess left, her black silk skirts rustling across the carpet.

Manon entered and held up a filmy negligee. "You will be irresistible in this, Miss Beckett." She laid the garment reverently across the bed.

A long length of creamy satin. Thin straps and lace insets. Pure seduction, the finest the countess could buy.

Manon brushed Charlene's hair. Twenty strokes. All the snarls gone. Fifty. One hundred. Waves of wheat-colored silk falling to Charlene's waist.

"The duke is very handsome and command-ing, *non*?" Manon's brown eyes twinkled. "Are you sure you can control him?"

Charlene bit her lip. "What if I can't control *myself*?"

Manon smiled. "Perhaps you shouldn't." She helped Charlene out of her shift and slipped the negligee over her head. The heavy satin slithered down her body and settled against her curves in a whispered caress.

Manon drew a cut-glass perfume bottle from her apron pocket. "This is from Paris." She dabbed scent onto Charlene's wrists, behind her ears, and in her hair.

Vanilla, jasmine, and something sharper and herbal. Almost like rosemary. More sophisticated than Dorothea's simple roses. A scent that would linger in a man's memory.

Charlene touched Manon's hand. "Thank you."

"It is my pleasure." Manon gathered the discarded dress, petticoats, and slippers. "You know? The duke, he doesn't stand a chance." She closed the door behind her.

Charlene ran a hand over her breasts, over peaks that stood out against the creamy satin of the negligee. Lower, over her belly and down, between her thighs, to a pulse that beat, faint but steady.

Would he touch her there?

And, if he did, would she be severed from the old Charlene forever?

Her sensible gray dress and worn leather boots had to be in the bottom of one of the trunks, waiting for her. She could find them right now. Run away.

Before it was too late.

She took a step toward the dressing room.

Satin swirled around her legs.

Jasmine and vanilla drifted in her hair.

*No fear, remember?*

She heard Grant's chilling voice in her mind. *Don't fight me, little bird. I've waited too long for this.*

She was no man's doxy. She would see this through. For Lulu. For her mother. For their freedom.

But also . . . for herself.

She wanted the duke's hands on her, where her hands had been.

She wanted him.

*For her.*

Charlene stared at the woman in the mirror.

Two women stared back.

One still closed and barricaded. Wary of her mission and of the duke.

One impatient and ready for sin.

She wanted to go to him.

*Hurry up*, the wicked self said. *Take your fill. Enough to last a lifetime.*

**O**utside the kitchens, Charlene breathed in the familiar scent of chocolate and spices.

The duke.

She stopped for a moment to pinch her cheeks and fluff her hair around her shoulders. Slowly, she pushed the heavy wooden door open, her stomach fizzing.

There was *someone* cooking chocolate on the range. But it wasn't the duke. Her throat closed with disappointment and she almost ran away, but Mrs. Mendoza turned her head and saw her.

"Come here." She motioned to Charlene with her head.

At Charlene's puzzled glance, the old woman smiled. "See what I'm making."

Charlene sniffed the mixture. Red chili peppers bobbed in the bubbling liquid. It smelled spicy and thick. The peppers made her sneeze.

Mrs. Mendoza laughed. Even though her face was weathered, and wreathed with deep wrinkles, her brown eyes shone bright and clear.

"Don't you want to take some chocolate to the duke?" She smiled slyly.

"Do you know where he is?"

Mrs. Mendoza stopped whisking. "Outside. He has been working on the cocoa press. We will make the finest drinking chocolate together. My family's cocoa beans will be famous in all of England."

She poured the mixture into a large stoneware mug, placing a towel over the mug and wrapping it tight. She handed it to Charlene and guided her toward the back entrance to the kitchens and out into the night air. "Hurry, or it will be cold. Follow the path. You see his light."

There was a light wavering in the windows of the structure where the duke had kissed her earlier today.

"But I—"

"Go. Quickly." Mrs. Mendoza clapped her hands. *"Rápido, por favor."*

Charlene clutched her dressing gown closed with her free hand. Was she really supposed to walk across the lawns and disturb the duke? The countess wouldn't know where to find them.

This was not the plan.

The door closed in her face.

She shivered in the cold air. Began to walk along the path, toward the duke's light.

His gardens were meticulously maintained. Moonlight glinted on a white marble fountain, and the trim hedges cast long shadows around her. No piece of bracken would dare poke sideways on these ruthlessly perpendicular hedges.

The pathway was lined with red roses. Char-

lene was more accustomed to roses bound together and stacked in piles in the wheelbarrows of
the flower vendors at the Covent Garden market.
Here they were rooted in the soil, able to whisper
to their sisters at night.

Soon, when the sun warmed them and the
rain fed them, they would open. Petal by petal.
Unfurling into the sun, offering what they had to
give. Color, scent, beauty.

The lives of the girls at the Pink Feather were
like those London roses—clipped too early, forced
to unfurl. How small their world was. Bordered
by soot-stained walls and doors that closed on the
commerce of lust.

Charlene wanted them to be able to put down
roots. Soak into the soil. They would have a
garden at the new boardinghouse.

The door to the duke's hideaway was closed,
but she could see smoke rising from a chimney.

She knocked.

No answer.

She tested the knob, and the door swung open.

The duke was at the far end of the oblong
room, heaping wood onto a roaring fire in an
iron grate. He didn't hear her enter because of
the grinding of a metal apparatus pumping and
whirring behind him.

The strange device bristled with angular pipes
and was connected by copper tubing to the stove.

"I've brought your cocoa!"

He didn't hear her over the clanking and
hissing.

There was a collection of knives hung along one

wall. Curved scimitars, primitive stone tools, jeweled silver daggers. The floor in one corner was covered with a red carpet and piles of cushions, as if he slept here sometimes.

"Your Grace," she shouted, louder this time.

He spun around.

Sweat dripped down his neck, and his white shirt stuck to his heavily muscled chest. He appeared perfectly at home here, in the flickering inferno, with oil lamps and firelight limning his powerful form.

He mopped a towel over his brow, leaving a streak of soot along his cheekbone that gave him a diabolical air.

He was more devil than duke.

She swallowed.

*Keep calm. There's no danger. The water is shallow.* She repeated his words from the boating accident in her mind as she crossed the long room, entering deeper into the devil's lair.


James wiped the sweat from his forehead.

He'd been thinking about Dorothea constantly and here she was, wrapped in a quilted pink silk dressing gown, with her hair unbound and streaming around her shoulders in a golden halo.

His thoughts made flesh.

She held out a mug. "I brought you some chocolate."

He blew on the hot liquid before taking a sip. Chili pepper burned his lips, dissipating quickly, leaving the chocolate liberally mixed with sugar and milk. "Josefa sent you to me?" he asked.

"Yes." Her eyes were unfathomable dark pools in the dim light.

"She likes you."

*He* liked her. Far too much. No use denying it any longer.

She eyed the steam press. "What is this?"

The press clanked and shuddered behind them.

He took another sip of chocolate. "It's supposed to be a steam-powered cocoa press. It uses the same principles as the steam engine you saw at the factory today. On a smaller scale, of course."

"You *made* this?"

"With Van Veen's help. We can't seem to get it quite right. It doesn't apply enough pressure. It's supposed to take the chocolate liquor, created from crushing the beans, and press out all the fat."

James showed her the thin trickles of amber-colored oil trailing into catch basins on either side of the tall machinery, which held a series of inter-connecting bowls designed to apply pressure to the chocolate liquor.

"Van Veen says if we can press the fat out, the cocoa left will be easily powdered and far more soluble. It won't go rancid so swiftly, either."

The amber liquid was cooling quickly into a yellow waxy substance. He dipped a finger into the catch basin. "This is the fat, called cocoa butter, because it cools at room temperature into a solid but melts on contact with skin."

He rubbed the butter between his fingers. "A

useful product in itself. Edible. And a natural moisturizer that women use to achieve a youthful glow."

"Really? May I try some?" she asked.

*Dear God above.* Her innocent request filled his mind with provocative images.

Dorothea. Naked. Slick with oil and desire. Moaning his name.

He'd been fighting the obvious until this moment, but when a beautiful woman—this *particular* beautiful, maddening, gloriously clever woman—invaded his inner sanctum, offered him chocolate, and then asked him to rub her with cocoa butter . . . there could be only one outcome.

He wasn't going to fight it any longer.

James brushed the back of his knuckles across her cheek, down her throat, and into the opening of her robe.

Blue eyes swirled with smoke.

She stepped away, and his heart lurched. *Don't leave.* But she stayed, gazing into his eyes, and slowly unknotted the sash at her waist.

The dressing gown slid to the floor, revealing a creamy satin-and-lace confection designed to capture a man's soul and bring him to his knees.

Burnished gold curls spilled over thin straps and bare shoulders.

A gilt-framed invitation to paradise.

Damnation. He wanted her.

Her spirit. Warmth. Courage.

Those full breasts that fit perfectly in his palms.

She wrapped her arms around his neck and

melted into him with a throaty moan that shredded the last of his control. He filled his hands with her soft breasts, kneading her nipples until they contracted into tight peaks.

The scent of her filled his nostrils, something floral with an herbal edge that drove him wild.

Wet steam in the air. The wetness of her mouth, her tongue and his, miming the thrust of the metal pistons convulsing beside them.

There was an ear-piercing whistle, and a cloud of steam erupted next to them.

*He'd forgotten the press.*

He wrenched free.

He had to stop the press from overheating and exploding.

# Chapter 19

The duke leapt toward the machinery, tearing off his shirt to use as a barrier between his hands and the searing metal while he unloosened valves and twisted knobs, releasing steam.

Charlene didn't know how to help. She grabbed a book from a table and started fanning the hissing contraption.

When all was quiet, he leaned against the table, breathing heavily. "That was close. But there's no danger now. I've stabilized it."

No danger. Charlene nearly threw back her head and burst into helpless laughter.

The press might be harmless now, but the duke was one hundred flavors of dangerous. With damp hair curling around his neck and condensed steam dripping down the daunting width of his bare chest. Down, across his firm abdomen, disappearing into buckskin stretched across muscular thighs.

He caught her staring, and a lazy smile lifted the corner of his mouth. Her cheeks grew warm. The satin of the negligee clung damply to her body, and the pulse between her thighs beat stronger.

"Why don't you come over here?" He patted the wooden table, his eyes gleaming.

The air was heavy with steam, fragrant with cocoa, replete with the promise of his invitation.

She hesitated. There was a nearly sick feeling in her belly. If she went to him, there would be no turning back. Maybe the countess wouldn't even find them. Charlene had to believe he was honorable enough to offer for her if . . . if she succumbed to her wicked self.

Oh, how she wanted to give in.

*He is yours tonight. Take your fill. Don't fear tomorrow.*

She ran damp palms down the fine fabric of the negligee, loving the way his eyes darkened and his gaze followed her hands.

He wanted her, but there was also a reverence in his gaze. He saw her as a promise, not something to be plucked and forced to flower early, tied in bundles, sold to the highest bidder.

He saw her as a living, breathing rose.

Or rather, he saw Dorothea as that rose.

Something to be nourished, tended, coaxed.

She wanted to be near him, as if he were the sun and the rain. She wanted to open for him.

"Come here," he growled.

She gave him an arch smile. Her wicked self gained more control with each step until she stood before him.

"Turn around," he commanded.

In her last defense test, she'd been blindfolded, and Kyuzo had attacked her from behind. She'd acted on instinct with an elbow jab to his gut, her senses alert and quick. She was trained to anticipate the unexpected. She had to will herself to trust the duke. Trust that he wouldn't hurt her.

He thought she was an innocent debutante. He would be honorable and ask her to marry him before anything spiraled too far out of control.

She turned and presented her back to him.

He hooked a finger under the flimsy strap of the negligee. Followed the line of the strap down her shoulder, sliding the negligee down several inches. Her neck and upper shoulders were exposed, naked.

Out of the corner of her eye, she watched him reach over, dip his fingers into the catch basin, and scoop up some of the butter.

When his hands spread the slick substance over her neck, she tensed.

"No need to be nervous," he said.

Her shoulders slackened as he kneaded her flesh in slow circles.

"That's right," he urged. "Relax."

There was the slight scrape of the calluses on the pads of his fingers. His hands knew guitar strings. The heft of an axe. They knew work. And they certainly knew pleasure.

The knots in her shoulders began to ease. He rubbed the balm into her shoulders and massaged until her tension evaporated.

She took a deep breath, marveling at the small cracks and pops of her bones moving within her skin. She'd never been so aware of her body. He dug his thumbs into a tender spot, and she startled.

"Shhh . . ." he soothed.

He shaped her, molded her into a new substance, pressing away doubt. He lifted her hair and lowered his head into the hollow of her neck. His lips found her neck, her cheek, her earlobe.

He tugged the negligee lower. It pooled around her waist, baring her back.

*Her back was bare.*

Abruptly she twisted away from him. Not fast enough.

"What's this?" He traced the small mark under her left shoulder blade. The place Grant had tried to brand.

She'd forgotten to hide her tattoo.

This is why she couldn't relinquish control. She had too many secrets to hide. When he saw his bride didn't have a mark, he would know without a doubt that Dorothea wasn't her. Ultimately it wouldn't matter, of course; he only needed a business partner, and sweet, feminine Lady Dorothea would be perfect.

She glanced over her shoulder, feigning confusion. "Oh, that? Only a . . . wager I lost."

"Must have been some wager. I've only seen these on sailors. How strange that a lady would have one." He traced the small, angular black characters. "What does it mean?"

*Warrior.*

Kyuzo had many similar marks on his arms from his years at sea. He'd said they were his way of proclaiming freedom, of immortalizing his will to survive and escape.

After Grant tried to brand her, Charlene asked Kyuzo to give her a mark as well, to symbolize that she would never be owned by the baron. Kyuzo had sterilized a needle in candle flame, dipped it in ink, and pierced her skin. It had hurt, but it had been a way for her to immortalize her resolve.

When Grant returned, she would be ready for him. She'd never be his plaything. Never sell her body for a man's pleasure. She was a warrior. Strong. Uncompromising.

*She was being compromised right now.* She shrugged the duke's hand away, repositioning her hair over her back.

"They tell me it means 'butterfly.'" She tried to make the lie sound flippant and careless. So many lies accumulating like soot in a chimney. She would never come clean.

He pushed her hair aside and outlined the tattoo with his tongue. The soft touch made her body turn liquid.

"What other secrets are you hiding, butterfly?" He nuzzled her neck. "Hmmm?"

*Don't ask me that.*

He wouldn't let her turn to face him. He held her against his body with one strong arm around her waist, while the other hand spread fragrant cocoa butter over her collarbone. Moved lower to shape her breast and rub butter across her nipple.

There was no way to remain passive. She

arched into his hand, a moan escaping her lips. He tugged gently on her nipple, and the pulse between her thighs accelerated.

Fingers slipped beneath satin, questing lower, smoothing her belly and thighs, moving perilously close to the source of her need.

"You're so exquisite," he whispered in her ear. "I've been dying to touch you."

His body rested on the table, supporting her weight. The hard length of his arousal pressed against her from behind. She dissolved against his solid chest, and her head fell back against his shoulder.

She gasped as he found the seam between her legs.

"Open for me," he murmured.

The pulse marched faster.

"Dorothea. Don't be afraid."

Even hearing the wrong name on his lips couldn't jar the pleasure away. It was too strong now, this need.

There was only his finger, not quite touching her, in that secret place. She tilted upward slightly. He rewarded her with a light flick that sent shocks rippling through her whole body.

"Oh," she breathed.

He rewarded her again, this time stroking long enough to establish a rhythm.

He stopped. Hovered. Teased.

No, *no*. "Please . . ." she moaned.

"Say my name."

"Please, Your Grace."

"My name is James," he growled.

"Please . . . James."

His breath rasped in her ear and his lips nipped her neck. "Very good."

He stroked hard and fast across her core.

Abandoning all control, she moaned aloud and rubbed against his fingers.

"Yes," he said. "That's right."

He rubbed with exactly the right amount of pressure. Faster now. Sure and true.

His other hand left her belly and traveled to her chin. He tilted her head around, and when his tongue found hers, his fingers slipped inside her.

First one, an exploratory expedition. Then two. Three. Invaded, ravished, by tongue and fingers, and by his hard thigh between her legs.

Alternately stroking across the apex of her pleasure and then sliding inside her body, taking her closer. She tensed her stomach muscles, racing toward a precipice that was around the corner.

A few strokes away.

He broke the kiss. "You're so wet," he moaned.

If he stopped now, her wicked self would beg shamelessly.

There. More pressure. So close now. Her mouth opened, but no sound emerged. She prayed wordlessly.

"Don't worry, I won't stop," he said.

She heard the amusement in his voice. Didn't care. Just wanted those skillful fingers to keep moving, to fill her, stroke her, faster, harder.

"Come for me," he urged. "I need to hear you come."

He played her body like a guitar, teasing music from her soul. When her belly clenched, he strummed faster, knowing exactly what she needed.

"Now," he said.

The command sent her over the edge.

"James . . . yes." The pulse between her thighs tightened and loosened to a new cadence as pleasure reverberated through her body in a shattering release.

He wrapped her in his arms, turned her so that she was cradled against his chest with her head nestled into the hollow of his shoulder. If she could remain Dorothea, have him a few months more, she could learn what books he liked to read. See if she could coax him to read to Flor, to admit he loved her. There was so much pain in him, a deep sense of loss that she could feel as if it had been a void in her own heart.

She wanted to wrap her arms around him and never let go.

James listened to her breathing slow, reveling in the slight tremors still racking her body.

When she'd climaxed, arching beneath his fingers and crying his name in a stuttering series of gasps, something inside him had shifted as well. Now, holding her in the dim lamplight, there was no driving need to find release.

He was content to stroke her hair, hug her close.

He felt raw somehow. As though she had pierced through his skin and left a tattoo on his heart. He told himself that she would be a good mother to Flor. Patient and kind.

She might not have been the perfect, blameless duchess, or even a prudent choice for a bride. She certainly wasn't a candidate for a bloodless business arrangement. But her family name would compensate for any social gaffes.

She was scorching fire and passion, but fire always burned to ash. Eventually this heat between them would go cold. And if it didn't, he'd be across the ocean, far from temptation.

At least that's what he told himself.

She nestled tighter against his chest, and her yielding curves immediately made him stiffen. It would be so easy to position her hips and drive home.

But he would never do that. Not with a young, trusting debutante. She could have no awareness that ruin twitched against her belly, growing an extra inch every time her lush breasts rubbed against his chest.

What was the harm in opening a few buttons? He wasn't going to ravish her.

Not tonight.

He reached down and opened the fall of his breeches. Took himself in hand. He turned her until her bum nestled against his stiffness.

Leaning back against the solid table, he placed his hands on her hips. He slid between her butter-slick thighs, under her sex. With the butter and her spending lubricating him, it was easy to rub back and forth without entering.

"Oh," she breathed. "That feels good." She rocked against him instinctively.

He smiled into her tangled curls, thinking about the months ahead, all the ways she would find pleasure. All the things he would teach her.

He tightened his grip on her hips and moved faster. Her wet sex cradled him, and the hot tunnel of her thighs quickly brought him to the brink. But it wasn't enough. He needed to be inside her.

To claim her.

One small adjustment.

His cock nudged her entrance.

No, he couldn't.

But she would be his duchess in a matter of weeks.

He stilled. "Dorothea," he whispered. "I didn't mean for this to happen. Not tonight, but I—"

He didn't complete the sentence because the door crashed open and Countess Desmond stood in the doorway, her pale eyes ablaze with righteous outrage.

"What is the meaning of this?" The countess's question echoed through the room.

James set Dorothea off his lap and handed her the dressing gown from the floor. She pulled her negligee up and covered herself with the dressing gown, knotting it around her waist. James swiftly adjusted his trousers.

How had the countess known where to find them?

Dalton's words echoed in James's mind. *You'd*

*better keep your door locked at night, or you might have
a debutante bent on ruin slipping into your bed.*

He shivered. The room was cold without Dorothea in his arms. He needed to rekindle the fire.
Find another shirt. Not finding anything within
reach, he stood with bare chest and pulled himself up to his full height.

"Lady Desmond."

The countess advanced, spine rigid. "Harland,"
she said, deliberately refusing to give him his
honorific.

Dorothea avoided his gaze. Guilt was scrawled
across her shadowy face. She'd known her mother
would come. They had planned the entire scene.

He'd been set up.

Ice settled in his gut, freezing emotion until he
felt nothing when he looked at Dorothea.

"I'm waiting for an explanation," the countess
said.

"You might ask your daughter why she came
here wearing only a scrap of satin and lace and a
liberal dousing of perfume," he said.

The countess swept an arm around Dorothea's hunched shoulders. "She's an innocent. She
doesn't know any better than to go wandering
about in her nightclothes."

He'd been on the verge of asking for her, but
having his hand forced in this sordid fashion
made him angry. "Did you have to resort to trickery?" he asked Dorothea.

She didn't answer, didn't deny anything, and
she still wouldn't meet his eyes.

"How dare you," the countess exploded, not giving her daughter a chance to respond. "She is sullied, compromised. I found her bed empty and was forced to go searching. This is a mother's worst nightmare."

"You win," he said.

The countess fixed him with a cold stare. "What is that supposed to mean?"

"You win. Lady Dorothea will marry me. I expect an heir within the year." He waved a hand toward the door. "Now leave."

Lady Dorothea stretched her hand toward him with tears in her eyes, and the tightness in his chest loosened a fraction. Then, as if a steam valve had been adjusted, she dropped her hand, exhaled, and met his gaze.

"I accept your proposal," she said coolly.

"Fine." He crossed his arms over his chest. "We'll be married in three weeks, by license, here at St. Peter's of Warbury."

"Three weeks?" The countess's eyes widened. "That's not nearly enough time to plan a wed—"

"I only have a few months left in London. I set sail before the hurricane season. Expect me to call upon Lord Desmond next week regarding the articles."

Lady Desmond regained her composure. She inclined her head. "My lord husband will be pleased to receive you."

"I'm quite sure he will," James said sarcastically. He sketched the barest of dismissive bows.

Dorothea opened her mouth to speak, but her

mother gripped her arm. "Come along, Lady Dorothea. There's been quite enough excitement for one evening."

"Goodnight, James," she whispered before her mother pulled her away, into the darkness.

# Chapter 20

The countess had won her prize. Lady Dorothea would be a duchess.

Charlene was nothing more than a guilty secret shrouded in black and smuggled out of the house before dawn, before anyone but the maid-of-all-work was awake. The countess sat in silence across from Charlene on the padded silk carriage cushions, and it was clear there would be no discussion of what had transpired.

The velvet green Surrey hills would soon give way to narrow streets hemmed in by gray stone and closed shutters. Every revolution of the carriage wheels carried her farther from James and Flor.

She told herself she didn't care. She tried to hate him. But he'd done those things. Those wicked, revelatory things.

*Did you have to resort to trickery?*

He'd been furious at their deception. Pain stabbed her chest when she thought of it, as if one of his knives was lodged there.

Would the reward be worth the price?

She'd repeat the question again after the debt to

Grant was paid, when her mother stopped coughing, and Lulu was happily up to her elbows in paint in Essex.

Charlene squeezed her eyes closed, imagining Lulu breathing pure country air and painting meadows dotted with purple flowers, like the meadow James had found after he'd rescued Charlene from drowning. He'd lifted her out of the river, only to throw her into something deeper, a treacherous current of longing that had eroded the embankment around her heart and swept her back into his arms.

She leaned her head against the cream silk brocade caught in festoons along the walls. Her world was toppled end over end. What was bad now? What was good?

Surrendering control could feel good.

Dukes were not all bad.

It was time to set her world back to order. This had only been a means to buy back their freedom from Grant and give Lulu the chance at a new life, away from the perils of the bawdy house. When Lulu was ensconced in her new life, Charlene would have the satisfaction of knowing she'd done what she'd had to do to provide for her sister's future.

"We've nearly arrived, Miss Beckett," the countess said. "I expect you to depart for Essex with your sister the day after tomorrow, before the duke arrives in London to meet with Lord Desmond. My family can have no further association with you."

Charlene gripped a silk tassel that hung near her head. "I doubt the duke and I run in the same circles."

"One never knows. Gentlemen of his ilk do frequent houses of . . . houses like yours. I can't run the risk."

Charlene hadn't even thought of that. "Of course." She matched the countess's wintry tone of voice.

The countess returned to staring out the window.

The situation was more complex than Charlene had anticipated. Now James was angry with Dorothea for manipulating him, when Dorothea had done no wrong. Charlene wanted the chance to explain everything to her half sister.

No, not *everything*. Not the lapses when Charlene had allowed her heart to open. But certainly she wanted to explain about Flor and about the workers at the duke's factory.

She wrapped her arms tighter around her chest. "I must speak to Lady Dorothea when we arrive in London."

The countess's head swiveled. "Out of the question."

"But I have so much to tell her."

The countess's blue eyes frosted over. "I can't have you associating with my daughter," she said, as if the very idea made her skin crawl.

Stung, Charlene's breath puffed out her veil. "I see. I was good enough for your purposes, good enough to impersonate your daughter, but I couldn't possibly be allowed to speak with her."

"Miss Beckett, do try to view matters from my perspective. Unfortunately, news of the duke's gathering spread, and I'm told wagers on the outcome were placed in all the clubs." She shuddered. "Utterly distasteful that my Dorothea was the subject of such lurid speculation."

"But I must speak with her, only for a moment."

"Absolutely not. Whatever you think you have to tell her is irrelevant. Your work is finished."

"Maybe he'll be able to tell she's a different person," Charlene muttered. "If I don't prepare her."

"What did you say?"

Charlene lifted the veil and swept it over her bonnet. "I said perhaps the duke may discern that Lady Dorothea is not *me*. Have you considered the possibility?"

"I expect he'll find her vastly improved." Lady Desmond's lip curled. "The refined duchess he always desired. Infinitely more suitable for his purposes."

"I'm sure you're right." Charlene couldn't keep the bitterness out of her voice. It coated her throat, like tansy tea. It might never wash away.

"Even if he does find her changed, that's only natural," said the countess. "People alter from one day to the next. They grow distant . . . keep secrets. Disappoint you."

Charlene sensed she wasn't talking about the duke anymore.

"The duke said he'd be leaving for the West Indies soon," the countess continued. "He will leave and Dorothea will remain in London, the duchess, with the respect and privileges she's due."

To the countess it was the ideal marriage—a husband who hid his infidelity across oceans, instead of flaunting it in her face.

"No one will laugh at my daughter now. No one will call her a wallflower. He may be uncivilized, but he's a duke." The countess slashed a hand through the air. "They'll have to genuflect and bow to her. It will be *'If it please Your Grace'* and *'Please attend our ball, Your Grace.'*"

"I'm sure you're right," Charlene repeated dully. She replaced the veil and sat back against the cushions. There was no use reasoning with the countess. She could never understand the urgency of Charlene's need to speak with Dorothea. The needs of illegitimate daughters weren't to be considered.

If she couldn't tell Dorothea about the conversations she'd had with the duke, he would marry a complete stranger who had absolutely no knowledge of Flor's fragile emotional state and need for sympathy and guidance.

Guilt cramped her stomach as familiar streets unfolded and the old watchfulness returned, sharpening her senses for the battle to come, steeling her for combat. She didn't know how Grant would react when she repaid the loan, and whether he would attempt to find another way to control them. Leaving London and traveling to the countryside would take Lulu out of harm's way, at least.

The carriage jolted to a stop, springs jouncing and horses whinnying. Charlene realized they were already on Henrietta Street, across the Covent Garden piazza from home.

The countess slanted her eyes at the carriage door. "You may keep the cloak and gown—Blanchard burned your old clothing. Good-bye, Miss Beckett."

*Never bother me again, Miss Beckett,* Charlene supplied to the end of the countess's cold dismissal as a footman handed her down. The carriage door slammed and the wheels began to turn.

The piazza was still uncrowded. Evidence of last night's festivities clogged the gutters. Empty gin bottles, theater bills, a lone white glove muddied by boot heels.

Vendors set up stalls overflowing with flowers and vegetables. As Charlene walked by, a bird seller tipped his broad-brimmed hat and smiled, revealing a row of rotting teeth.

"'Ere, miss, see the pretty goldfinches." He pointed to a cage. "If you don't like finches, try a lark."

Charlene slowed, her mind racing. She stared into a cage. Finches with red masks and velvety-white underbellies balanced on perches, their small heads bobbing and tilting in constant motion, except for one little bird that cowered in a corner of the cage.

She'd taken the employment for Lulu's sake, and now she would be able to change her sister's life.

"Them finches are a bob apiece, and thrupence for the cage," the seller said, sidling up to her, a hopeful glint in his eyes.

"Why do the other birds peck at that one?" she asked, watching as one of the birds swooped down to peck at the poor bird shivering in the corner.

"Dunno." The seller shrugged.

One of the birds burst into an aria. "teLLIT-teLLIT-teLLIT," it sang.

"That's a champion, that one," the man said.

Yesterday flying free over a meadow and today beating their wings against a wooden cage, sold for sport.

"I'll take the lot," Charlene said, following a sudden impulse.

"You won't be sorry, mum." The seller pocketed her coins and handed her the cage full of finches. She took a few steps, then set the cage down on a pile of crates and opened the hatch.

" 'Ere now, what you doing?" the seller called after her.

Charlene reached into the cage and shooed the birds toward the door. They burst through the opening in a flurry of gold and red, warbling as they rose into the wide sky.

Even the injured bird escaped. He was soon a speck over the rooftops of Covent Garden.

The seller cursed and his friends laughed.

Charlene hurried across the piazza to set her sister free.

She reached the house and paused on the front

steps, gathering her resolve. When she entered, she would be Charlene again. She'd scrub the last trace of roses from her skin, remove the fine muslin, and never dream of glittering green eyes again.

Lulu's soft hazel eyes filling with joy would be her reward.

She took a deep breath. Inside, all was quiet. Charlene saw the house as if for the first time. The overstuffed pink chairs gossiping in the front parlor. The gaudy gold paint peeling from the staircase banisters. The way the stairs groaned and wheezed as she climbed. Everyone except Lulu was still abed at this early hour, even Kyuzo.

Lulu sat in her sitting room, thin shoulders bent over the wooden artist's box that doubled as an easel. As Charlene watched, Lulu dipped a slender brush into a porcelain palette, choosing a vivid blue to paint sky onto the back of the playing cards she used for backings, since they couldn't afford ivory for her miniature paintings.

Charlene didn't want to startle her and make her brush slip. She quietly set her bonnet and cloak on a chair, struck by the way the morning sun caressed Lulu's russet hair, stoking it to the crimson of autumn leaves.

A rush of love and pride flooded her chest with hope. After her apprenticeship, Lulu would be able to make an independent income from her painting.

Lulu set her brush down and turned her head. "Charlene!" She leapt from her seat and flung herself into Charlene's arms. "You've been gone so long."

"Only a few days," Charlene laughed, stroking Lulu's soft head. "How are you, my love? What are you working on?"

"The Wellington portrait, only I can't make his eyes come out right. They're not nearly noble enough. At least not as noble as I imagine them to be."

"I'm so glad you are safe." Charlene breathed in the familiar sharp smell of paints and the heavy scent of the linseed oil her sister used to clean her brushes. She never would have forgiven herself if Grant had harmed Lulu while Charlene had been at the duke's estate.

Lulu's eyes clouded. "Why wouldn't I be safe?"

"No reason, sweetheart." Charlene kissed the top of her head and set her at arm's length. "Now cover up those paints and let's have some tea."

Lulu tilted her head, for all the world like one of the bobbing finches. "You look different somehow." She contemplated Charlene's face. "There's something about your eyes. I'd have to use new colors to paint them. They have mysterious shadows. As if you know a secret."

Charlene tried to laugh, but the sound stuck halfway. She'd always marveled at how Lulu was so intuitive and sensitive to emotions and so completely oblivious to the reality of their lives, preferring to live in the worlds she conjured in her paintings. "Same old Charlene," she said. "Nothing mysterious about me."

"But where did you go? Mother wouldn't tell me. You *must* have a secret."

Charlene smiled. "You caught me."

"I knew it." Lulu's eyes danced with curiosity. "You finally found a handsome suitor, and that was his mother I saw you with the night you left. He took one look at your heavenly blue eyes and golden curls and was hopelessly smitten."

Charlene shook her head. "Guess again."

"No handsome suitor?"

"Not a one."

"Hmm." Lulu tapped a finger to her lips. "A benefactor, then? A distant relation who bequeathed you a vast fortune and a crumbling old castle haunted by hundreds of ghosts. Oh how I should love to live in a castle." She sighed, her eyes shining. "Tell me I've got it right."

Charlene laughed. "You've been reading too many novels, sweetheart."

Lulu wrinkled her nose. "I give up."

Charlene took her sister's hand. "Remember when I said I wanted to find you a painting apprenticeship?"

Lulu's eyes widened. "Yes," she breathed.

Charlene squeezed her hand. "I found a perfect one."

Lulu stared at Charlene, a million questions shining in her eyes.

"You're to be apprenticed to Mrs. Anna Hendricks," Charlene said. "An elderly painter with failing eyesight who needs you to help her complete her paintings. You'll be able to learn from her tutelage, and she may be able to help launch your career."

"Is it really true?" Lulu breathed.

"Absolutely. I'm to take you to her in Essex. She has a lovely stone cottage and a pretty garden." Charlene had received more details from the countess about her situation. "You'll have ivory and fine French pigments, and you can take rambles in the countryside. It will do you a world of good. I'll stay with you for the first weeks."

Lulu clasped Charlene's hand even tighter. "I can't believe it. It's more than I ever dreamt of . . . but . . ." Her face fell. "Mama is worse, Charlene. She coughs all night long. I can't leave her."

Charlene kissed her sister's knuckles. "Don't worry, sweetheart, I'll take care of Mother. She wants you to have this chance. She'll be so very proud of you."

Lulu wavered between concern for their mother and joy at the chance. "Are you sure?" she asked tentatively. "Oh, Charlene. Are you sure?"

"Quite sure. There's nothing to be decided. Everything is settled."

Lulu smiled, unable to contain her elation any longer. She danced over to her paint box and grabbed a brush, flourishing it at her painting. "Do you hear that, Your Grace?" she asked the half-finished portrait of Wellington. "I'm to live in Essex, and I can finish you on real ivory, as befits a war hero."

She turned back to Charlene. "Will there be meadows full of flowers in Essex?" She set her paintbrush back in the box. "Will there be crumbling castles?"

Charlene smiled. "I'm sure there will be billions of flowers and heaps of ruined castles. Now come downstairs, sweetheart. I'm famished."

As the sisters descended to the kitchens, Charlene's heart was lighter than it had been in a long time. Lulu would have a safe, uneventful girlhood, away from the sulphur and coal smoke of London. She'd never climb the stairs to the Aviary and learn the sordid truth.

"You'll need a smart traveling dress," Charlene said as she poured their tea. The ladies Lulu painted always wore silk and jewels, but she donned the same gray dress and smudged shapeless painter's smock every day.

"Will Mrs. Hendricks be very fine? She won't think me hopelessly plain, will she?"

"No one could ever find you plain." And that was another reason Charlene had to send her sister off to the countryside. With all that red-tinged hair and those wide hazel eyes, her sister's budding beauty would attract too much attention from London gentlemen very soon.

Dangerous men like Grant.

The good, strong black tea was bracing. No more rich chocolate or impossible dreams for Charlene. No more tempting green eyes.

No more kisses.

"You have a faraway air," Lulu said. "There's something you're not telling me. Something mysterious. Are you certain a handsome suitor isn't going to appear and spirit you away on a magnificent stallion?"

Charlene steadied her hand as she poured more tea. "Don't be silly. That only happens in fairy tales."

In real life, the prince married within his rank, and the serving girl swept ash the rest of her lonely life.

James had been eager for the officious mamas, fawning daughters, and trunks full of feathers to leave. He'd wanted his solitude back. So why did the house feel too empty now?

He went down to the stables and saddled a horse, then mixed himself a mug of cocoa, but it tasted burned and bitter.

He paced up and down the echoing hallways, startling unsuspecting chambermaids. Catching sight of his reflection in a hall mirror, he realized why they shrank from him. He'd refused to shave, and there was dark stubble shadowing his jaw. His hair was unkempt, his eyes wild, and he was still wearing the same rumpled clothing from the night before.

He must be losing his mind.

As he strode through the oppressive passageways of his ancestral home, he circumnavigated the same mental circle. If Dorothea had plotted to be compromised, it followed that all the rest of her actions and words could merely have been a skillful act. If it had all been an act, maybe she didn't care for him, or Flor, as she had seemed to. And if she didn't care for him . . . why did that rankle? Had he been so arrogant as to expect his bride to fall in love with him, when he wanted to keep his own heart remote?

He paused outside of the Jonquil Suite. Maids had stripped Dorothea's bed of its linens. He resisted the urge to enter the room to see if the scent of tea roses lingered. Instead, he walked quickly away, not caring where his feet carried him.

Last evening, waltzing with Flor and Dorothea, something had eased inside his chest. A wall had begun to crumble. He'd envisioned the three of them together . . . as a family.

This house preyed on his mind, made him feel trapped and helpless. What did it matter if she cared for him or not? He needed an heir. Flor needed a mother. Nothing more was required.

Even if Dorothea *had* orchestrated the sordid moment of discovery, he'd been about to offer for her, so it didn't change the inevitable outcome. Shouldn't this simplify matters? He'd wanted a bloodless business arrangement. He should be applauding her cold-blooded ambition. The way she and the countess had left so hastily after achieving their goal, with no good-bye, besting him at his own game.

Or had Lady Desmond plotted to trap him and Dorothea had been an innocent accomplice to her mother's deviousness—as innocent as a woman could be with that much wicked wit lighting her eyes.

He had no one to talk to about his suspicions. Dalton was ensconced back at the club in London. James had tried speaking with Josefa, but she hadn't understood why there was a problem.

*She will bear you many strong and healthy sons and her important father will lower the taxes,* she'd said to James, as if that settled the entire matter. She approved of his choice.

Would his mother have approved of Dorothea?

The question caught him unawares, halting his forward motion. He gripped a brass door pull, bracing himself as the memories descended, too fast and vivid to stop.

The day he'd left for Eton, his mother, Margaret, had hugged him so tightly he'd nearly choked. *How big you've grown,* he heard her say in his memory. *How strong. Oh, James, I love you so much.*

Fourteen-year-old James had been embarrassed by all that emotion. He'd pulled away, clearing his throat manfully and folding his arms across his chest to ward away a further embrace.

It had been the last time he'd seen her. He'd never let another woman hold him in her arms.

"Your Grace, are you well?"

James hadn't even noticed Bickford approach. "I'm fine." He swiped a hand across his eyes.

Bickford nodded at the door in front of James. "Are you thinking of . . . *her*?"

James unclenched his fingers from the door pull, staring at the rose pattern imprinted deep into his palm.

With a start, he realized he was standing in front of his mother's chambers in the east wing.

"We've kept the rooms intact, you know," Bickford said, his narrow face solemn. "May I show you?"

James backed away from the door. He couldn't go in there. But brisk, efficient Bickford was already opening the door. He bustled about the room, drawing the drapes and running a finger along the mantelpiece. "No dust," he said with satisfaction.

James took a tentative step inside. Everything was exactly how he remembered. Curving draperies, plump chairs, and small round tables covered with lace. James half expected to see his mother sitting in her favorite rocking chair by the fireplace, a baby stocking forming below her whirring knitting needles.

As a young boy, James had thought her the prettiest woman in the world, with the Harland family diamonds around her slender throat and in her lustrous blonde hair, and a sweet smile for him on her lips.

When he grew older, she stopped wearing diamonds and dressed in high-necked black gowns. He'd been too young to understand, but now he knew that after him, she'd given birth to six stillborn babes. She'd died birthing the seventh.

"I'm told you made a choice, Your Grace?" Bickford asked.

James pulled himself back to the present with an effort. "Yes, I'll be marrying Lady Dorothea."

Bickford gave a rare smile. "A young lady with a great vivacity of spirit, if I may be permitted to say so. She reminds me of the duchess, when she was the same age."

James stared at Bickford. "She does?"

"Oh yes, the duchess was always racing willy-nilly across the lawn. With no bonnet at all."

This was news to James. "Really?"

Bickford nodded, his eyes twinkling. James had never seen him so animated. Apparently Dorothea had managed to charm even his staid, dignified steward.

"You wouldn't have noticed, you were only a child," Bickford said. "But she was quite spirited, your mother, until . . ."

James clenched his hands. Bickford didn't need to continue. They both knew why his mother had lost her spirit. His father had placed his wife in danger again and again, even when it had become clear she would never bear another healthy child.

If she wasn't producing more children, she was of no further use. The deaths of her children had crushed her. After every birth, every funeral, she'd faded more, until she'd been a shadow haunting these chambers. Crooning to the ghosts of her children. Knitting mounds of tiny slippers.

James could never become the duke his father had been. Obliterating all that was good and pure with impossible demands, stony silence, and an iron fist.

"I hope you won't mind me saying that your mother loved you very much, Your Grace. Yours was the last name she spoke before she left us." Bickford wiped away a tear. "But that's so long ago now. How wonderful that you are marrying. She would have been so proud."

Bickford stared at him expectantly. James felt paralyzed, as though his lips had forgotten how to form words. "Such a long time has passed," he finally managed to say.

"Yes."

They stood in silence.

"I've kept her jewels polished for just such a happy occasion, Your Grace. Shall I fetch them?"

James nodded, not trusting himself to speak again.

Bickford bowed and disappeared into the adjoining room.

Had the mournful Duchess of Harland truly been as impulsive and unconventional as Dorothea? It seemed impossible. James searched his memories for moments of impropriety. He did remember her laughter . . . silvery and unrestrained, pealing in his ears like church bells.

Bickford returned and opened the lid of the teak and ivory jewel box.

James waved him away. "You choose something suitable."

Bickford lifted out a string of pearls with a faint peach tinge. They were worn from contact with his mother's skin. "These were her favorites. She was rarely without them."

James remembered the pearls glowing against the austere expanse of his mother's mourning blacks.

"But they are rather subdued," said Bickford.

"Perhaps this would be more suitable for Lady Dorothea, Your Grace?" He opened a small blue velvet box and held a ring up to the light coming through the windows.

Rose-cut diamonds sparkled in an openwork filigree gold setting.

Sturdy, yet delicate. The same intriguing combination he'd sensed in Dorothea.

James made a sudden decision. He hadn't thought to travel to London until next week, but he wasn't going to wait that long. He needed to confront his fiancée, demand answers to all the questions buzzing through his mind.

He rose from the seat and pocketed the velvet box. "Thank you, Bickford. Please send word to the staff in London. I arrive tomorrow."

# Chapter 21

"**Y**ou've been keeping secrets from me." Charlene's mother patted the bed next to her. "Come tell Mother all about it. What took you to Surrey? Your note was so mysterious."

Charlene's mother, Susan—or Madame Swan, as she was known in most circles—reclined in bed wearing frothy lace around her throat and wrists. She was still luminously lovely, but there was a feverish tinge to her cheeks.

"Hello, Mother." Charlene bent to kiss her cheek and sat down beside her.

"Mr. Yamamoto told me what happened with Lord Grant," Susan said. "I had no idea he was back from Scotland."

"It doesn't matter . . . we have the means to pay him now."

Susan pushed herself up on the pillows. "How did you manage that?"

"I met a duke."

"A duke?" Susan clasped Charlene's hands. "How wonderful!"

"It wasn't wonderful, or the answer to all your prayers. It was only this once. Never again."

"But it *is* wonderful, darling. My first was only a lowly baronet. You've far eclipsed me. You'll be the most brilliant demimondaine London has ever known."

"Stop, Mother." Charlene took her hands away. "We're not going through this again. I'll never be a courtesan. We're going to repay Grant and close the Pink Feather, just as we agreed. I even found Lulu a painting apprenticeship."

A coughing fit shook Susan's slender frame like waves battering a boat hull. Charlene hurried to the bedside table and opened the laudanum bottle. The hacking cough made her chest ache in sympathy and her throat raw.

When her mother was finally able to swallow some medicine, the cough eased, and she fell back against the cushions.

"I'm sorry," Susan murmured. "I don't know what comes over me."

"Hush," Charlene said. "We'll talk tomorrow. You need to rest." She laid a hand on her mother's brow, tracing the fine lines that etched deeper every day. Her mother's breath rattled in her chest, threatening to erupt into another coughing fit.

"You need a physician, Mother."

"I don't want to hear what he'll say," she whispered.

Charlene smoothed the thin skin of her mother's hand. "You must. Please. For me. For Lulu."

Her mother nodded. Her eyelids drooped, and her voice grew dreamy as the laudanum took effect. "What was he like, your duke?"

"He's not *my* duke, and if you must know, I hate him." Charlene's heart thumped an erratic, contradictory cadence. "He's arrogant and unfeeling."

"Darling, dukes are *always* arrogant. Why shouldn't they be? They've got the whole world on a tether." Susan's lips curved up. "But was he handsome? That's what I want to know."

Charlene crossed to the window. It was raining. Sheets of silver driving against the cobblestones and flooding the gutters. She traced the path of a raindrop down the windowpane.

"He has the most vivid green eyes," she said. "Every time he looked at me I felt like I was standing in a tree-lined avenue, and the branches had interlaced into a canopy above me, surrounding me. It was the kind of green that told the sun what color to be as it filtered through the leaves."

"Oh, gracious." Susan smiled weakly. "It's worse than I thought."

"I don't like losing control, Mother."

"You never did, even as a babe. You always rearranged the covers and ordered me around in your forceful baby language. But there are ways to bring a man to his knees, Charlene, ways to ensure he never leaves you, until you want him to."

"The earl left you."

"Your father was a mistake. He plied me with jewels and flattery, but the second he found out I was with child, he cast me off, denying your claim, when anyone can see very well you are his. I would have given you up if it meant you could have been raised a lady."

Charlene crossed back to the bedside. "I've had a taste of luxury these last few days. I can safely say that wealth and social position don't equal happiness, or even basic decency."

"Still, why not let the duke provide for you?"

That was the best life her mother could conceive. To be owned. Set up in an apartment in a fashionable district, with a maid and three footmen and a generous allowance for gowns and jewels.

Exactly the bondage Grant sought for her.

"I told you," Charlene said. "I hate him."

"If you insist." Her mother wiped the corners of her eyes with the handkerchief. "Just remember that sometimes hate has a strange way of feeling an awful lot like love . . ." Her voice trailed off and her eyes closed.

"Is she sleeping?" Diane, or Dove as she was known to the patrons of the Pink Feather, poked her sleek, dark head around the door.

Charlene nodded. She tucked the covers around her mother and kissed her forehead.

In the hallway, Diane hugged Charlene. "Welcome home. Everyone's dying to hear where you've been."

"Nowhere in particular."

"Don't give me that. Come upstairs with me and tell us."

Charlene followed Diane down the hallway and through the door that hid the back staircase to the Aviary, where her mother's exclusive beauties entertained their clientele.

"I heard what happened with Grant. God, how I loathe him." Diane shook her head as they climbed the stairs. "Do you know he's hired us to dance at an entertainment tonight? We daren't say no. He's in a rare bad temper these days."

Charlene faltered, nearly missing the next stair. "You'll never have to dance for him again, Diane. I promise you that."

"How can you be so sure?"

"I can't tell you now. Soon, though. Trust me."

The tables and chairs had been cleared to the sides of the Aviary, and the ladies were trailing after Linnet, like geese learning to fly in formation.

"Remember, you are Birds of Paradise. Flitting from branch to branch." Linnet flapped gracefully around the room, her long white-blonde hair floating behind her.

"This is for the performance," Diane explained. "One of Lord Hatherly's notorious Cyprian affairs."

"Will Grant be at the ball tonight?" Charlene asked.

"Of course. He has to make sure we perform to his standards," Diane said bitterly. "The audience will be mostly peers, so we're sure to find new admirers, and Grant will secure new investors for his schemes."

This could be Charlene's opportunity. She'd been thinking that it would be best to find a way to give Grant the payment outside of the house. Catch him off guard. She didn't want to be alone with him ever again. If he refused to take the money, Kyuzo would convince him, but first she would face him on her own.

"I'm going with you to the Cyprian's ball," she announced.

Linnet stopped floating. "What was that? You're coming with us?"

All five ladies stopped dancing and stared.

"Are you certain you want to go to such an affair?" Diane asked.

Charlene nodded. "I need to give something to Grant in a public setting. I don't want him knowing I'm there until the last second."

Diane lifted a pink satin mask lined with pink and white feathers and pearls from a table. "We'll all be wearing these. No one will recognize you."

"Perfect," Charlene said.

Diane fit the satin mask over Charlene's face and tied it in back with the long pink ribbon. One of the other ladies brought a mirror. The mask made Charlene's eyes tilt up. She looked entirely un-Charlene-like.

In the disguise, she wouldn't have to worry about encountering someone such as Lord Dalton. And the duke had said he wouldn't visit London until next week. She'd be in Essex with Flor by the time he arrived.

"Did I overhear you saying something to your mother about a duke?" Diane asked.

"I don't want to talk about it."

Diane's eyes widened. "That bad? I'm sorry, darling."

"I'm not thinking of him. There's work to be done." She wasn't thinking about green eyes and charcoal hair. Playful lips. Strong, calloused hands, rough against her skin, stoking the blaze in her belly.

The more Charlene tried not to think about the duke, the faster the memories came. The one-sided quirk of his lips when he smiled. What his hands felt like sliding down her spine and smoothing the curve of her hips. The taste of chili and chocolate on his tongue. The low hum of his voice.

Her defenses had frayed around the edges, unraveled. There were cracks in the shuttered citadel of her heart. Longing swirling like dust in a piercing shaft of sunshine.

She'd just have to shut the blinds, close her heart, and block out the memory of his eyes.

"**Y**our Grace, we weren't expecting you in London for several days yet." Lord Desmond offered his hand. He was fleshy, florid, and had a high-pitched voice that grated on James's nerves. But when he'd determined to make a suitable marriage, James had known there would be one of these in the bargain. An avaricious father-in-law, hungry to secure his daughter a duke.

"Lord Desmond." James accepted a cigar and a glass of port. "I'm here to speak with Lady Dorothea."

Desmond shook his head. "Won't be possible,

I'm afraid. My lady countess claims there was a bit of unpleasantness. Says you're not to be allowed near Lady Dorothea until the wedding."

"I only require an hour. The countess may chaperone."

"So sorry." Desmond's jowls quivered when he shook his head. "There's nothing that moves that woman once her mind is made. Not even a ducal visit. I do believe she thinks you'll ruin the girl. Tarnish her lily-white reputation and all that." He winked. "Bit of rogue, are you?"

"I'll hardly ravish your daughter in plain sight of her mother."

Desmond cleared his throat. "Again, I'm terribly sorry, but Lady Desmond was even making noises about taking Dorothea to the country, to visit her aunt until the wedding."

James raised his eyebrows. There was something odd here. First the countess was throwing her daughter at him, and now she wanted to whisk her away to the countryside.

"I knew your father well, you know," Lord Desmond said, changing the subject. "Such a damned shame. Gone too soon. And your brother, too." He gestured for a footman to pour more port. "But you're the duke now, eh? There's something to be said for that."

He raised his glass. Lowered it when James didn't join him in the toast.

"Heard you were engaging in a bit of commerce?" Desmond asked. "Not short on capital, I'm sure?"

Desmond's greedy squint made James's stomach roil. He settled back in his seat. "Not at all."

Desmond heaved a sigh. "Glad to hear it." Obviously his affection for his new son-in-law was contingent on solvency.

"That's part of the reason I came to speak with you, though," James said. "I need someone looking after my interests in Parliament when I'm back in the West Indies. The duty import tax on cocoa is outrageous. I trust now that our families are allied, you will take up my concern. I would see the tax lowered on cocoa grown specifically on farms that don't use slave labor."

"Decrease duties on cocoa. I shall make it my personal mission next session." Desmond raised his glass. "To a partnership of mutual interest."

This time James raised his glass. He disliked Desmond, but unfortunately he had need of him.

"Lady Dorothea is young and fertile." Desmond swallowed his port. "I daresay you'll get your heir, and several spares, and she'll have . . . say, six hundred pin money per annum?"

The old weasel. That was highway larceny, but James didn't care to argue. If he couldn't see Dorothea, he wanted to stay as briefly as possible.

"Fine," he said. "But I'll expect her to adhere to my rules of conduct. It will all be outlined in the contract."

"No trouble there. Lady Dorothea is as pure and meek as they come. Never given us a moment's worry."

That didn't sound like Dorothea, but her father would hardly suggest otherwise.

"I'll also ask that you monitor the progress on my gravest concern—the abolition of slavery," James said.

Desmond steepled his fingers and leaned back in his chair, his waistcoat buttons straining to contain his ample belly. "The abolitionists are causing quite a storm. Quite a storm. I support the cause, don't misunderstand me, but I have interests in the African Company and would not wish to see anything hasty occur."

James gripped his cigar so tightly that it nearly snapped in half. And so it was with the men who profited from the trade—willful bigotry and ignorance. "You are wrong, Sir. Slavery must be abolished throughout the world."

"Come, come, let's not talk of our differences," Desmond said. "You say you're going back to the West Indies soon?"

"I'll return to England only rarely. I've grown accustomed to life in Trinidad."

"Wish I could move abroad, sometimes. Escape my darling wife." Desmond winked.

James couldn't stomach any more of this conversation. It would be better to conduct his future business with Desmond through intermediaries. Murdering his father-in-law wouldn't help his reputation.

James slammed his glass down. "I must visit my solicitor and some of my old set. There's an affair at Hatherly's tonight." And every night from what Dalton had told him. Their old friend Nick, Lord Hatherly, had become quite the hedonist.

Desmond stood as well. "Hatherly? Now there's

a fellow who knows how to throw an affair." Desmond walked James to the door. "I'd join you, but there's some tedious charity event. Always something with my wife."

"You'll inform Lady Dorothea I was here."

Desmond nodded. "I daresay there'll be time enough to talk to the gel after the wedding. Only two weeks away, is it? You should be off enjoying your last days of freedom. I was no better at your age." He winked again. "I remember the week before my wedding . . ."

"I'll be on my way then—"

" . . . or rather I should say I *don't* remember. There was a great deal of rum involved. If I recall, we ended up in a jolly nunnery in Covent Garden . . ."

James accepted his coat and hat and made his escape before he learned more nauseating details.

As he climbed into the barouche, he glanced up at the house. A curtain rustled in an upstairs window. He caught a brief glimpse of flaxen hair. Dorothea had been watching him.

How strange that they wouldn't let him see her.

He still had a swarm of unanswered questions.

And now he was even more convinced she was hiding secrets from him.

# Chapter 22

Charlene hid at the back of the group, staying close to Diane as one of Grant's scowling guards escorted them into Lord Hatherly's estate through the servant's entrance. The man was barrel-chested and had a jagged scar running across one cheek. The guard looked dangerous and difficult to throw.

Charlene held the heavy black silk purse stuffed with pound notes under her cloak, ready to give to Grant.

The baron was waiting for the girls behind a red velvet curtain on a stage that had to overlook the ballroom. Charlene could hear male voices from beyond the curtain, an occasional high-pitched female laugh.

"My birds," Grant said. "Your adoring audience awaits."

He'd been drinking. Charlene could tell by the way he swayed, almost imperceptibly, on his feet, and by the sharp juniper scent of gin mingled with the bitter orange hair pomade.

Grant reached for Linnet's cloak and pulled her toward him. "What do you have under these long cloaks, eh? Pink feathers, like I asked?" He groped her breast through the black silk. "I like the masks. Nice touch."

He bent Linnet's head back by the hair and kissed her, thrusting his tongue into her mouth noisily.

Gorge rose in Charlene's throat as she remembered the feel of those lips on her own mouth. She hadn't meant to give him the purse until the girls were on stage, but she couldn't wait now.

"Lord Grant," she called, her voice ringing strong and clear.

He lifted his head. "Who's that?"

Charlene slipped between the girls and lowered her hood. She lifted her mask for a moment, before dropping it again.

"Charlene? What the devil?" Grant released Linnet and stepped toward Charlene. "What are *you* doing here?"

She drew the purse from under her cloak, squaring her shoulders. "I came to repay our debt and secure our freedom."

Turning to the scar-faced guard, Grant guffawed loudly. "Hear that, Mace? She wants her freedom." Mace laughed, rough and mean.

Charlene extended the purse.

Grant's face lost its mocking smile. "Go home now. I'll visit you tomorrow." He slapped Linnet on the bum and pushed her toward the stage. "Time for the performance. Go show 'em your feathers."

"No one's going anywhere until you accept this

purse." Charlene raised her chin, staring straight into his eyes. She took another step forward, away from the group, until she was standing close enough to touch Grant.

"Where did you find the money, Charlene?" His voice took on a sharp edge. "Been whoring on the side? By God, if that's true, I swear to you that I'll mur—"

"Take the payment." Charlene held the heavy purse outstretched, even though her arm ached with the strain.

He folded his arms over his chest. "Birds, if you don't head for the stage this instant, Mace here will become angry. And you don't want to make him angry."

Mace's scowl deepened, the violet scar puckering across his cheek.

"Have you ever thought about our feelings?" Charlene asked. "Have you ever given one moment's thought to the consequences of your actions?"

Grant scoffed. "Why should I care? I purchased these birds. I own them. And they have a dance to perform. Now out of my way." He knocked her aside.

She stumbled but swiftly regained her footing, raising the purse again. "You don't own us," she said. "You never did."

Mace cracked his knuckles. He was favoring his right knee. An old injury? Could give her an advantage.

Diane stepped out of the group and came

to stand beside Charlene. She folded her hand around Charlene's elbow, propping up the outstretched arm that held the purse. "Take the payment, Baron," she said, her gold eyes flashing.

"Go on stage now, Dove," Grant said. "There's a pretty bird."

"I'm not a pretty bird. And my name is Diane." She narrowed her eyes. "Not Dove."

Charlene smiled at her gratefully. "Thank you."

Diane nodded.

"What a touching scene," Grant jeered. "What do you call it? Mutiny of the Whores?"

Mace grinned. "I know how to deal with mutineers. Should I take 'em outside, my lord?"

Charlene took a deep breath, preparing to drop the purse and assume a defensive posture.

"This is becoming ridiculous. Do you hear them cheering, birds?" Grant gestured toward the curtain. "There'll be a riot if you don't appear soon."

The other ladies drifted closer, forming a tight semicircle behind Charlene and Diane, glaring at Grant. Charlene's heart swelled. They were so brave, these women who came from nothing, with only their bodies to sell. They stood beside her. Supporting her. Giving her the strength she needed.

Charlene shook the purse. "Accept our payment."

Grant nodded at Mace, but before the guard could take action, a tall man in a well-cut black coat stepped out from the shadows of the velvet stage curtains. For one heart-stopping second, Charlene thought it was James.

But he was still in Surrey.

This man was tall and broad-shouldered, true, but his hair was chestnut and hung past his collar, far longer than fashion dictated, and his eyes were gray. "We're ready for the performance, Grant—" He stopped. "What's happening here?"

Grant's face reddened. "Nothing, nothing at all. Bit of a domestic squabble, Lord Hatherly. Give me a few minutes to sort it out and the performance will begin."

So this was their host, Lord Hatherly. He looked at Charlene, his gray eyes turbulent. "Is there something wrong, Miss?"

Charlene nodded. "Lord Grant is refusing our repayment of a loan."

"Quiet!" said Grant. "Lord Hatherly won't be troubled by such trivial matters."

Lord Hatherly glanced at the baron. "Why won't you accept it?"

Grant sputtered, his face reddening even more. "This is all a misunderstanding."

"No." Charlene shoved the purse at him. "There's no misunderstanding. We want our freedom."

"How dare you humiliate me," Grant hissed. "Go home. I'll deal with you later."

Lord Hatherly rounded on Grant, his silver eyes glittering in the backstage gloom. "You should take the purse."

Grant glanced from Lord Hatherly to Charlene.

"Now," said Lord Hatherly, low and commanding.

Grant accepted the purse.

Hatherly flicked a finger, and two large footmen materialized from the shadows. "Escort Lord Grant and . . . companion"—he glanced disdainfully at Mace—"to his carriage."

"But these are my birds!" Grant said. "You can't throw me out."

With incredible speed, Lord Hatherly crossed to the baron and grabbed his collar. He pulled his face close. "I don't like you. I never have. You will leave this house and never return."

The footmen caught Grant as he reeled back from the strength of Lord Hatherly's forceful shove.

Lord Hatherly held his arms out to Charlene and Diane. "Ladies?" They hooked their arms in his, and he escorted them toward the curtain. "Shall we dance?"

Grant's furious shouting was drowned out as they neared the curtain and the din of the crowd grew louder.

Charlene smiled up at Lord Hatherly. "Thank you, my lord. That was kind of you."

Silver eyes met hers. "Can't think why I invited him. Suppose it was for the benefit of your charming company."

Charlene waited with the girls for their musical cue. She'd hide in the back of the group and slip out while everyone was watching their performance.


James glanced around at the decadent chaos of Hatherly's ballroom. Monkeys in red fez caps with black tassels swung from chandeliers. A peacock roosted on a pile of silk cushions. Plush divans dotted the room, occupied by poetic types with tousled hair, quoting bad rhymes for buxom tarts.

The air was thick with amber-scented smoke and a cacophony of laughter, philosophical arguments, and animal noises—a dissolute Babel tower, presided over by Nicolas, Lord Hatherly, heir to the mad Duke of Barrington. They'd been friends since childhood—James, Nick, and Dalton, and compatriots in pranks at Cambridge.

James caught sight of Nick climbing down from a stage at the far end of the room. James walked toward him, through the crowd of men gathered around the stage.

"Well, if it isn't His Disgrace, in the flesh." Nick clapped him on the back. "I like the beard. I was beginning to think you were just a story mamas made up to scare their daughters into behaving at balls."

Heads swiveled. Whispering began.

"Where's the duke?" James asked Nick. "Doesn't he mind his ballroom being turned into a menagerie?"

"Rotting upstairs. Doesn't even know who I am. Claims I'm his friend Sir Pemberton. He's always trying to kiss the nurse. Thinks she's Mother. Mother's abroad, you know, she can't bear to see him like this."

Nick swiped a bottle of brandy from one of his adoring followers and took a long swallow. "I was sad to hear about William. Hell of a way to go."

James nodded. "He would have made a damn fine duke. I'm sure to make a debacle of the whole thing."

Nick shook his head. "Heard about your marriage plans from Dalton. My condolences."

"Where is Dalton? Not here tonight?"

"He's disappeared again. He's always disappearing. Probably off in the arms of some foreign princess. He told me—"

Blaring brass horns drowned out Nick's next words as a pack of musicians wound their way through the crowd. Several women in long black cloaks and pink feathered masks floated across the stage to the appreciative calls of the gathered gentlemen.

"Extraordinary creatures," Nick shouted, indicating the girls with his head. "From a place called the Pink Feather. Obviously."

The line of black-cloaked women swayed seductively. One of them stepped to the front and slowly shed her cloak.

Long midnight-black curls hung to her waist, and bold gold eyes flashed behind the mask. Her costume was pink feathers and white gauze, and hid nothing. Curving hips and high, rounded breasts.

Nothing.

An enticing beauty, nearly naked, and James's body had no response. Instead, his mind traveled to Dorothea's petite curves and gold curls. What was she doing tonight? He couldn't quite picture her staying home and embroidering.

"Hello!" Nick waved a hand in front of James's face. "What do you think of the dancers?"

"They're lovely, I suppose. If you like that sort."

Nick stared at him. "Dalton told me you'd been captured by Lady Dorothea, but I didn't believe it until now."

"Don't believe everything Dalton tells you."

The band played a slow tune, and the women, as one, swept away their cloaks, revealing more pink feathers and gauze that left little to the imagination.

They danced for the men, baring a thigh here, a delicately arched instep there. All lovely, all curved and luscious. The crowd cheered and surged around them.

One of the dancers had kept her cloak on and was edging down the stairs, her shoulders hunched. Something about the way she walked drew his eye.

"That one," he pointed at her. "The one descending the stairs."

Nick followed his finger, nodding when he saw the woman. "Good choice, but she appears to be leaving."

Oh no she wasn't. Not until James had a closer inspection. He wove through the crowd of cheering spectators. The woman glanced around the room, obviously searching for an exit.

It couldn't be her. Not *here*.

She caught sight of him, and surprise opened her lips. Before she could run away, he grabbed her arm and pulled her to face him.

Stormy eyes glinted behind pink satin.

He knew those eyes.

She struggled against his grip.

He ripped the feathered mask from her face.

It *was* her.

Dorothea. His duchess.

*She'd gone too far.*

Outrage quickened his pulse.

He scooped her up, ignoring her protests, flung her face-first over his shoulder, and strode from the room.

# Chapter 23

**"P**ut me down!" Charlene beat on his back with her fists, but his arm was an iron band around her lower back, his other arm pinioning her thighs against his chest.

He only grunted in response, plunging out onto a balcony and down some steps to the gardens.

If she found the right point in his neck, he'd have to release his grip. But no, then they might both go tumbling down the steps. Better to conserve her energy for what lay ahead. There was no possible way he'd believe she was Lady Dorothea now. Finding her at a Cyprian's ball wearing a feathered mask.

Charlene took a breath. There was a searing sense of relief in knowing her lies would be exposed. Until she recalled that exposure would jeopardize everything she'd worked so hard for.

The countess would demand the reward back because Charlene had violated their contract. The money Charlene had already given to Grant.

All the pain would have been for nothing.

Lulu would lose her apprenticeship.

Flor would be left with no mother at all if he didn't marry Dorothea.

*Think, Charlene. Think. Could you claim complete ignorance? You don't know who he is, or why he's here. You've never heard of Lady Dorothea.*

He carried her down a garden path, stepping with the surety of a mountain lion in the darkness lit only by a bright yellow moon. Where was he taking her? She craned her neck. A dome of glass and metal appeared ahead of them, the glass reflecting the moonlight.

He kicked the door to the domed structure open with his boot and carried her inside.

Abruptly, he dropped onto an ironwork bench, pulling her down with him and shifting her weight until she was draped across his knees, facedown. Her fingers brushed leaves and dirt.

There was the sound of trickling water. The smell of loam and flowers. The air was warm and humid.

She could hear him breathing, heavy and thick. She dangled over his knees, knowing that if she needed to, she could roll away in an instant, crouch on her heels, ready for anything.

"What am I going to do with you, Dorothea?" he asked. The anguish in his voice was as palpable as the soil beneath her fingers.

Wait. He'd called her Dorothea.

The countess's clipped tones intruded into her thoughts. *People see only what they expect to see. A duke is no exception.*

"Why are you here?" he asked. "I went to your house today, and your father refused to let me see you. And now I find you *here*. You can't break every rule under the sun! I need a respectable duchess, damn it. And I find you dancing for a crowd of leering men."

Hands clamped around her shoulders, holding her down across his knees. "It won't do. Do you hear me? My duchess can't parade about in front of my friends like some . . . *demimondaine*."

He still thought she was Dorothea. He'd gone to Lord Desmond's house but hadn't met her half sister.

The charade continued.

Charlene quickly adjusted her response, unloosening her muscles, rippling from coiled to coy in one imperceptible shift.

She tilted her head and glanced up at him. "Papa wouldn't let me see you, but I need to talk to you. I heard you would be here, and I arranged to meet you. They think I'm at Vauxhall with my friends, and I must go back soon. I need to explain, you see. You were so angry with me the other night . . . in your workshop."

"I want to talk to you about that as well. Did you plan to be compromised?"

"It was Mother's idea. I wanted to stop her. I knew . . . I knew you were honorable." She worked a catch into her voice, with a hint, just a hint, of challenge. "I know it was bad of me. I'm so sorry. I . . . deserve to be punished."

In the dim moonlight, his eyes went nearly black.

She dropped her head, hiding her face with the fall of her hair. It wasn't difficult to feign trembling.

A hand reached around to unclasp her cloak, tug it out from under her hips and off her body. Underneath was Dorothea's dove gray muslin gown. Modest. Not provocative, like the gauze and feathers the dancers had worn.

"You're sorely in need of reform, Dorothea." His large hand settled over her bum, and a new batch of tremors started in her belly. "And I've never been one to shirk a difficult challenge."

He used her own words, almost making her smile. "And I suppose you're precisely the big, bad duke to attempt such a fool's mission?"

She'd thought she would never see him again. And here they were, flesh to flesh. How easily she fell back into the role. Being Dorothea again.

"Yes, *my lady*. I am. I know exactly what to do with recalcitrant debutantes." He smacked her bum.

"Oh!" She startled. It hadn't hurt, only surprised her.

She was intensely aware of her position. Over his knees, her face hidden in her hair. Completely exposed. Under his control. Fingers slid down her calves, searching for her hem. She wasn't wearing any drawers. If he lifted her skirts . . .

He lifted her skirts, sliding layers of muslin up her body until she was naked.

He could see her.

*There.*

She pressed her thighs together.

His hand smoothed across her backside, stroking and soothing. Then it left. Came down again.

*Smack.* His palm impacted.

Wetness and heat pooled between her thighs.

This was a secret, depraved pleasure she never could have imagined.

She should put a stop to this. Run away before more lies accumulated. But how could she leave now, with his arousal pressing against her belly and his palm smacking her bare arse, making her heart race and her mind cloud with desire.

He smoothed his hand over her again, inching his fingers down, closer to the seam between her thighs. She squirmed against his fingers.

She heard his sharp intake of breath. Knew a rush of heady power.

He increased the frequency of the glancing blows, striking with a gentle yet firm touch. The perfectly calibrated impact made her skin tingle and her insides turn liquid.

The sweet, heavy ache between her thighs increased.

"Dorothea," he groaned, "what are you doing to me?"

In one swift, powerful movement, he lifted her, settling her thighs on either side of his body, cupping her bottom with his hands and pulling her tight against his chest.

He'd stopped shaving. The stubble of his black beard scraped against her cheek and jaw as he kissed her, hot and fast, with a hunger that left her breathless, panting, and needing more.

"I'm sorry," she breathed when he finally broke the kiss. "I'm here for you, only you."

His body shook, an ominous rumble like distant thunder on a summer day.

She rubbed against his stiffness, her thighs wide and wanton, knees pressed against solid iron on either side of his body. She'd been given one more night of pleasure. She knew it would only mean more pain. But she had to take it. She had to. There was no other choice.

He captured her mouth with his and kissed her, over and over. A coil of vines unfurled in her stomach. His hands molded her breasts.

She kissed him, pressing her body into his, wanting to imprint this feeling so deeply that she would never forget. He stopped to rip off his coat and cravat, giving her access to his smooth chest. The heat of him.

He kissed his way down her neck, pulling at her bodice until her breasts spilled free over the half-stays and the hard ivory busk. He lowered his mouth and suckled her breast, his tongue flicking over her swollen nipple.

The wall behind them teemed with waxy green leaves and lacy yellow flowers. He reached behind, to the wall, and broke off a flower, brushing it down her cheek and across her lips. Her teeth pierced a petal. Faint taste of honey. Scent of lemons.

He trailed the petals down into the valley between her breasts. He followed the petals with his lips, teasing and sucking, swirling his tongue around her nipples until she was panting and breathless.

The flower found her belly, slipped lower. He

parted her legs even wider and pressed the cool, smooth petals against her core.

She would give herself to him, for one insane moment. She would open for him, let him pleasure her.

He spread her wide with his fingers, and then the flower brushed softly over her center, the place that throbbed for his touch. His fingers replaced the petals, flicking over her, softly at first and then harder, more demanding.

She found his lips again and his tongue entered her mouth in the same rhythm as his fingers.

He undid his trouser flap and his sex sprang free, finding her core, sliding against her belly.

"Oh." She hadn't been able to stop the startled sound from escaping her lips.

She wasn't ignorant. She'd heard the girls at the Pink Feather describing the act of sex, the varieties, the possibility for pain . . . and maybe even pleasure, with the right person. Someone you chose. Not a customer.

The hard length of him. As unrelenting as the iron bench biting into knees.

She reached between their bodies, circling the root with her hand.

"Ah," he groaned. "Yes. Touch me." He closed his fingers around hers, showing her what he liked. She moved up and down in between their bodies, and he was completely in her control, his head thrown back, muscles in his neck cording. "Yes," he moaned. But then he said, his breathing ragged, "We'll be married soon. We can wait."

He would do that for her. Deny himself pleasure. She felt his restraint all the way down her
body, deep in her heart.

She shifted her hips and brought his flesh in
contact with hers. She opened a little wider, nudging his hardness with her core.

"We don't have to wait," she said. "I need
you, James," she said. "Here." She showed him
where with her body, pressing down, vulnerable,
open . . . lost forever.

"Are you sure?" he asked. "There are bedrooms
upstairs. At least we could—"

No time for pretty words. Only raw wanting.
"I'm sure," she said. "Here. Now."

*Now. Do it now.*

He lifted her hips. The tip of him stretched her
wide.

"Move down onto me," he said. He held his
breath beneath her, straining with the effort to
remain still, as she slid down, inch by silken inch.

It was uncomfortable at first, the girth of him.
The unfamiliar sensation. The heat and pulse of
him inside her.

"Dorothea." He buried his face in her neck. His
voice shivered down her spine.

*Not Dorothea. Charlene.* The words nearly erupted
with a need so overwhelming that she bit her lips
hard enough to draw blood.

His large hands gripped her hips as he began
to move inside her. Slowly, at first, and then faster.
Pushing . . . pulling . . . steering her. Propelling
them forward.

Green eyes glinting. Dark hair falling over his brow.

He closed his lips around her breast and suckled. She threaded her hands into his hair as they moved together. She'd known it would be like this. That he would sweep her away and never let her come up for air.

He was almost all the way inside now. It stretched and stung, but then he shifted a little so he could reach around and touch her. His thumb found her sensitive flesh, and soon she was moaning above him, her wetness easing his passage, a string held taught, vibrating, the pleasure building in slow, sensuous waves.

All her life she'd lived beneath a canopy of leaves, crawling through darkness. Now, in his arms, she knew what life was like for the hawk soaring above the trees. The weightless feeling of leaving the earth behind and climbing to some impossible new height.

When she thought she might die, when her stomach muscles clenched until it was painful, she flew over the edge of the forest into a sunrise of pleasure so intense it burned her to cinders in his strong arms.

**S**he was hot as tropical sun, hot and wet around him, her climax still contracting her inner muscles around his cock.

"Wrap yourself around my waist," he said. And she did. Circling him completely. Her legs hooked

behind his back, his hands cradling her sumptuous arse.

He plunged all the way inside, then lifted her
hips, almost sliding all the way out.

Then slid home again.

Faster now. Keeping her exactly where he
needed her to be. Angling up, into that place so
far inside her. The one that knew his name. And
would never know another.

She was his duchess. His passionate, impulsive,
outspoken duchess.

"I can't believe I found you in cold, old England," he whispered into the decadent silken
waves of her hair. He thrust again, loving the way
she clenched around him, took him in, and asked
for more with her eyes and those soft moans.

"You'll never dance for anyone but me," he
commanded.

"Never," she gasped.

"My duchess only dances for me."

"Yes. Only you."

Now the pressure was building, the pleasure
mounting.

"Good," he panted. "Feels . . . so . . . good." He
pumped faster, pushing up into her silken heat.
She moaned and raked her nails down his back,
through the linen of his shirt. He moved hard and
fast. So close now.

Her eyes screwed shut, as if she was holding
back tears. He slowed. Used every reserve of
strength to stop. She was an innocent. This was
her first time. Outdoors, with her skirts rucked

up around her waist. He hadn't even removed his clothing.

"If this hurts," he gasped, "if you don't want this, all you have to do is say so."

Her eyes flew open. The blue of wide open seas engulfed him.

"I don't want you to stop. It stings . . . a little. But it's . . ." She smiled shyly. "Fierce and melting and dangerous and . . . beautiful. All at once."

He remained still, while his prick jerked inside her, begging for completion.

"*You're* beautiful," he said. He kissed her cheek. "I never want to hurt you. Ever."

She adjusted her hips. Relaxed around him. Sliding tentatively at first, then with bolder movements, using the leverage of the bench beneath her knees, she found a rhythm that had him clawing for the last shred of his control. "Oh," she moaned, taking all of him inside her and rubbing against him.

That one small sound was almost his undoing. He had to fight for control. Find strength so deep inside he hadn't known it existed. He clung to the edge of his climax, needing her to be there with him.

He reached between them, using his thumb in exactly the right place.

The bench shook beneath them. James's boot kicked into a new position, startling a bird, who flew away with a shrill protest.

Scruples be damned.

She was his duchess. And he wasn't going to

wait a moment longer to claim her. He threaded her arms tighter around his neck and pulled her legs more firmly around his waist. He gripped her arse, feeling his orgasm closing in like a tropical hurricane, gathering heat and energy, spiraling so fast there was nothing but this driving need.

She clenched around him, her breath coming in rapid, shallow gasps. When the storm broke, and he came inside her, it was melting and dangerous and all the things she'd said.

He leaned his head against her soft breasts, listening to the rapid fluttering of her heart. He loved the feel of her curves pressed against him. Loved how her cries had rung natural and untutored. With no artifice.

Tupping one's own fiancée at a Cyprian's ball. Not the usual outcome of such an evening. Usually he ended up in the arms of a worldly courtesan.

Probably, that would have been much safer.

A courtesan would know the score. Would expect him to give her a gift of jewelry and leave.

He'd said he didn't want to hurt her. But wasn't that exactly what he was going to do if he married her and then left her alone in England? He set her off his lap, adjusting his trousers. She nestled against him on the bench.

Tenderness rose from some untapped source inside the dark well of his heart. He stroked a lock of damp hair away from the smooth curve of her cheek and tucked it behind her ear. He wanted to make wild promises about staying by her side forever.

He wanted to tell her what she wanted to hear.
But he couldn't do that.
He had to remain silent.
Do what he always did. Give expensive jewelry and leave.

It was killing her, this silence.

Cracking her heart into pieces inside her chest. There would be a hollow, rattling sound when she stood up. She'd had her moment of insanity. The fire in his eyes and the heat of their bodies together. She would remember it forever.

But now she had to tell him. Even if it ruined all of her plans.

"James," she began, but he didn't hear her. He was already moving off the bench, walking into the shadows.

Charlene heard him strike tinder against steel. Soon he had a candle lit. It must have been so lovely here once, but now the plants had grown wild and vines twisted everywhere, cracking the stone pillars and sprouting through the flag-stones. With all that plant life, the air was warm and humid, still holding the day's sun in a riot of green limbs.

She could wait another few minutes.

"What is this place?" she asked.

James sat next to her, folded her into his arms again. "The duke's orchid conservatory. It was his obsession. He'd spend hours every day out here, growing new exotic varieties."

He glanced up at the cracked glass ceiling. "They call him 'the Mad Duke' now. It looks like no one's been here in years. Nick and I used to play out here when we were boys, pretending to be explorers."

Nick had to be Lord Hatherly, the man who had banished Grant.

"We've been friends since childhood," James continued. "I left for the West Indies. Explored real jungles. England's too tame for me, too set in its ways. I could never be happy here, Dorothea. I hope you understand that."

Yes. She saw that. He was made for open spaces, not ballrooms or tearooms.

"James, I have something I must tell you," she whispered, the words wrenched from her lips.

He stroked her cheek. "First let me show you something."

He pulled a small, blue, velvet-covered box out of his discarded jacket pocket.

*Blast. Please don't let it be—*

"This was my mother's," he said, opening the box.

*Diamonds.*

"Her name was Margaret. She would have liked you. She wanted me to be happy. And you make me happier than I ever thought I could be."

It wasn't ostentatious. Just a small cluster of diamonds fashioned into a flower, set in delicate, twining gold.

"You're so quiet," he said. "You don't like it. You can select something better, more fitting for—"

"I love it."

*She loved him. No, no she didn't.*

"Then try it on." He caught her hand, but she resisted. If he slid the ring onto her finger, she would dream for just one second that he was giving this ring to her. To Charlene.

He frowned. "You don't want to wear it?"

"Oh, James, of course I do."

He slipped the ring onto her third finger and kissed her knuckles. "I know I said I wanted a business arrangement, but then you tumbled me arse over ears onto my own carpet. What was I supposed to do?"

She smiled, remembering that moment. The horror on the countess's face. The flapping steward.

"There," he breathed, brushing his thumb across her lips. "That smile. That blinding smile. A man could make that his life's ambition, to produce that smile."

"James. Don't."

"Why? I need someone like you, so full of light and life and conviction. What you said about me having a responsibility to create a new kind of manufactory. I think you're right. I'm having an architect draw up plans."

That was something, at least. Some glimmer of good in the accumulated soot of all the lies.

"I'm willing to try. I'm willing to learn how to be a better father. A better man. Flor hasn't screamed once since she met you. I don't know what you told her, but she actually sat down and completed all her lessons. I sacked that awful governess. You can choose a new one."

Just for the space of an instant, Charlene imagined a different world. One where they could be a family. James, Charlene, and Flor. In this world, she'd been born the legitimate daughter of the earl. In this world, she could wear his mother's ring.

It was a seductive dream.

And it could never happen.

But he was willing to change. For *her*.

No, not for her. *For Dorothea.* For the woman he thought she was. Pure. Good. Pedigreed.

"I won't be the husband you deserve," he said. "I won't even be here most of the time. But when I am, I will always try to make you smile. And I will never stop attempting to win your heart."

She turned her head away from green eyes that glinted like emeralds among the vines and flowers.

He caught her chin in his fingers and turned her back to face him. "Damn. I'm making a mess of this."

"No. You're not. It's me. I'm not . . . her. The woman you're talking about. I'm not . . . Why are you saying these things, damn you."

He smiled. "See? No proper debutante would say something like that." He drew her in closer, dropped a kiss near the corner of her mouth.

*Because I'm not proper, or a debutante, or any of the things you need your duchess to be.* She should just blurt it out, or she'd never say the words.

She couldn't. What did she think was going to happen? Did she think he'd renounce Dorothea and marry her? Dukes never married illegitimate girls who'd been raised to be courtesans.

Charlene would lose Lulu's apprenticeship, and James's eyes would lose that reverent glow.

"So, what did you need to tell me?" he asked, nuzzling her neck.

Her heart beat faster, thumping against the cage of her chest.

Water dripped from a leaf above and landed on Charlene's cheek.

In St. James's, Dorothea shook out the contents of her trousseau trunk, fingered fine linen and lace. Prepared for her wedding.

At home, Lulu dreamt of painting ruined castles in fields of wildflowers.

Charlene closed her eyes. "Only that I must go back. My friends will be worried," she whispered.

*Coward.*

"I'll take you to Vauxhall." When she tensed, he smiled and stroked her cheek. "Don't worry, I'll leave you near the entrance. No one will see you with His Disgrace before our wedding." He loosened a candle from the sconce, took her hand, and led her outside, into the cool air and starry skies. She shivered and wrapped the black cloak tighter.

In the bloodred leather interior of his carriage, bordered by his strong arms, the wanting settled around her so thick she could taste it. The sweet lure of honey and the bitterness of tansy tea. Brewed with salty tears.

He drew her closer against his warmth. His mother's ring was heavy around her finger. Now the pain of losing him would be so much worse.

But she'd never had him. Not really. What she'd had had been built on a foundation of lies.

She had to find a way to give the ring to Dorothea early tomorrow morning.

They were in sight of the stone archways of Vauxhall.

"Stop the carriage," she said. "Please." She was so close to breaking down and sobbing in his arms. She had to leave.

He waved the footman away and helped her alight from the carriage himself. "Lady Dorothea." He bowed, tall and commanding, every inch the duke.

She walked a few steps. Turned around. She didn't care that there were people about. She ran back to him and stood on her tiptoes, slipping her arms around his neck.

His lips found hers, and he kissed her until she was breathless. Until she forgot her name. Until there was nothing but heat and urgency and sweetness.

It would have to last, this kiss. Their last kiss.

It would have to last a lifetime.

Finally, he broke away. "I will call for you tomorrow evening," he said. "They can't keep me away from you, Dorothea."

He climbed back into the carriage.

"Good-bye, James," she whispered, knowing there would be no tomorrow.

# Chapter 24

**J**ames would not wait weeks to marry Dorothea.

Not after what had happened last night. Someone could have recognized her. She'd promised to behave like a proper duchess from now on, but he'd been thrusting inside her at the time. She probably would have promised anything. It was best to marry her swiftly and spirit her away from the eyes of the *ton*.

Into his bed, where she belonged.

Picturing what they would do in the enormous island of the ducal bed, marooned for days . . . weeks . . . made his heart beat faster and his palms dampen.

He took a sip of too-bland hot chocolate. "I've decided to roust the archbishop and obtain a special license," he said to Nick, who was seated across from him in a breakfast room at Brooks's.

Nothing had changed here in the ten years James had been absent. The white-whiskered porter had recognized him immediately when James and Nick had arrived last night. This morning, the breakfast room was as tomblike as ever, with discreet waiters gliding noiselessly across thick carpeting, serving hot rolls and coffee to club members nursing brandy headaches and reeling from losses at the gambling tables.

Nick peered over the edge of his newspaper. "Come again?"

"Why should I wait and marry in Surrey? I'll be married here in London by special license." Saying that out loud made him feel happy. Not that he wanted to examine the feeling too closely. It was just there, like a hidden vein of gold in a granite mountain.

"That's what I thought you said." Nick set down his paper and lifted an eyebrow in the direction of a thin, elegant waiter, who hastened to their table. "Morley," said Nick, "fetch a skilled physician, a bucket of ice water, and a strong draft of laudanum. His Grace is unwell."

Morley bowed and snapped his white-gloved fingers at a young waiter. "I shall see to it immediately."

James shook his head. "That won't be necessary—I feel fine. Hatherly's only having a bit of fun."

"Very relieved to hear it, Your Grace," Morley said, his long face carefully expressionless. He bowed and returned to his station.

"You should have helped me with that bottle of smuggled whisky last night," Nick groaned. "If your head pounded like mine, you wouldn't be contemplating anything as rash as marriage."

"Lady Dorothea inspires . . . reckless acts."

"Nothing would inspire me to marry save a pistol held to my chest."

James finished his chocolate. "You'll see when you meet her tomorrow, since you'll be one of our witnesses. She's no common debutante. She's extraordinary . . ."

With the most intriguing blend of passion, intellect, and beauty James had ever known, although it wouldn't do for him to spout. Not in a breakfast room at Brooks's, where wives were strictly off-limits.

Nick nodded. "Fine. But I won't stop giving you arguments in favor of bachelorhood until the moment the curate sounds the death knell."

"You know I have to marry." James attempted a blasé shrug of his shoulders. "May as well be tomorrow."

"You don't fool me, you know." Nick tore apart a roll and slathered it with butter. "Leave it to you to do something as disreputable as fall in love with your own wife."

Love? James hadn't thought of it in those terms. He'd sworn off love after his mother died. He would admit to feeling different, somehow. Probably just the remaining glow from the extraordinary night they'd shared.

If she behaved, he would treat Dorothea with respect and gentleness while he was in England. He had no doubt that she would, in turn, be a caring mother to Flor, and their future children, while he was abroad. Even if Dorothea's conduct was far from impeccable, he believed that she genuinely cared for his daughter, and he hoped that her family reputation, coupled with her new title, would smooth Flor's road into society.

"Scoff all you want," James said, "but never say never. You might find a woman one of these days who's willing to overlook your many faults."

"Not going to happen." Nick attacked another roll. "Wish Dalton was here to talk some sense into you. Remember our oath? We were never going to marry, and, above all, we were never going to become our fathers."

"I will never become my father," James said. "You know I didn't plan any of this. Life threw me this bend in the road, and I'm only making the best of it." It was far more than that, but James wasn't going to admit that Dorothea was very nearly making him rethink his aversion to intimacy.

"I know." Nick sighed. "Forgive me, I've a demon of a headache. Best to go and sleep it off." He rose and threw down his napkin. "Give my regards to the archbishop."

James finished his breakfast alone, his mind returning to the orchid conservatory and Dorothea, where it had been ever since he'd left her at the entrance to Vauxhall last night. It was against his moral code to ravish an innocent debutante, even if she was his fiancée. That's why he had to marry her immediately. She could already be carrying his heir.

Lady Desmond had been absolutely right to refuse to let him see Dorothea, because he couldn't control himself around her. And he didn't want to. He was going to claim her again and again.

The thought ignited sparks in his mind.

She wouldn't leave his bed until he'd exhausted every single way to make her smile, moan, and cry his name.

The duke's diamond ring was knotted inside a plain cambric handkerchief, concealed in the pocket of Charlene's cloak. She turned her head toward the main entrance for the hundredth time. She'd sent a note to Manon asking her to bring Dorothea to St. Paul's Church on the west end of the piazza, in secret, on a matter of urgency.

They were nearly a half hour late.

Charlene couldn't afford time to sit and think. She needed to be out doing things, keeping her mind off Ja . . . dukes. She had arrangements to make for Lulu's apprenticeship. A physician's appointment to force her mother to keep.

She had to stop thinking about green eyes that stared into her soul and uncovered her deepest longings. Silken flower petals trailing over her lips. The sore place between her thighs that throbbed with the knowledge of him, the pulse that still beat his name.

She couldn't blame him for taking what she had freely offered. He'd thought she was his future duchess. So here she sat, draped in black, possibly carrying a duke's illegitimate child. She was her mother's daughter after all. Her carefully constructed defenses had crumbled like foolscap in his embrace.

The church's great carved door swept across

stone floors. Sunlight pierced the gloom, illuminating a marble angel reclining on a pedestal. Manon appeared. When her eyes found Charlene, she opened the door wider and stepped aside. Lady Dorothea glided across the floor in a straw bonnet covered in a white dotted veil and a pale pink gown trimmed with embroidered lilies and seed pearls.

Charlene's jaw clenched. How could anyone have mistaken her for this picture of fair English maidenhood, swathed in shell pink—graceful, dainty, and demure? Charlene rose, but Dorothea motioned her back onto the oaken pew and took a seat next to her.

Manon stood guard behind them, ready to alert them if anyone entered the church. She gave Charlene an encouraging nod.

Dorothea turned to Charlene, the summer-sky blue of her eyes visible through the pale gauze of her veil. "Miss Beckett?" she whispered.

Charlene nodded. "Thank you for meeting me, Lady Dorothea."

Dorothea peered at Charlene through her veil. "Are we truly so alike? I've been so curious ever since Mama told me what happened." Her eyes searched the galleries before she untied the ribbon holding her white veil in place.

When she lifted her veil, Charlene's heart pounded. It was like looking in a mirror with slightly wavy glass that distorted the image almost imperceptibly.

Charlene lifted her own veil.

"Oh!" Dorothea's hand flew to her mouth, stifling the exclamation. "Extraordinary," she whispered. "We could be twins."

The two girls stared at each other in fascination. No wonder the deception had worked.

"We shouldn't be seen together," said Charlene, replacing her veil. "The countess would be furious. I have something I must give you."

Dorothea covered her face again. "I had no idea you existed. Why did Father keep you from me? I can't express how very discomfiting it is to arrive home after a long journey and find that not only do I have a sister but my mother paid you to procure me a duke." She smiled. "I certainly wasn't producing any prospects . . . but still."

Charlene wanted to take her hand, but she stopped herself. She had to give her the ring quickly. They couldn't be seen together. "I hope I haven't caused you any pain."

"I've always known my parents would choose a husband for me. I'm the dutiful daughter. That's me."

There was a hint of rebellion in her voice that warmed Charlene's heart.

"Sometimes I feel like a marionette at Punch's Theatre and Mama is pulling my strings. Have you ever felt that way, Miss Beckett?"

A feeling like vertigo nearly knocked the breath out of Charlene's chest, pushing her over the edge of a new awareness. "I know exactly how you feel," she said. She'd grown up envying Dorothea, but her sister's life hadn't been a fairy tale. She had a domineering mother, a foolish, philandering father, and the burden of society's expectation to make a brilliant match.

"Everyone says the duke is brutish and disreputable," said Dorothea. "Is it true?"

Charlene shook her head vehemently. "Don't listen to them. He likes to be shocking, that's all. He carries knives around in his boots and plays Spanish guitar. You'll never know what he's going to do next . . . but he's not at all unkind. You'll see. He's strong . . . and *good*."

Dorothea's head tilted to one side. "You sound as though . . . I don't know . . . as though you admire him."

"I admire his unconventionality."

"You don't have feelings for him?"

The laugh Charlene mustered sounded false to her ears. "He'll be kind to you."

"You didn't answer my question, Miss Beckett."

There, she sounded like the countess for the first time. It was good to see Dorothea had some of her mother's spine without the ruthlessness. "Of course not," Charlene said.

Dorothea grew still. "You're lying. I can hear it in your voice." She gripped Charlene's fingers. "Can I marry someone my sister loves?" she whispered. "Can I?"

Charlene blinked away unexpected tears. "The countess hired me because I was raised to be a . . . courtesan." She rushed her words, feeling as though she was polluting Dorothea somehow, even by saying them. "The duke requires a respectable, suitable bride. I *want* you to marry him.

You'll be a perfect duchess . . . and I hope you will be a good mother to his daughter Flor."

Dorothea searched her face through the gauze. "Mama told me about the daughter, and I know I could never fault her for being born on the wrong side of the . . . that is to say . . ."

"It's all right." Charlene knew Dorothea hadn't meant to offend her. "I'm relieved to hear that you are sympathetic." And now her work was done. She knew that Flor would be in caring hands. And James would be pleased with his suddenly sweet-tempered and respectable bride.

"Here." Charlene thrust the linen-wrapped ring into Dorothea's palm. "This was meant for you." She rose. "I must go."

"Wait." Dorothea caught her arm. "There's something else. The duke sent word to my father this morning that we are to be married by special license tomorrow. Why is there such a rush?"

Charlene's gut clenched, as if someone had struck her. They were marrying tomorrow.

"Miss Beckett?"

"The duke and I . . . last night . . ." Charlene began, but the words wouldn't come.

"Yes?" Dorothea prompted.

Charlene could see her brow furrow through her veil.

"Oh," Dorothea breathed. "I see." She tucked the ring into her reticule. "In that case, do you truly think he'll believe we are the same person? What if he guesses the truth and sweeps *you* off to one of his castles in Northumberland?"

Charlene turned away. "That will never happen."

She smiled, even though she felt more like crying. "Marry him, and be happy." She was surprised to find that she meant it. If circumstances had been different, perhaps she and her half sister could have been friends.

Lady Dorothea rose, and Charlene followed. "I'll try," Dorothea said. She hesitated, stretching out her hand for a shake and then impulsively giving Charlene a brief hug. "I wish you the best, Miss Beckett."

Charlene and Manon exchanged a smile before Charlene hurried back toward the bustle of the piazza. Her hand involuntarily patted her empty pocket.

Dorothea would marry the duke tomorrow, and there would be no more diamonds for Charlene.

Just as well, she told herself. Diamonds were only a way of saying, *I own you*. And Charlene could never accept that.

# Chapter 25

❧

"**T**here's still time to stop the wedding," Nick said.

James shook his head. No there wasn't. Not when Dorothea could already be carrying his child.

He'd wanted to hold the ceremony in his town house, where Flor and Josefa would be arriving soon, but the countess had insisted on a church, saying something about her cousin being the curate.

Standing in front of a gold-draped altar, with an elderly clergyman in black robes, white cravat, and white curled wig presiding, all James could think about was the orchid conservatory. The scent of crushed petals and the sound of Dorothea's soft moans.

Sunlight danced across the red carpet. The wedding party entered the church.

James's heart nearly galloped out of his chest. Dorothea was radiant in pale rose silk shot with gold threads that shimmered in the sunbeams filtering through the round stained-glass window.

*So beautiful.*

*She'll do.*

She wore a broad-brimmed bonnet trimmed with pink tea roses that shaded her face, but he could tell she was nervous and unsmiling. She walked down the aisle with small, tentative steps.

He willed her to hurry, needing her standing next to him, joining with him in name, and then in body. He craved the heat of her smile, the challenging glint in her eyes. He even welcomed her talent for infuriating him, the way she flouted propriety, the mocking way she said his title.

When she finally stood beside him, James took her hand. Her eyes widened, and she snapped her head straight, her bonnet brim hiding her from him.

Something was wrong.

She seemed . . . different. It was probably just wedding-day nerves.

"Dorothea?" he asked. "Is something wrong?"

"No, Your Grace," she whispered.

He craned his neck to see her face. Why didn't her eyes tilt at the right angle? They were clear blue, with flecks of flinty gray, but they were rounder. Were her cheekbones sharper? Was her lower lip thinner?

Was he hallucinating?

He bent closer. "You *are* Lady Dorothea?" What a question to ask one's bride.

A small muscle pulsed at the crux of her jaw. "Of course I am." Her voice sounded wrong—higher, less smoke.

The doddering clergyman began reading from

the Book of Common Prayer, oblivious to their conversation.

This had to be Lady Dorothea standing beside him, since her parents were here. But James would be willing to wager his estate that she was not the woman he'd made love to in the orchid conservatory. He couldn't say how he was sure, he just knew.

His stomach heaved.

Lady Dorothea turned to face him. Her large blue eyes searched his face. Her gloved fingers tightened around the bouquet of white roses and sage, nearly snapping the stalks in half.

The clergyman droned on about mystical unions and reverence.

Lady Dorothea took a deep breath. "Stop," she said.

When the clergyman continued reading, not hearing her, she raised her voice. "Please stop."

He lifted his head from the prayer book. "My lady? Is anything amiss?"

"Would you give us a moment, Vicar?" she asked, lifting her chin bravely, reminding James for the first time of the woman he'd held in his arms among the flowers.

White eyebrows rose. Watery eyes searched for the countess in the first pew.

James gestured to the clergyman. "We need a moment." He drew Lady Dorothea to the side of the altar.

Behind them, the countess drew a quavering breath.

"Er, what seems to be the trouble?" Desmond's voice bounced around the vaulted ceiling.

Lady Dorothea glanced back at her parents fearfully. She set her bouquet on a railing and removed her glove. "Here," she whispered, sliding something from her finger. "Take this."

Her eyes brimmed with tears. Diamond and gold filigree flashed in her palm. His mother's ring.

"I don't understand," he said.

"You gave this ring to someone else."

James felt as though his head was going to explode. "It wasn't you at Hatherly's?"

She shook her head, her face paler than the flowers in the bouquet.

"And at Warbury Park? Was that you?" he asked.

Lord Desmond rose from his seat, his hand resting on his dress sword. "I'm warning you, Harland . . ."

The nightmare moment bowed and strained like the mast of a ship about to crack in a storm.

Lady Dorothea's shoulders trembled. James stared at her, feeling nothing but a sick sense of dread. He had a notion of what she was about to say.

She drew a shuddering breath. "It wasn't me, Your Grace, on both occasions. It was my half sister."

"I see." He couldn't seem to feel anything. His body was numb, as if he'd been sinking beneath an arctic sea.

"Her name is Charlene Beckett," Dorothea

said. "You'll find her at number fifty, Rose Street, Covent Garden." She pressed the ring into his palm. "I can't say more."

Alarm bells built to a clanging chorus that filled his head with pain.

*Lies. Trickery and lies.*

Dorothea placed a hand on his sleeve. "Please don't be angry with her."

James brushed her hand away. "I have to go." He turned his back on her and faced the earl and countess.

Nick gave him a quizzical look.

"I will not be married today," James announced.

The countess's hands flew to her cheeks.

Lord Desmond raised his dress sword. "The hell you won't," he roared.

James strode down the aisle.

Nick leapt for the earl, restraining him from following. He should have let the earl follow. James would have welcomed the chance to squash Desmond like the bloated tick he was. James had been holding back the tide of anger and frustration, attempting to be civilized enough for London society, but no longer.

They wanted His Disgrace? He'd give them the scandal they craved, just as soon as he found the woman who had played him for a fool.

He burst through the church doors, startling his grooms.

"Rose Street, Covent Garden," he yelled, vaulting into the barouche.

With a bone-jarring lurch, they were off and racing down the street.

# Chapter 26

**K**yuzo dropped his arms. "You're not yourself today."

*I may never be myself again*, Charlene thought.

Not when the duke and Dorothea had to be standing in front of a curate somewhere in London, promising to love and cherish, till death do them part. She shouldn't have cared, but she did. It made her feel helpless, and that made her angry.

She rolled to her feet, ready to defend against the next attack. They were sparring in a basement room at the Theatre Royal on Drury Lane, where Kyuzo knew one of the managers. He allowed them to practice here, in a small room that he'd furnished with bamboo floor mats.

The smell of sweat braced her. She adjusted the fabric of the cotton gown she'd tied into a loose approximation of male trousers.

"Again." She straightened her back, finding her center of balance and hugging her elbows close to her sides.

Kyuzo's bare foot snapped out. Charlene twisted and tried to block the kick, but she lost her balance and crashed to the floor.

"Emotion makes you weak, Charlene," Kyuzo cautioned. "Breathe. Empty your mind."

The *duke* made her weak.

Damn him to hell.

Kyuzo threw an uppercut punch. Charlene blocked the blow with her left forearm and stepped in for an arm lock, but she miscalculated Kyuzo's trajectory and ended up strangled, his elbow around her throat.

She tapped on his arm and he released her.

"Are you ready to stop now?" he asked. "Your mind is somewhere else."

In a church. Where a clergyman was asking the duke and Dorothea to confess any impediment to their lawful union. And Charlene wasn't there to ruin the wedding in any of the outrageous ways she'd imagined in her lonely bed last night.

Drape herself across the altar and perform *seppuku*, the ritual suicide Kyuzo had told her about, where dishonored Japanese warriors took their own lives by slashing a knife into their bellies with one smooth, left-to-right slice.

That would surely stop the wedding.

Charlene sank to the floor, crossing her arms over her knees.

"So," Kyuzo sat beside her. "Are you going to tell me what this is all about? You won your reward, did you not? You paid back Grant and Louisa will have her apprenticeship."

"Yes."

"Is it the duke?" Kyuzo's face grew fierce, the lines around his mouth deepening. "Did he hurt you?"

"No." Charlene hugged her knees against her chest. "Not the way you mean."

"What way then?"

Charlene pressed her forehead to her knees. "Have you ever been in love, Kyuzo?"

"Oh." Kyuzo smiled. "So it's love, is it? Well you have the right of it there. Love can hurt."

"Yes."

"I fancied myself in love when I was your age. Her name was Yuki and she was the daughter of a wealthy merchant. I was a humble fisherman's son. I loved her in secret for years."

"Did she return your affection?"

"It doesn't matter. You know the rest of the story. The boat that captured me. I never saw Yuki again."

*The boat that captured me.*

Five small words to describe so much suffering. He'd been a slave on that boat for six years before he'd made his escape into the streets of London. Charlene's heart ached for the young man Kyuzo had been. Penniless and foreign in a strange land.

"I didn't know," she said. "I'm so sorry."

"Not your fault." He stared at the wall. "My bloody fault for getting drunk that night, thinking of my hopeless love. I wasn't watching when they drugged me."

"You have to go back to Japan. Maybe she still loves you. Maybe she's waiting for you, staring out to sea every day, faithful to your memory."

Kyuzo snorted. "Too late now. She's forgotten about me. And I have a new life here in England

and I've had new loves." He stared straight into her eyes. "It's not too late for you, Charlene. You are still very young. You will find love again."

"Never. I'll never let this happen to me again."

Kyuzo smiled. "Always so dramatic."

Charlene stared at the painted scenery panels propped against the storeroom walls. Bright blue skies. Fluffy white clouds.

The fantasy of a world without coal smoke.

"I will give Lulu a perfect life," she vowed. "I'll live only for her."

"Honorable," Kyuzo said. "But dramatic." Still smiling, he rose and offered her his hand, helping her stand. "Go home. You shouldn't practice today."

Charlene untied her skirts and donned her plain straw bonnet. "Thank you."

Kyuzo nodded and began his *katas*.

Charlene walked slowly across the piazza. Kyuzo was wrong. There was no chance that she would find love again. She would devote the rest of her life to her sister's happiness.

She was so engrossed in her plans for Lulu's future that she didn't notice the carriage outside their house until it loomed in front of her face.

With a queasy stomach, she registered the rampant lion worked in gold on the side.

Lord Grant. Inside the house. With Lulu.

She ripped off her bonnet and slammed the front door open, immediately recognizing the sound of Grant's voice coming from the front parlor. There was no time to run back for Kyuzo.

She had to face this on her own, before Grant hurt Lulu. She raced down the hall and burst into the parlor, counting on the element of surprise.

The baron was seated in a chair by the fireplace. She lunged for him, but strong hands caught her arms from behind and wrestled her into submission. She twisted her neck to see the identity of her captor. It was the scar-faced guard, Mace. He must have been waiting beside the doorway, with instructions to subdue her upon entry.

So much for the element of surprise.

"Ah, Charlene, at last," Grant said. "Join us, won't you?"

Diane and Lulu were sitting opposite him on a sofa. There were tears streaking Lulu's cheeks. Charlene's heart clenched.

She relaxed in Mace's arms, feigning docility.

Beside Mace there was another guard, equally muscled and scowling.

Charlene prayed Kyuzo came home early. There was no way she could defeat three men.

She realized with a sinking heart that Grant was idly turning his branding iron in the flames, until the iron glowed orange.

"Charlene, tell him it's not true," Lulu blurted.

"Yes, tell her, Charlene," Grant said. "Tell her this is a respectable boardinghouse and Dove here is a virtuous boarder."

If Charlene's hands had been free, she would have struck the ugly smile from his face.

"Sweetheart, I didn't want you to find out like this," she said.

"What are you saying?" More tears escaped Lulu's eyes.

"Don't be coy, Charlene." Grant lifted the brand, evaluating the color. "Tell her the whole truth. This is a brothel. The girls are whores. *You* are a whore."

Charlene turned to Lulu in anguish. She should have prepared her. This was the worst possible way for her to find out. Charlene had been so concerned with keeping her sister innocent that she hadn't even taught her how to defend herself. She'd been so wrong.

"Diane," Charlene said briskly, with a confidence she didn't feel, "please take Lulu upstairs. This is not a conversation for her ears."

Diane glanced fearfully at Lord Grant.

"I'm the one you want, Baron," Charlene said. "Here I am. At your bidding."

Grant regarded her with half-lidded eyes. "I've waited a long time to hear you say those words."

Charlene schooled her face into an expressionless mask. "If you let Lulu leave, I'll be yours."

Lulu's hazel eyes swam with tears. "I can't leave you here."

"Everything will be fine, sweetheart. I'll be up soon."

Grant nodded, and Diane gathered Lulu and hurried from the room. Charlene heard their footsteps running down the hallway and up the stairs. When she was sure they were safe, she faced

Grant. "Our guard will be home any moment," she lied. "I'm sure you remember him?"

"I do indeed." Grant smiled. "Only I happen to know he's in the Drury Lane theater right now and won't be back for an hour."

*Damn.*

"You shouldn't have humiliated me in front of Lord Hatherly," Grant said. "I was hoping for his patronage. Instead you made me a laughing-stock." He struck the iron against the stone of the mantel and sparks flew.

"You shouldn't have done that," he repeated, rising and walking toward her.

Keeping an eye on the glowing iron, Charlene allowed him to grab her collar and march her to the mirror over the mantelpiece.

Grant stood behind her, using his free hand to force her to look into the mirror. "You were fashioned for a man's pleasure, Charlene," he whispered in her ear. His fingers closed around her throat. "See these plump lips?" He squeezed her cheeks until her lips popped open. "And this glorious hair . . ."

He released her face and tugged at her chignon until her hair tumbled loose. His breathing quickened.

Desperation and anger threatened to boil over. She had to remain calm and search for the best opportunity to strike.

"Come to the point, Grant." She spoke with as much bravado as she could muster.

"You want the point?" Grant pulled her back

against his hard length, holding the branding iron inches from her neck. "I have two points for you."

The guards guffawed loudly.

"Did you know that your mother was the first female I ever had?" Grant asked. "My father bought her for me when I was only fourteen. Oh, she was a skilled teacher, your mother. I was so grateful for her instruction that when I came of age, I helped her fund this little venture."

"And we repaid your loan," Charlene said. "We owe you nothing."

"You don't know the whole story," he said calmly, as if he'd been discussing the weather. "I purchased this building, and I never once charged rent."

That couldn't be true. Charlene always set aside three hundred pounds per year. True, she'd never met the landlord and didn't even know his name . . . oh, God.

"Charlene." Grant sighed. "I invested so much, and received so little. I was grooming you to be my private songbird. To grace my apartments and make me the envy of every gentleman in London. How disappointing. You could have been such a success."

He pushed her away from him and she stumbled against Mace, who grabbed her shoulders.

"Now I have to break you, instead," Grant said softly. "I was going to brand your shoulder, but now I think I'll find someplace more . . . visible."

Mace stuck a hand down her bodice and ripped

the gown off her chest and over her shoulder. Charlene struggled, but he held her in an iron grip.

Grant made a mocking approximation of a bow. "Please excuse my associate. He's only a rough sort with no schooling."

Despair choked the anger from Charlene's heart. She was outnumbered, outmaneuvered.

*Emotion makes you weak*, Kyuzo had said. But how could she remain calm when she was about to be branded?

Grant ran a finger down her neck and over the top of her breast. "Here?" He traced a circle on her breast, just above her nipple.

His finger continued across her shoulder, down her arm, and over the sensitive skin of her inner wrist. "Or here?"

Mace brought both of her wrists together in one of his enormous paws. He smiled nastily. "The wrist would hurt something awful." He used his strength to force Charlene onto her knees.

She assumed the *shikko* posture. Heels together, crouching in preparation to strike. She bowed her head. Mace thrust her arms out to their full extension.

Grant was wearing polished boots. Charlene bowed her head further, until she could see her wavy reflection in his boots.

She knew what she had to do.

When he lowered the branding iron, she would block and deflect it, forcing the iron back toward him. He'd be so worried about marking his handsome face that he'd drop the iron, and she'd use the chaos to run for help.

It was her only chance.

She looked up at Grant. Smiled.

He frowned. "Why are you smiling?"

Because he had no idea what she planned for him.

# Chapter 27

*Lies and trickery, trickery and lies*, the carriage wheels chanted mockingly as they ground along the worn cobblestones of Covent Garden.

James punched the leather upholstery, welcoming the pain that blossomed along his knuckles. He knew this area well. He and Dalton had misspent quite a bit of their youth drinking cheap ale in the basement taverns that doubled as brothels on Maiden Lane. By half past four this afternoon, there would be no respectable females left on the streets.

The woman he sought, this Charlene Beckett, was no respectable lady.

She'd impersonated Dorothea, clearly with the goal of cheating him into marrying a complete stranger, for reasons he had yet to fathom. The countess must have been complicit. That was the only conclusion to draw about why she hadn't let him see Dorothea before the wedding.

But why?

Why was this happening to him?

*Because every single time you allow yourself to care about someone, it all goes to hell. Haven't you learned that bloody lesson by now?*

How would he explain to Flor that the woman she thought of as her new mother was a fraud and imposter? It would break her heart. Again.

James groaned aloud. The old duke had to be laughing from his special place in hell. James had managed to land himself in a tangled mess of grand proportions, proving his father right yet again.

Pieces of the puzzle fell into place: the fact that no gently bred debutante could possibly know professional wrestling moves. He'd known that but hadn't seen through the ruse. He'd been so blind. Also, the cryptic comments she'd made in the conservatory, after he'd given her the ring.

*I have something I must tell you . . . I'm not her. The woman you're talking about.*

He'd been so addled by lust that he'd completely ignored her warnings. There would be no more half truths, no more evasion.

The door to number fifty was ajar. He heard voices coming from a nearby room.

He heard *her* voice.

He walked swiftly down the hall, pausing outside the door of a small parlor. The first thing he saw in the room was a tangle of blazing gold hair falling around rain-drenched blue eyes. Charlene was kneeling in the grip of two unsavory-looking characters, and a man James recognized as Lord Grant was brandishing a glowing fire iron over her wrist.

What the hell was happening here?

"You won't be smiling when I'm through with you," James heard the baron say. The tip of the fire iron pulsed orange.

James's stomach dropped into his boots.

She was in *danger*.

Instinct took over, obliterating thought. He charged into the room and lunged at one of the men, smashing his fist into his nose. The man toppled to the floor with a crashing thud. The scarfaced man came at James. James feinted right and swung with his left, impacting the man's jaw and snapping his head back.

He caught a glimpse of Charlene grappling with Grant. She blocked the burning iron with her arm in a surprising blur of motion.

Scarface lunged, and his fist connected with James's gut, momentarily knocking the wind from his lungs. James gave a gasp of wild laughter. It would take a lot more than that to fell him.

He lifted his head. Two brutes stared at each other.

Scarface didn't like what he saw. His face whitened, and he abruptly turned on his heel and fled from the room.

James flexed his stomach muscles and took a breath. Bruised. Not broken. He was well acquainted with the difference.

*Now for Grant.*

James spun around.

Grant was watching him, his elbow collaring Charlene, with the heated iron nearly brushing her cheek. "Don't come any closer," he warned.

James stood still, not daring to breathe.

"James," Charlene said, her lips twisted with anguish. "What are you doing here?"

Grant tightened his grip around her neck. "Not another word," he spat. "Whoever you are," he said to James, "this is a private matter . . ." He craned his neck, disbelief contorting his face. "Harland?"

"Seems we have a mutual interest, Grant. Release the woman. There's no need for violence." James gave him a smile that told him in no uncertain terms what would happen if he didn't follow instructions.

"Bit late for that, wouldn't you agree?" Grant extended his boot and poked at the heap of flesh and muscle that had been his guard. The man remained down. "Is he dead?"

"He'll live," James grunted.

Charlene tried to speak, but Grant's fingers closed around her mouth. James nearly lost control and made a move, but he had to wait for the right moment. The branding iron was too close to her face. She'd already been burned. He could see an angry red weal snaking across her bared forearm.

"I own this woman. She's mine to mark." The baron's arm trembled, and the iron bounced near Charlene's face. She bent her neck away from the heated metal.

James sucked in a breath. He'd have to risk it. If he was quick enough, he could put himself between the iron and Charlene.

He took another step forward.

"Don't come closer," Grant shouted. "Why do you care? What's she to you?" He squeezed his elbow tighter around Charlene's neck. Her fingernails clawed at his arm as she struggled for breath. "I knew you couldn't be as high and mighty as you pretended." He bit her earlobe, and she cringed. "Deeper pockets opened her legs, eh, Harland?"

"Drop the iron and give me the woman, or I'll kill you," James replied. "Simple choice. Life. Or death."

"You wouldn't dare," hissed Grant. "You're the duke now. You can't go about murdering peers."

"That's right, I'm the duke. And believe me, the arrogant despots glowering on my ancestral walls have nothing on me. My heart is darker, my fists bloodier. The only difference is I fight on the side of justice. I'd have no problem sending a coward like you down to hell to meet the other dukes of Harland."

Grant blanched. His hand wavered, lowering the iron a fraction. It was all Charlene needed to swivel and break his grip. She put several paces between them, drawing deep, gasping breaths and clutching the mantelpiece.

Grant flicked the back of his wrist at her. "I don't want the duke's leavings. When he tires of you, and you're whoring on the streets for shillings, I'll spit in your face."

He spat on the carpet, so intent on humiliating her that he didn't notice James stalking closer. James shattered his fist into the baron's long, straight nose with the full force of his fury.

The baron's nose wouldn't be straight any longer.

Grant tottered for a moment, a nearly comical expression of surprise frozen on his face, then he hit the floor with a thud that shook the floorboards.

A barrel-chested older man with black hair and black eyes bolted into the room.

"Kyuzo," Charlene shouted.

She seemed happy to see him so this couldn't be another of Grant's men.

Scarface lumbered to his feet, lunging at the newcomer, but was felled instantly with one perfectly timed blow to his jaw.

Charlene caught James's eye. "This is Mr. Kyuzo Yamamoto," she said.

"You have an excellent left hook, Mr. Yamamoto," James said.

"Thank you. And you must be Charlene's duke," Yamamoto said.

"Kyuzo," Charlene exclaimed, her voice hoarse and weak.

Yamamoto frowned down at the three large men sprawled across the carpet. The baron's nose bleed was turning the carpet red. "We should take these vermin back to the gutter where they belong, Your Grace."

"Indeed, Yamamoto. My thoughts exactly."

Yamamoto crouched down, hoisted the baron by the armpits, and began dragging him out of the room.

"I'll be right back," James told Charlene.

She nodded. The depths of her blue-gray eyes brought all the questions swirling back, like ocean waves closing above his head.

He wrenched his gaze away and dragged a slumbering brawler out of the room.

There would be time to seek answers later.

Charlene rested against the mantel, leaning her head back in search of more air. She'd been about to attack Grant when the duke had appeared, huge and raging and lethal. And so distracting that she'd stopped for a split second to stare at him. That's when Grant had wrapped her in a stranglehold.

Why was the duke here? Shouldn't he be with Dorothea?

"Charlene?" her mother called.

"In the parlor," Charlene croaked. Her throat still ached where Grant's fingers had severed her air supply for those endless, terrifying seconds.

Her mother entered, followed by Lulu and Diane. "Charlene, what happened? We heard such noises."

Lulu ran to Charlene and hugged her waist.

Charlene winced when Lulu touched her burned arm.

"Are you hurt, Charlene?" Lulu asked, her eyes wide with concern.

Charlene smiled through the haze of pain, her legs wobbly. "I'll be fine," she whispered.

The duke and Kyuzo reappeared. Suddenly the pink-and-white parlor seemed much smaller with the great beast of a duke standing in its center in his blood-spattered linen.

"Oh," Charlene's mother exclaimed. "Who's this, then?"

"James, Duke of Harland, at your service, madam."

"That's your duke?" Diane whispered to Charlene with a sly, secret smile. "No wonder you were pining for him. He's dreamy."

Charlene's mother recovered her aplomb. "Your Grace." She curtsied skillfully, ever the fashionable lady, even pale and thin from her illness. "I'm forever in your debt for rescuing my daughter." She fluttered her eyelashes. Then she nudged Charlene. "Offer His Grace some tea, Charlene."

"I don't think he wants tea, Mama."

She knew that what he wanted was answers. He'd found out about her deception. She'd seen the accusations in his brilliant green eyes as he'd entered the parlor. He'd come to demand answers, and instead he'd ended up rescuing her.

But the questions would come soon. She'd have to tell him the truth and face the betrayal in his eyes.

"I would love some tea." The duke's deep voice reverberated in the small room. "Yamamoto, would you like some tea?"

"Love some." Kyuzo grinned. Apparently he and the duke had bonded while hauling away the bodies of the men they'd pounded to the floor.

Lulu tilted her head. "You're ever so much handsomer than the Duke of Wellington, even with all those cuts and bruises, Your Grace."

"Thank you."

"I don't suppose you'd let me paint your portrait?" Lulu asked.

His lip quirked in the lopsided way Charlene loved. "I would be honored, Miss . . ."

"Luisa. But Charlene calls me Lulu." She made a square with her fingers in the air, framing the duke's face. "Yes." She nodded. "I'll paint you on a rearing black stallion. It will be my most magnificent portrait ever."

"Lulu!" Charlene said. "His Grace doesn't have time for tea or portraits. Can't you see he's injured?" He was bleeding from a cut above his eye, and every time he took a breath, Charlene noticed he winced slightly. "Besides, he was married today. I'm sure he wants to return to his bride."

The duke raised one eyebrow in that sardonic, expressive way of his.

He ran a hand through his thick black hair, his green eyes searching her face. "I did go to a church today . . . but the wrong woman was at the altar. And so I left."

Charlene's heart pounded.

*He hadn't married Dorothea.*

The room started spinning. She clutched Lulu's shoulder for support.

The duke was at her side in two long strides. "You're the one who's injured."

"It's nothing."

He lifted her arm, examining the burn. His touch hurt her blistering skin. "This needs to be treated immediately. It could fester."

"Oh, Charlene, sweetheart." Her mother fluttered her hands.

"I'll send for a physician," Kyuzo said.

"I don't need . . ." Charlene began, and stopped. Her mind thought the words, only her mouth wouldn't form them. She tried again. "I . . . don't . . ."

She didn't need to be rescued again. And she wasn't going to swoon in the duke's arms.

She wasn't the swooning type.

The room spun faster.

And then the world went blank.

# Chapter 28

**M**aids ran to fetch water. Footmen tore strips of cotton for bandages. The household whirred like well-oiled clockwork, as it had for decades, regulating the lives of the dukes of Harland. James was grateful for the efficiency in a way he'd never been before.

Charlene was small and fragile in his huge bed, her face as pale as the linens, her determined chin slack as she slept deeply.

James ran a finger along the inside of her wrist, searching for a pulse. "Shouldn't she be waking by now?"

"Don't worry," Josefa said. "She's had a shock. That's all." She crushed herbs into a bowl of water and dipped cotton strips into the mixture. "Help me cut off her sleeve," Josefa said.

James used his knife to slash the torn cotton sleeve from her arm, revealing the angry red burn that slashed from her elbow nearly to her wrist. Josefa dipped Charlene's arm in a basin, gently sloshing cool water over the burn. She dried her arm with a clean towel and pressed pungent comfrey leaves to the wound.

Charlene moaned when Josefa wrapped bandages around her arm. Her eyelids fluttered but didn't open.

Josefa passed a cool, wet cloth over Charlene's brow. There was the soothing smell of chamomile.

"I don't know anything about her," James said.

Josefa shrugged. "She makes you happy." She rearranged the cushions and drew the covers up Charlene's sleeping form. "What more do you need to know?"

It wasn't that simple. Nothing would ever be simple with a woman like Charlene.

James paced the room while a maid helped Josefa remove Charlene's dress beneath the covers and replace it with a clean cotton nightgown.

Josefa shook her head. "You need some rest. You are injured as well."

"It doesn't matter, only a few bruised ribs." He rubbed his hand across his eyes. "What if she contracts a fever?"

"Please don't worry, she's very strong and healthy. There's no danger." Josefa's eyes twinkled. "She'll live to bear you sons."

James frowned. "You don't understand. She's not the woman I thought she was."

"Who is she then?" Josefa asked.

"I don't know. She's not Lady Dorothea." He'd just rescued her from what was almost certainly a bawdy house. The most likely explanation was that she was a courtesan. But that wasn't what tied his stomach in knots. It was the fact that she'd lied to him, to his face, for days.

Had it all been an act?

"She's not from a respectable family," he said. "There will be no lowering of the duty taxes."

Josefa narrowed her eyes. "What's stopping you from staying here with her and lowering those taxes yourself?"

"She lied to me," he said.

"She had her reasons."

Whatever her reasons, she'd stormed into his life and laid waste to his careful plans.

He thought about that moment when she'd blocked the glowing brand with her arm. There was no frame of reference in his experience for a female that fierce and brave. Who was she?

Her breathing sounded normal now. He could see her chest rising and falling in a slow, regular rhythm. He'd witnessed too many people dying from fevers. Some of them from a small scratch they'd received that had gone on to fester.

Even now, knowing she'd lied to him, he still wanted to touch her, comfort her. If her breathing changed, if she became restless, or her skin grew flushed, he would send for the Prince Regent's own physician to save her if necessary.

"You listen to me, you duke of a long line of dukes," Josefa said. "I need to return to my family, my home. But you should stay here. With Flor. And this woman, whatever her name is."

"Charlene."

"You should stay with Charlene. She's a good woman with a big heart. Big enough to love Flor. Even big enough to love you."

That made James pause. Love him? Did she love him or was she only a skilled actress?

Josefa shook her finger at him. "If you don't forgive her you will regret it the rest of your life. You will think of her always."

"I could never trust her again."

"Then you are a fool." Josefa planted her fists on her hips. "*A bloody* fool of a duke."

Now she was learning to swear in English. Wonderful. She stalked out of the room carrying a bowl of water-soaked towels.

James sat and rested his head on the high-backed chair. Watched the light fade from the sky to a faint purple bruise through the tall, mullioned windows.

Charlene slept on, her breathing rhythmic and regular.

She was under his skin, in his blood. Ignoring her wasn't an option. But forgiving her seemed impossible as well. He wanted to slip under the covers and hold her, bury his face in her tangled curls. Tell her how beautiful and strong she was, even when injured.

And then shake her until she told him the truth.

Charlene's eyes flew open. She was in an unfamiliar room. A single beeswax candle had dripped over the wooden nightstand and was nearly spent. It was nighttime. She was in a large bed with whisper-soft linens. There was a long, dark shape draped across an armchair by the fire.

The duke.

The pillows smelled like pine needles. She was in his bed.

"You're awake." His voice rumbled from the chair. He shifted, stretching his long legs.

"How did I get here?" she asked. "What happened?"

"You fainted. I brought you here, and Josefa prepared a poultice for your burn. How does your arm feel?"

She flexed her arm experimentally. Not as much pain as she'd expected. "Surprisingly painless."

"Josefa is very skilled."

There was no avoiding their conversation any longer. Charlene pushed the covers down and swung her aching legs out of bed. Someone had clothed her in a modest nightdress that covered her from neck to toes. Dragging the counterpane with her, she sat in a chair opposite the duke, tucking her knees under the soft flannel and wrapping the covers tightly around her.

He added more logs to the glowing coals, and flames soon licked at wood. He was wearing a midnight blue velvet dressing gown over his trousers. Instead of making him more civilized, the sumptuous fabric only served to bring his brute masculinity into sharper contrast.

The immense breadth of his shoulders made her feel light-headed, as if the fire had stolen all the oxygen from the room.

His jaw was dark with stubble. He hadn't shaved, or bathed. He looked tired, but dangerous, with bruises shadowing his cheekbones and a cut slashed across one eyebrow.

His expression was difficult to read in the dim light, but the way he sat, with rigid back and clenched jaw, told her all she needed to know.

The interrogation was approaching.

"I want to know how you could—" he began, but she cut him off, rushing into her explanation before he had a chance to speak.

"My name is Charlene Beckett. I'm the illegitimate daughter of the Earl of Desmond and a courtesan. I was groomed for my mother's life, but I refused to follow in her footsteps. Mr. Yamamoto taught me how to defend myself." She paused to take a quick breath. "I know you have no reason to believe me, but it's true. Lady Desmond paid me one thousand pounds to impersonate her daughter."

Disbelief, pain, fury. Charlene imagined she could recognize each of the emotions grappling in his eyes, tightening his jaw and constricting his throat.

"But why?" he choked. "Why would she hire you?"

"Lady Dorothea was on a ship back from Italy when the countess received your invitation." She hugged her knees closer, seeking protection. "The countess was desperate. And I'm her daughter's near twin."

"One thousand. Is that all I'm worth?"

Was that a hint of amusement she heard in his voice? No, it couldn't be. It had to be bitterness. Sarcasm.

"I accepted the terms of her proposal in order to purchase my sister a painting apprenticeship and to repay a large debt to the baron. You saw the outcome of *that*."

The fire crackled and popped, punctuating the tension in the room. Charlene stared into the yellow flames tinged with blue at the base and locked her fingers around her ankles.

"He's tried to brand me before," she whispered. "It plays tricks on your mind. Makes you wary of everyone."

James's huge hands gripped the chair arms. "I should have killed him."

"I almost thought you were going to. You had a murderous look in your eyes." Charlene shivered despite her warm wrappings.

"So you needed the money to pay Grant."

"Yes. I was going to close my mother's business and open a respectable boardinghouse, a refuge for vulnerable young girls."

"Are you sure you're not lying again? That seems an unusual goal for a woman who was raised to be a courtesan."

Why did her dream sound so flimsy and unrealistic when she spoke it out loud? She'd thought it all through carefully, how she would repaint the house, purchase all new beds, how she would go out into the streets of Covent Garden and search for the newly arrived girls, the ones driven there out of desperation. It was solid and real in her mind. But now, with the duke's sharp gaze slicing through to her soul, it sounded implausible, impossible.

"Why didn't you tell me the truth at Hatherly's?" His voice made her shiver again. "You had every opportunity."

"Believe me, I tried, so many times. Every time I started to speak you kissed me, or my throat closed. I just couldn't bring myself to say the words."

"You should have told me. Given me a chance."

"A chance for what?"

"To make my own choices."

"You never made me think there was a choice to be made. What did it matter if you never met Dorothea before you married her? The message was that you didn't care who you married, as long as the bride met your requirements for lineage, propriety, and the political influence of her father."

He stood up abruptly and tightened the sash on his dressing gown. She had to close her eyes, because he was too beautiful, standing there in front of her.

She heard him walk to the fireplace. Heard the thud of metal striking wood as he jabbed at the half-burned logs.

They were in the same room yet worlds apart. The feeling was palpable and heavy, like coal smoke smothering London streets, lodging in eyes and throats, choking out the sun.

He hated her for lying to him.

She hated herself for loving him.

"When I arrived in Surrey, I thought you would be like all the other peers I'd encountered," Charlene said, keeping her eyes squeezed shut. "Arrogant and selfish. You *did* invite four women to your house to compete for you, after all."

More thudding iron against wood.

"And when I met Lady Dorothea, I wanted to hate her, too," Charlene said. "I was envious that she'd lived the life I never had. But she's sweet, kind, and intelligent, and she's willing to protect Flor. You have to take her back, James."

Iron scraped against stone this time. "Take her back?" he asked. "Are you honestly asking me to marry your sister?"

Humiliating tears gathered in the corners of Charlene's eyes. She squeezed her eyes closed even harder to keep the tears from spilling. "Yes. She will be the perfect duchess. Go to her." It cost her dearly to say those words, but it was the right thing to do.

"You want me to marry her." The sense of betrayal in his voice made the tears gather faster. "Was it all an act then? Was I only a means to an end for you?"

She swallowed. She hated being vulnerable. She never allowed anyone this much power over her. But whatever he said to hurt her, whatever he did, it couldn't be worse than the last twenty-four hours, when she'd believed he was marrying Dorothea.

"It started as an act," she whispered. "But you were so different than I expected. You played your guitar for Flor, you acknowledged her . . . and you cared about the laborers in your factory. It wasn't an act in the end, Your Grace."

"James" was the answer.

She hesitated. She'd vowed she would never think of him as James again.

All of a sudden she sensed that he was there in front of her. She opened her eyes. He dropped to his knees and buried his head in her lap.

"Say my name," he said, threading his arms around her hips.

"James," she whispered. She stroked his head. She couldn't not touch him.

"And your name is . . ." He caught her good wrist in his fingers and kissed the sensitive inner skin. " . . . Charlene." It was the briefest of touches, but that one soft kiss, and the way he said her true name, made her melt with longing.

"James." She pulled her wrist away, finding a hidden source of resolve. "We need to talk. I have more to tell you."

In one sweeping movement he stood and lifted her out of the chair and into his arms, silencing her with kisses. He wasn't going to let her breathe, let alone speak.

He carried her to the bed and laid her gently down, lowering himself beside her. He kissed her eyelids, her nose, her tightly closed lips, shaping her body with his hands, loving her until her lips opened and his tongue entered her mouth.

They kissed for so long that she stopped breathing; he was breathing for her, filling her so completely.

"We can talk later," he said when he finally broke away. "I need you, Charlene. Now."

Hearing him say her name rendered her protests useless.

There was a swift intake of breath, a hiss like a pot of water boiling over, and then his hand was behind her neck, pulling her into the tempest of his lips. It lasted a minute, or an hour, and there was no time for thought.

The stubble on his chin tickled her chest, and his lips moved inside her bodice, seeking her breasts. A light touch on her nipple, and then an ache that tugged sweetly and made her arch her back.

"No," she said. "We shouldn't." Even as she closed her eyes and offered her breasts to his exploration.

He stopped and pressed his head to her chest. "Your heart is saying yes."

He stroked her breasts, reaching under cotton and filling his hands with her, rolling her nipples until they were swollen and heavy and she was moaning beneath him, the pain in her arm forgotten.

He shifted both breasts to one hand and slid his other hand down her belly and thigh, finding the hem of her nightgown and urging it up to her waist. He eased her thighs apart and dipped his finger between them.

"You're so wet and ready for me, Charlene," he said in a low, husky voice.

Every time he said her name, she grew wetter.

Careful to avoid her bandaged arm, he kissed his way down her body, stopping to worship her breasts and belly and then each hip bone. Then he parted her thighs wider.

"I want to taste you," he growled, his breath rasping against her thigh.

He wasn't going to kiss her . . . *there*, was he?

She startled off the bed when his lips descended.

He *was*.

She gasped as his tongue touched her, licking and nibbling until her breath came fast and ragged. He lapped and sucked and made her belly quake. His fingers slid inside her while his tongue urged her toward the precipice.

When she needed him to close his lips around her and suckle, she told him with hands in his hair, pressing him to her, and he answered her silent call, hands cradling her buttocks, sucking with his lips and flicking with his tongue at the same time until she was panting beneath him.

He was strong and slow and steady, and his hands moved to circle her waist, then closed around her nipples, while his tongue never stopped moving on her.

Desire eddied through her mind and spilled into her heart. This time the pleasure swooped down without warning, bursting like ripe strawberries on her tongue, flooding her mind with sweetness.

When he slid back up her length and found her lips again, she tasted herself on his tongue. Honey and brine.

While she was still humming with bliss, he

ripped off his dressing gown and trousers and positioned himself between her thighs.

In the candlelight his eyes were nearly black. His hands were everywhere, running down her side, tracing the curve of her hip, cupping her breasts.

He pinched her nipples and Charlene moaned.

"Take me," she said. Whose voice was that?

The room was dark except for the faint glow of the fire's embers and the dying candle.

He pushed her nightgown over her head and moved her hips up until she was cradling him between her thighs. The first touch of her sensitive flesh against his hardness sent sparks of pleasure streaking through her body.

He slipped inside her, only a few inches.

"I thought I would never see you again," she whispered.

"I thought I would marry you today." He pushed all the way inside, kissing her while he claimed her with slow, controlled thrusts.

He clutched her hand to his sweat-slicked chest. Spread her fingers over his heart. She felt it beating beneath her palm.

*This is the rhythm. Follow it.*

She understood, going still under him, relaxing and letting him guide her into the push and arc of it, the steady, building chorus of beats and pauses.

Sensation built again in her belly and he increased the speed, moving above her, his breathing harsh and guttural.

She'd never known she needed this. She tensed, her thighs clenching his hips.

There was the faint slapping sound of their

bodies meeting and parting. The slippery sheen of sweat. She discovered that if she nipped at his neck, he breathed faster, moved faster.

His lips found her eyelids, eyelashes, the tips of her fingers.

She already spoke this language. She didn't have to learn it. There was no doubt. No fear. She wanted to laugh. Cry. Both.

"That's so good, Charlene. Yes. Come with me." He thrust one last time, shuddering in her arms as his release came. He sank against her, covering her, the weight of him stealing her breath.

This coming she experienced with him was almost violent. She clenched and held her breath until her stomach muscles hurt, then the tipping point came with a sudden release. The involuntary spasms were nearly frightening in their intensity.

Charlene knew that for every coming, every arrival, there was a leave-taking. The pleasure could never last long enough for her to forget that. She knew that women like her were only useful for limited purposes. Temporary diversions. Illicit liaisons.

She might be in his arms right now, but eventually he'd marry his perfect duchess. And leave England. Leave both of them behind.


Charlene was having the loveliest dream. James was in her bed, warm and solid, with his arm wrapped around her waist and his lips against her neck. He fit so nicely, cocooned around her back. She tightened his arm around her and wriggled back against his warmth and . . . hardness.

Rigid, marble-carved hardness.

Her eyes flew open.

"Mmm . . . you're awake," he murmured, nibbling the tip of her earlobe. "So am I." He pushed against her thighs in case she hadn't grasped his meaning.

"James, we can't. It's not right. Please, we must talk."

"We'll talk in the morning," he said. He turned her over, rolling her onto her stomach. He swept her hair off her neck and over the pillow.

Gently, he lowered his weight onto her back, and she was completely pinned against the soft, crisp linens. He took his time, nudging her legs apart, slowly kissing the back of her neck, telling her she was beautiful and that no one had ever made him feel like this before.

He stroked her, reached underneath her body to knead her breasts. She was half asleep and pliant under his fingers, allowing him to shape her. Her moans were swallowed by the pillow as his large hands lifted her hips and his knees nudged her thighs apart.

He was completely in control, so huge on top of her, pressing her into the bed. But she knew that he only did what she allowed him to do.

Searching fingers explored her thighs and discovered the source of her longing. Shamelessly, she spread her legs and lifted her bum off the bed, grinding against him.

She loved surrendering like this. Loved that her

thighs were spread so wide they trembled with the strain. He grasped her waist with both hands, circling her, preparing her. Then he was sliding inside her. So easily. Her body already knew his girth.

The pillow muffled her cries, and, as he drove her into the bed, she cried his name over and over again as unseen tears soaked the linens.

She gave herself to him. *Please don't ever stop. Don't let the moon fade and the sun rise again.*

Afterward, Charlene rested her head on James's chest, and he clasped his arms around her. She traced the roughness of his cheek. He was falling asleep; she could feel his body loosening.

They shouldn't fall asleep again, but her eyes were so heavy, and his breathing was so deep. She would rest her eyes, just for a few moments.

Later, she would hate herself for allowing this to happen. Right now, all she wanted to do was nestle into his arms, find that perfect hollow between his neck and shoulder to shelter her.

She wound him closer, knowing that once she let him go, he would be gone forever.

# Chapter 29

It was the same nightmare. The one James had been having nearly every time he fell asleep since the voyage back to England.

He stood in front of a mound of earth heaped over a wooden door frame. It was a church, although no one in England would have recognized it as a place of worship.

A priest wearing a brightly striped wool shawl crouched beside the door's dark maw. He lifted his gnarled hand, crossed the air, and began to keen in Latin mixed with some language that was only guttural clicks and soulful whirs to James's ears.

In his nightmare, James walked past the priest and entered the church. Inside, it was damp and dark. A table was laden with fruit, fermented corn beer, water, and bread.

Then he saw them.

Mother. Brother. There, hovering around the table. Faded and shimmering.

*Muertos frescos.* The freshly dead.

Another phantasm floated next to them, its back turned. Long gold hair, loosely braided. A thin white nightgown.

The spirit turned around.

*Charlene.*

He rushed toward her, tried to touch her, but his fingers went right through her arm.

*She doesn't know she's dead. I can't let her know.*

The priest walked under the wooden mantel. He dipped his fingers into a mug of beer and sprinkled some over the bread. When he began to chant, Charlene stared at James.

"Where am I?" she whispered. *"Where am I, James?"*

James bolted upright, wide awake. His chest was drenched with sweat. The fire had burned to ash. He'd fallen asleep.

Did Charlene have a fever?

He touched her brow. Slightly warm, but not feverish. He bent down, listening to her breathing. Slow and measured.

He let out a breath he hadn't known he'd been holding. He got out of bed and lit another candle.

Light from his candle danced over wicked curves. Her hair was alive, absorbing the candlelight until all he saw was twining golden curls.

He set the candle on the nightstand and slipped under the covers, burying his face in her hair. There was no girlish scent of tea roses. She smelled of sun-warmed lavender and the comfrey leaves Josefa had applied to the burn. Practical, soothing scents.

She sighed as he nestled her against him, wrapping his arms around her. She fit so perfectly in the cradle of his arms.

Propped up on his fists, he gazed down at her with wonder and a touch of fear. To care about someone was to face the knowledge that they could be taken from you. It was bittersweet, like cocoa nibs coated with honey.

Golden hair spreading over his sheets. Full breasts above a small waist and flaring hips. Remarkably, he was already stiff and ready for more.

He nudged her thighs apart.

"Oh, James," she sighed, keeping her eyes closed.

He stroked her sex with his finger, watching the flush spread from her cheeks down her neck and over the tops of her breasts.

He found her mouth and lost himself in sweetness. Her fevered response made his blood simmer and his brain cloud. Her tongue danced with his. He'd never felt this sense of wonder before. This feeling that they belonged together.

"Charlene," he moaned. "You're not biddable, or prudent, or even polite most of the time. But you're mine. The first day I met you, when we were sitting in the salon and the others were playing cards, I pictured you standing next to me on the deck of a ship."

"That's. Odd," she gasped.

He pushed two fingers inside her, loving the noises she made in the back of her throat. So fierce. She was very close to finding release. Her belly contracted. "I want to travel with you, Charlene. I want us to climb ancient stone terraces carved into precipices. Feel our lungs working and know we're alive. Civilizations rise and fall . . ."

His fingers rose and fell inside her, riding the swell of her passion. She ran her hands down his back, urging him on.

"The wide sky," he said. "The stone steps. They will wend into our hearts and create wider, steeper thoughts."

"Yes," she breathed. "Oh James, yes." She was very close now.

"Later we'll go to a dim, raucous tavern and drink homemade spirits flavored with cardamom seeds. I can see it so clearly, you're wearing a thin silk gown, which keeps slipping off one shoulder. It's driving me mad."

He kissed her shoulder.

"I'm longing to touch you . . . *here* . . ." He moved his hands to her breasts, lightly pinching her nipples. " . . . only I have to wait until later. I can kiss your fingertips, one by one. Something I'd never be able to do in public in England."

He followed his words with action, capturing her fingers and kissing each one.

"I pull you to your feet," he said. "We dash through the warm rain. We swim nude in the ocean with the sun on our backs."

"Nude?"

He resumed stroking her sex. She was so close now.

"Completely nude. And then . . ."

"Yes?" she gasped. "Then?"

"I make love to you as the sun sets over the ocean." She came undone beneath his fingers, moaning and shuddering. Only then did he claim her with his cock, pushing inside her with slow, measured thrusts.

There were no more words.

Only the familiar pleasure of losing himself in sensation and the new, unfamiliar desire for more than mere physical communion.

He clasped her head in his hands and kissed her with deep, strong intention. He wanted her to know how much he needed her. How he couldn't imagine leaving her. Her hair swirled against the pillow as she called his name.

He wouldn't last much longer.

She arched beneath him, urging him to move faster. "James," she gasped. "Come. Climb with me."

And he did.

And she was right there with him.

Where she belonged.

# Chapter 30

**I**n the morning, when the light streaming through a crack in the drapes woke her, James was gone.

He'd told Charlene they would talk, but he was gone.

This was how it would be in her luxurious apartments in a fashionable neighborhood with her maids and her footmen and her diamonds. He'd visit her in the evening, warm her bed, and then leave before dawn.

While she was in his arms, she'd tell herself it didn't matter. She would allow him to weave more fantasies, to lull her into complacency. When he left, the world would go bleak and cold, with nothing but her dreams to warm her.

She couldn't do this. Leave Lulu, leave her mother. Become his mistress.

She had to leave before he returned and broke down her defenses. It was better this way. She'd avoid the moment when he offered to set her up as his mistress and she searched for the fortitude to refuse.

Her arm was stiff and sore, but the herbal compress Josefa had used was still easing the worst pain. She rose, found the water closet, and tied her hair into a knot as best she could. She discovered a plain cotton dress on a shelf in an adjoining room, with her petticoats and boots brushed and neatly laid out.

She had managed to struggle back into her gown, although impeded by the bandages around her arm, when she heard a small voice behind her.

"Lady Dorothea?"

"Flor? I didn't know you were here."

"Papa brought me here for your wedding. I'm so glad you'll be my mother." She narrowed her eyes. "You're not going to die, are you? Josefa told me you were sick, and I couldn't come to you last night." She sniffed. "Please don't die."

"Oh, sweetie, I'm not dying."

"Good. Then you can read me more Swiss Family." Flor recovered swiftly, pulling the book from her pinafore pocket. "Papa read me some, but he can't do the voices as well as you."

"Flor, I have to tell you something." Charlene pulled her to a chair and knelt in front of her. "My name isn't Lady Dorothea."

Flor cocked her head. "It's not?"

"No, my name is Charlene."

Flor regarded her steadily. "It was a game. You were pretending to be Lady Dorothea."

"That's right."

"Sometimes, when I'm reading my history book, I pretend I'm Mistress Anne Boleyn and I cut off that mean old King Henry's head before he can cut off mine."

Charlene smiled. She was going to miss Flor so much. "I'm quite sure King Henry wouldn't have stood a chance."

"Did you know that Papa sent Miss Pratt away?"

"Did he?"

"Yes, and you're to choose my next governess." Flor leaned toward Charlene. "If you ask her questions first, don't forget to find out how she feels about bonnets."

Charlene patted her cheek. "You're not understanding me, dear. I'm truly not Lady Dorothea, and I can't be your mother."

Flor's lower lip jutted out. "Why?"

How to explain the tangled lives of adults to a six-year-old judge and jury?

"Remember how King Henry had so many wives? Well, instead of chopping off my head when he tires of me, your papa won't marry me in the first place."

Flor shook her head. "That doesn't make any sense."

Charlene sighed. The girl was too precocious for her own good. "You're right. Let me tell you a story then, about a very foolish girl and a dangerous duke with broad, strong shoulders and piercing green eyes."

"Oh," Flor breathed. "A romantic tale."

"Yes, but this one doesn't have a happy ending."

"What? Those stories *always* have happy endings," Flor informed her with the duke's self-assurance.

"This duke must marry a highborn lady with a spotless reputation."

Flor tossed her head. "Why must he?"

"Because he's not free to marry anyone else."

Flor shrugged. "Why?"

Charlene could tell this conversation was going to go around in circles, and she needed to leave before James returned. But she didn't want to hurt Flor.

Why did life have to be so heartbreaking?

James made some important realizations as he rode through the early-morning mist in the gray stone jungle of London. He saw everything so clearly, as if he'd emerged from a fog after being half blind, as if his thoughts were rendered in brilliant detail.

The first realization was that he'd fallen in love with Charlene, and he didn't give a damn that she'd been raised in a bawdy house.

The second was that this bone-deep longing would never, ever flag. It was an elemental pull, as if she'd been the north pole and he'd been a compass needle, and he'd sailed across the globe until he'd finally arrived home. Into her arms.

The third flash of blinding clarity was that he truly didn't care where he lived, as long as she was there. He could appoint Josefa and other trusted associates to manage his affairs abroad. If he stayed in England, he could take his seat in Parliament and argue for the abolition of slavery in person, just as Charlene had suggested the first night he met her.

So wise, his future duchess. And scorchingly passionate. England would never be too cold with her arms around him.

What he didn't know was whether she felt the same way. He couldn't bring himself to believe that she'd been pretending last night. No one was that skillful an actress. If she loved him, if she would have him, he was going to marry her and never leave her side again, as long as he lived. He'd wanted to buy respectability by marrying the right woman. But James didn't have to be respectable.

He could be both the renegade and the duke. That was the fourth, and final, realization. The one that made him turn his horse around and head for home. He guided his mount around a jagged hole in the paving stones. He'd rather have been in an open field, able to give the stallion a long lead, of course, but if they had to learn to navigate the narrow London streets, they would.

She would be his refuge in England or in the West Indies.

When he reached his town house, he handed the reins to a groom and hurried upstairs. There were voices coming from his room, so she had to be awake. He couldn't wait to tell her everything he'd realized. He opened the door. Charlene was kneeling in front of Flor, who was seated in a chair by the fire.

"Sweetheart, the duke doesn't love the foolish girl," he heard Charlene say.

"You mean Papa doesn't love you?" Flor's brow wrinkled. "Why not?"

"I don't know . . . life is complicated."

"But you love him, don't you? You love me?" Flor's voice caught, and she sounded close to tears.

"I do love you, so very much," Charlene said. "But I have to leave."

"Because you're not Lady Dorothea?"

"Something like that." The hurt and frustration in Charlene's voice was real, and it was all the proof James needed.

"I have to leave, sweetheart," Charlene repeated.

James strode into the room. "Why?"

"Yes, why?" Flor's eyes were ferocious.

Charlene turned from one pair of green eyes to the other.

"Because you're a duke and I'm a . . ." She raised that sharply pointed chin and stared at him defiantly. "I will never be owned. You can't tempt me into it. I will never be your mistress."

"What's a mistress?" Flor asked.

Charlene gasped. "Oh, sweetheart." She brushed aside her skirt hem and rose. "I have to leave," she blurted, and ran from the room.

"Charlene," Flor called. "Don't go!"

Her eyes narrowed, and she put her fists on her little hips. "Papa, run after her!" she commanded. "Bring her back."

James bent to kiss his daughter's adorable, imperious head, and then he did exactly that.

# Chapter 31

"**W**ho's running away now, Charlene?" she heard James shout.

He caught up with her at the gate and gripped her shoulders, breathing heavily.

Charlene looked up at the gray sky, blinking away tears. It was going to rain soon.

"James, let me go." She easily twisted out of his grasp. "You make me weak, and I can't have that."

"You're the strongest person I know," he said, with wonder in his eyes. "No one can make you weak."

"You do," she cried, beating on his chest with her fists. "You make me weak with wanting. And I can't . . . I can't be your mistress. Please don't ask me."

James shook his head. "Who said anything about making you my mistress? I've no idea where you got that notion."

"You said you would bring me to a tavern in a scanty dress. What is that, James? What is that if not a mistress?"

He struck his forehead with the palm of his hand. "I wasn't asking you to be my mistress, Charlene."

"But I can't go to the West Indies, can't you see that? I need to stay here with Lulu, and with my mother. You can't tear me apart like this."

"Oh, Charlene, God, I'm an idiot." He placed his forehead against hers. "I do want to travel with you, it would be the most amazing experience. But we can wait. We can stay in England for now. You were right. About everything. I was scared of connection, of letting myself feel love. Scared of losing Flor . . . and you. I thought if I closed my heart, I wouldn't be hurt."

Charlene held her breath. She reached up to touch his chin, where several days' worth of black stubble had already appeared. "I'm so happy you've realized how much Flor needs you."

"Do *you* need me?" he asked, his eyes vulnerable.

Charlene tilted back her head and stared at the gathering clouds. "I do," she whispered. "But it doesn't matter. We're too different."

"I'm not cut out to be a duke," he said. "At least not the kind of duke my father was. And you're highly unsuitable to be a duchess, but you suit me, Charlene. You're strong, caring, and you're not scared of me, not one bit."

She was scared of him right now. Because he was saying the exact script she'd written for him, word for word.

"James, please, I know you think you mean what you're saying, but it's only this wild attraction we have. In a few weeks you'll thank me for releasing you. Nothing has changed. I'm still illegitimate, born in a bawdy house."

"Everything has changed," he said. "I've

changed. I'm never going to be the duke my father was. Or the duke my brother would have been. But you've shown me the path to becoming something new."

She looked up into the green archway of his eyes.

"The manufactory is nearly finished," he said. "I want it to serve as a refuge and a school for vulnerable young girls, exactly as you described."

"That's wonderful, James."

"I want you to oversee it."

"How could I? When you were gone this morning, I thought how it would be when you left me. When you tired of me. I will never be owned."

"I left because I needed to think, Charlene. It was a lot to take in. Finding that you had lied to me, and that you would have let me marry Dorothea. I had to be sure, I had to be sure that you loved me. Because I love you. With all my heart."

"Oh, please don't say that."

She tried to leave, but he pulled her back, held her against his chest.

"Why not?" he asked.

"Because I lied to you. How can you love me?"

"What if I thank God that you lied? That it was Charlene, not Dorothea, who stormed into my life, threw me on my arse, and captured my heart?"

His heartbeat was steady under her hand. Could he be telling the truth?

"Can you forgive *me*?" he asked, stroking her hair. "I wasn't ready to find you. No one could be ready for the force of nature that is Charlene."

"I'm a force of nature? I'm . . ." Charlene blinked

her eyes. "You're the one who always looks like you're standing on the prow of a ship, heading into a squall."

"Then picture me shouting into the gathering wind, trying to find the words that will save us both from despair. Listen, please listen."

He touched the tips of his fingers to her fingers where they lay on his chest. That gentle contact unloosened her moorings and set her adrift in a sea of possibilities.

What she heard.

Carriage wheels creaking outside the gate.

Her mother saying that hate had a strange way of feeling like love.

Kyuzo telling her not to give up on love. Telling her to breathe.

*Wait.*

*Listen.*

She closed her eyes. Inside the still center of her heart, there it was. So new it could be easily missed. A tiny tendril of hope. Pushing up through the cracks of the brick and mortar she'd used to wall off her heart.

"I hear it." She opened her eyes. "But I still have to leave." She wrenched away. "Please, let me leave. You can't marry me. You're a *duke*."

"You're right."

*Blast.* Charlene didn't want to be right. "Then . . . I should leave."

James tilted her chin up. "You're right," he said. "And you're wrong. Dukes don't marry illegitimate women raised in bawdy houses. Fact.

However, I'm hardly a duke. I'm His Disgrace, a degenerate, uncivilized excuse for a duke. And I'm also a man who's terrified of losing you."

He cupped her cheek. "I could ask you this question that I'm about to ask, and you could say no. And that would kill me."

Charlene stopped fighting. If he thought she could ever say no to him, he was wrong.

"I don't want to own you or control you," he said. "I'm proud of your strength. You'll make a thoroughly disgraceful duchess, and a challenging, exacting business partner."

Charlene laughed, because if she didn't laugh, she was going to sob. "I don't suppose we'll be invited to many parties."

"No, I don't suppose so."

Charlene sobered. "Poor Dorothea. She'll be ruined."

"Not necessarily. No one has to know that it was you at my estate. They can think that I met you at the Pink Feather. Let them think I'm being monstrous, that I jilted her at the altar. I'll be even more disgraceful, and she'll be the injured party. I'm quite sure the countess will never set anyone straight."

"You're right. I hadn't thought of it that way. So when people ask us how we met . . ."

"We'll say we met at a Cyprian's ball, and I threw you over my shoulder and carried you outside and gave you a thorough tupping."

She swatted his shoulder. "But Flor . . . she won't be able to enter society with a mother like me."

"Are you still inventing obstacles? I want Flor to have every advantage, I want her to be a fine lady, but what would all that be without a mother who truly loves her? Nothing. Life is nothing without love. That's what you've taught me."

"They will cut us, ostracize us."

"I have friends. And so do you. I'm willing to stay here in England with you until our children are grown enough to travel."

"Oh, so now there are children?" Charlene laughed.

He nodded. "They'll have my green eyes, and your stubborn chin."

"James."

"Yes, my love?"

"You haven't asked me any questions yet."

"Damn it! You're right."

He dropped to one knee, on the hard paving stones.

"Charlene Beckett of Covent Garden, will you be the most disgraceful duchess London has ever seen? Will you toss anyone who cuts you to the ground, and place them in a stranglehold? Will you be Flor's champion and love her no matter what?"

Her heart threatened to spill over along with the clouds. "Sometimes I'm sad, James, and I can't hide it. Things make me angry. Girls abused, thrown out, beaten. Such a harsh, difficult world, and I want to do something about it, but I can't save them all. And it weighs on me."

"Then let's do something about it together. If

you imagine it, I'll make it happen. All this ill-gotten fortune can be good for something."

She closed her eyes. A raindrop splattered against her cheek. A teardrop followed.

When she opened her eyes, James had opened a velvet box. He held out his mother's ring. "Marry me, and polite society can go drown."

More raindrops skittered across diamonds.

Charlene's heart stopped. And then it started again, with a new, galloping rhythm.

"Yes, oh, James. Yes."

He rose and swept her into his arms, kissing her as the heavens opened and the rain baptized their promise.

It was a gale-force kiss.

The first kiss of the rest of their lives.

# Epilogue

*Three months later*

The bell rang on the east side door at the cocoa factory near Guildford at noon. Charlene answered. Outside shivered a girl with frightened brown eyes and cold-chapped nose and cheeks. Her coat was woefully thin, and she had no trunk with her. They rarely did.

"I 'eard I might come 'ere if I didn't 'ave nowhere else to go," the girl whispered, her teeth chattering.

"Come in." Charlene put an arm around her slight shoulders and brought her into the newly completed parlor, with its blazing fire. "What's your name, dear?"

The girl ducked her head, staring shyly at her mud-crusted boots. "Mary, miss."

"Where did you come from?"

"I walked from Bramley, miss."

"You must be freezing. Here, sit down, I'll fetch you some hot cocoa."

Charlene left the girl on a sofa near the hearth. "We've a new one," she called.

A few minutes later, Diane ran down the steps carrying a warm woolen shawl, and Linnet arrived with a tray laden with biscuits and cocoa in a silver pot with a wooden handle and a long, slender spout.

The three women stopped for a whispered conference.

"Her name's Mary," Charlene said. "She looks between fifteen and seventeen."

"Obvious bruises?" Diane asked.

"Thank heaven, no. But she's afraid of something."

"We'll soon fix that," Linnet said with a determined nod.

In the parlor, Diane draped the shawl around Mary's shoulders. "How did you find us, Mary?"

"I 'eard from a working girl at the Angel Posting House. I've nowhere else to go." Her shoulders hunched under the cheerful yellow shawl. "Papa died, sudden like, and they sold the farm. I'll be on my way to try my luck in London if . . . if there's no work 'ere." She bit her lip.

"You have no family to turn to?" Charlene asked.

"None, miss. Papa was all I had . . ." Mary grabbed handfuls of her coarse homespun skirts, obviously staving off tears.

She would be easy prey on the wintry streets of London. A naïve country girl, sweet-faced and alone.

Charlene would have to tell James they needed more beds. The girls kept coming. Running from danger, poverty, abuse. There were fifteen now. Wary at first, they soon learned that the cocoa factory offered them shelter, training in useful skills, wages, and some very unusual lessons in the art of defending themselves.

"And who's this, then?" Charlene's mother entered the room swathed in a red wool shawl. Her cough was nearly gone. Charlene smiled with satisfaction every time she noted a new improvement. Sharp cheekbones disappearing. Silver-blonde hair regaining its shine. Steady hands and brighter eyes.

"This is Mary." Charlene smiled at the girl encouragingly. "She'll be staying with us tonight, and as many nights as she needs."

Mary visibly relaxed as they chatted and drank chocolate, but her eyes retained the hunted look of any girl who had faced hopelessness and couldn't quite believe there was such a thing as a free cup of chocolate.

Charlene left Mary warm and fed and in the care of Diane and her mother. As she walked toward the experimentation chamber to find James, Lulu and Flor barreling down the corridor to meet her.

"Charlene," they cried in unison.

"Come quick," Flor said, her dark eyes dancing.

They tugged at her hands, dragging her with them. Laughing, Charlene surrendered to the tide of their excitement. They complemented each other so well, as she'd known they would, Flor's impulsive headlong rush to experience life balancing Lulu's inclination to escape into her imagination.

At the door to the experimentation chamber, the two girls exchanged anticipatory glances.

"What's all this about?" Charlene asked.

They only smiled, opening the door with a flourish and standing with arms extended, ushering her into the room.

For a moment, Charlene couldn't see anything in the steamy, cocoa-scented air. Then a tall, imposing figure emerged.

"Charlene," James said, drawing out the *shh* sound in his deep, seductive voice.

White linen clung damply to a formidable chest, and dark eyebrows arched over green eyes. He'd shamelessly rolled up his shirtsleeves and undone the top buttons of his shirt.

Because he knew what that did to her.

Charlene swallowed. "Duke." She inclined her head demurely, but her stomach performed somersaults.

"Show her, show her," Lulu cried, darting around his legs.

Charlene noticed for the first time that he stood next to a red-velvet-draped easel. She never would be able to see anything except him when he said her name in that wicked way.

James caught Flor by the skirt and dropped a kiss on the top of her head. He was so much more loving with her now. And for her part, Flor was learning to control her temper and use more subtle means of persuasion to make the world dance to her tune.

James bowed to his audience. "I hereby present to you the most tempting, the most enticing cocoa in the entire world." He plucked the red velvet cloth off the easel, revealing a hand-lettered advertisement.

"Duchess Cocoa," Charlene read out loud. "Pure. Concentrated. Delicious." The red letters scrolled over one of Lulu's whimsical paintings of the Guildford castle ruins.

Flor and Lulu burst into loud clapping.

"What a lovely painting, Lulu," Charlene said.

Her sister smiled. "I'll never tire of painting that castle."

"But James, you can't call it Duchess," Charlene scolded.

"Why not?"

"Because you may as well call it Scandalous Cocoa, or Disgraceful Cocoa, for all that people will buy it with even a hint of association with me."

James laughed, an exquisite sound that she'd been hearing more and more. "I did consider both of those names, but I settled on Duchess. And anyone who wouldn't buy it because of a name isn't our preferred customer."

Charlene glanced at him from under her lashes. He was always so sure of himself. It took her breath away.

Flor giggled. "What about Bonnet-less Cocoa?"

James chuckled. "I daresay little girls named Flor would buy that one." He tugged at her braid. "But I'm staying with Duchess. The most daring, delectable name of all."

His green eyes made Charlene a promise that just as soon as they were alone, he was going to show her how daring duchesses could truly be when properly encouraged. Her cheeks flushed with anticipation.

"Now run along, girls," James said. "Charlene needs to taste my new formula, and if she pronounces it ready, I'll make a pot for you."

"Oh yes, please!" Lulu said. She took Flor's hand, and the two of them skipped out of the room.

"We'll be moving to London soon for you to take your seat in Parliament," Charlene said. "Do you truly want to provoke them with this?" She gestured to the advertisement. "There will be gossip and rancor enough."

"I'll clothe you in scarlet and kiss you on the floor of Parliament if I so choose. They can't dictate our lives."

She couldn't help grinning at that.

"You're terrible," she said without conviction. "I don't care about myself . . . but Flor, Lulu, and . . . other reasons."

He wrinkled his brow. "Other reasons?"

She brought his hand to her belly. "This other reason."

He stared into her eyes. "Really?"

"I'm not sure . . . but I think so—"

"Oh, Charlene." He dropped to his knees and kissed her stomach. "My disgraceful duchess."

Charlene ruffled his hair and held him close. The life they'd chosen would never be easy. But it was theirs. And they were happier than any two people had a right to be.

He kissed his way back up, stopping to sample her breasts before claiming her lips.

He tasted of cocoa, rich and spicy.

She would never have her fill.